# K. L. HAWKER

# EYE OF DARKNESS

## A DREAM KEEPER NOVEL

# EYE OF DARKNESS

Eye of Darkness / K.L. Hawker

ISBN: 978-1-7753011-3-4

Written by K.L. Hawker

www.klhawker.com

Cover Design by Design for Writers

www.designforwriters.com

Published by Pages & Stages Publishing

www.pagesandstages.com

*For Reed, Ryan, Fiona, and Leo . . .*

*For summer shenanigans and sleepovers at the camp.*
*For making me laugh and inspiring me with all your*
*awesomeness and antics.*
*I hope you can always find an adventure between the*
*pages of a good book.*
*Preferably one written by your awesome aunt. xoxo*

"To accomplish great things, we must not only act, but
also dream; not only plan, but also believe."
~ Anatole France

# K. L. HAWKER

# EYE OF DARKNESS

## A DREAM KEEPER NOVEL

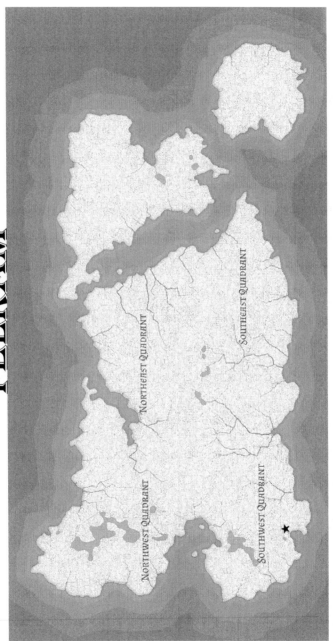

# PROLOGUE

# A Visit with Luke

## ~ MADDY ~

THE HALLS WERE dark, but they didn't scare me like they used to. With the dreamcatcher above my head, I knew nothing *really* bad would happen to me here, and besides, I had to believe that Luke was still my friend.

I turned down the next corridor, running my fingers along the cold stone walls. No one ever guarded these halls, which always seemed strange to me. I guess there weren't many dreamers Luke allowed to enter the palace. I was one of the lucky ones. Or unlucky ones, depending on the mood I found him in.

His door was closed, and I hesitated before knocking, remembering the time I walked in on him and Ella when

I thought he was lying to Sarah. I took a deep breath. That was in the past. I had to do this again. For Sarah. I knocked hard on the door and waited. A minute later the door opened, and Luke stood in the doorway wearing nothing but an old pair of jogging pants that hung low on his hips. I looked down, avoiding his chiseled abs and rippled pecs. I swallowed.

"What are you doing here?" he asked, his voice low and dark. "Is something wrong?"

"I . . . uh . . ." I looked from the floor to the fireplace behind him to the window. "Can . . . we talk?

He pushed the door open further and stepped back to let me in. I averted my gaze and walked in as he shut the door behind me.

"What's wrong?" he asked again. "Is it Sarah?" There was concern in his voice, which I couldn't quite understand given his hiatus.

"Can you please put a shirt on?" I blurted.

"Really?"

"Yes," I said. "I find it hard to . . . *focus* when you're half naked."

"It's your dream," he said. "Maybe I did have a shirt on before you got here." He chuckled, but I knew this wasn't true.

"Maybe," I said. "It very well could be a nightmare." I grinned as I took a seat on the sofa next to the fireplace. The seat was warm, and the glass of clear brown liquid with ice cubes told me that Luke had been busy trying to forget.

He returned to the fire a minute later wearing a white v-neck t-shirt and grinning. "Better?"

"Much."

"So why are you here?" He took a seat in the chair next to me and picked up the glass.

"Well, we haven't seen you in a while, and . . . I was wondering if you planned on ever coming back?"

"Is there a reason to? Is everything okay?"

"You mean with Sarah?"

He reached for the glass and took a drink. "Or whatever."

"You still love her, don't you?"

"And why would you think that?"

"Because I saw the way you looked after her enchantment broke. You thought she didn't love you anymore, and it hurt you."

He was silent.

"Why are you pretending it doesn't hurt?"

"Because it doesn't."

"Why are you lying?"

"Because I don't feel hurt, Maddy. Pain empowers me because I'm a dark lord and that's just how it goes."

"But you're not happy."

"Of course I'm not happy."

"Then why are you doing this? Why are you staying

away?"

"Because I *have* to, okay, Maddy? Because Sarah is better off without me."

"How can you say that?"

"Look at me, Maddy!" he shouted, and his eyes were blacker now. They were sunken into a paler face than I remembered. "I'm no good for her." He downed the rest of his drink and set the glass abruptly on the table.

"What's happening to you?"

"Being around Sarah made me a better person. I was taking light from her."

"Well, then you should definitely see her again. You look like shit."

He ignored my joke. "And guess what happens when I take her light? . . . She becomes darker."

I considered the impact of that statement. "And that's why you've been avoiding her."

He nodded. "Until she finds that cure, she can't surround herself with someone like me."

I went to him and took his colds hands. His eyebrows puckered, and I could tell he didn't enjoy my touch.

"Luke," I said, keeping my hands on his, "she's been a mess. She won't open her world. She doesn't sleep. She needs you."

He pulled his hands from mine and turned away. "That's where you're wrong. She needs Drew."

"What?"

"She kissed him. Did you forget about that?"

"I know." I flinched, the pain of this memory was like a slap in the face. If he thought he was the only one tortured by that kiss, he was wrong. "But that was a mistake, Luke, and it was their enchantments that connected them. That's over now."

"But now she has the darkness in her, which fills her with a greed and need that she won't be able to control, and that darkness gets stronger when she's around me, so why would I subject myself and her to that?"

I took a deep breath and exhaled slowly. "Fine," I said. "Suit yourself. But just so you know, she's miserable right now."

"I can't fix that."

"Maybe not, but you could help us find the cure."

"As soon as that world is open, Maddy, what the hell do you think I'll be doing?"

"What do you mean?"

"The minute she crosses over into Yelram, she unlocks her world for the rest of us." He clutched the key at the end of his necklace and said, "Take me to Yelram." Nothing happened. "See? She hasn't opened her world yet."

"Then you do care."

"Of course I care. I want her to find the cure, but I don't want to be the reason she turns before she does."

"That's not going to happen," I said, dismissing his

concern without a second thought. But of course I had thought about it. So had Drew, which was why we had been trying so hard to convince her to open the world so we could start the search for the cure.

"What is she waiting for?"

"Why don't you ask her yourself?"

"Maddy," he began, "I can't be around her. If she hasn't turned already, it won't take much to send her to the dark side."

"Luke," I tried one last time as I felt myself waking, being sent from his world, "you're our last hope."

# CHAPTER 1

# *Moving Out*

## ~ SARAH ~

MADDY WAS FINALLY starting to stir, and I let her assume she was still alone as I laid quietly next to her. Finally, her eyes opened, the fog of her last dream all over her tired face.

"Damnit," she said when she realized where she was.

"It's nice to see you, too," I teased. "Good morning."

"He sent me out of my dream," she grumbled, her voice hoarse from a full night of sleep.

"Who?" My breathing ceased as I waited for her response. "Where did you go?" I asked.

"Nowhere," she said, but it was a clear lie. Maddy never lied well.

"Maddy," I warned.

"Etak," she finally admitted.

"Why?" I sat up, not taking my eyes from hers for even a second. I needed to know every single detail of her dream, but I couldn't let on that I cared. No, that was a sign of weakness, and she couldn't know how much it hurt to have him gone.

"I thought I could convince him to convince you to start looking for the cure."

"And let me guess, he doesn't want to."

"No, it's not that," she began, but I could tell she was protecting me from something. "He's just been . . . dealing with some stuff."

There was more to the excuse, but she was guarding her thoughts well, so I didn't push any further. Besides, I didn't want to hear that he didn't love me anymore. I was just finally starting to be able to breathe without the crippling pain of loss in my chest.

"It's alright," I said. "The enchantments changed all of us. It's better that we just get on with life separately."

"Okay," Maddy said, "and are you ready to actually do that then?"

"No." I lied back down and rolled away from her so that she wouldn't see the pools of water forming in my eyes.

"Sarah, it's been two months." Her voice was soft with sympathy.

Fifty-eight long, agonizing days to be exact. But that didn't change the fact that I still wasn't ready. I had just found out that my mother sacrificed herself to hide the key for me inside a beast that nearly killed me and my friends. And now I had to go into a world that was overrun with monsters that were sent there to kill my family and my people. More beasts that wanted my blood.

Was I ready to die? And if I didn't go, what was the worst that could happen to me here? I would slowly turn into a dark lord. Like Luke. I missed him so much that it hurt every time I thought about him. I squeezed my pillow tighter, willing for the memory of him to be gone.

"Sarah," Maddy tried again, "the longer you wait, the harder it will be. You're more ready now than you were on the quest—you have all seven crafts now."

"I know," I said, but saying it didn't make it any easier.

"What are you waiting for?"

I blinked, and my eye leaked over my nose and dripped onto my pillow. "I don't know. A sign, maybe? Motivation?"

"Is it not motivation enough to know that you could die if you don't get that cure?"

"I won't die," I said. "My key heals my body."

"But not your soul."

"My soul won't die."

"It'll just turn black," she said, insinuating that this was as bad as death.

A knock came to the door right before it was abruptly opened.

"Sarah? You awake?" It was my foster mother and she didn't care if I was awake or not, she was coming in.

"What is it?" I said as I quickly wiped the tears from my face.

"Just dropping off some more boxes." She came in and looked around. "I see you haven't started packing yet."

I felt Maddy's eyes on me, but I ignored them. "No, I haven't. But don't worry, I'll get it done."

"It's Thursday, Sarah. We have another child moving in on Monday, and I need at least a couple of days to paint the walls that you destroyed with pictures."

"Darlene, I'll be gone by my birthday. Don't worry."

She sighed heavily, rolled her eyes, and then left my room, closing the door behind her.

I threw my blankets off and went to my closet. I plucked off a row of shirts and tossed them into a box.

"What's going on?" Maddy finally asked.

"I'm eighteen on Saturday."

"So?"

"So they no longer get money for me."

"Yeah, but are they really kicking you out?"

"It's fine," I said. "I don't want to be here anyway."

16

"Where will you go?"

"I don't know."

"Are you okay?"

"I'm fine. I'm used to being abandoned."

She didn't ask any more questions, but a minute later I heard her re-packing my clothes. And ten minutes later, Drew walked into my room, smiled sympathetically, and began peeling pictures off my walls and packing them neatly into a box. No one said anything, but that was how I wanted it. I kept my face turned toward the closet as I secretly wiped the tears that silently fell. When each box was packed, Drew quietly left the room with it. This continued for most of the day until the room was empty and the three of us stood there together staring at the bare walls.

"You'll stay with me," Drew said, then wrapped his arms around me and let me quietly cry into his chest. Maddy's hand was on my back, and I heard her sniffle, which let me know that I wasn't alone in my sadness.

MY BOXES WERE stacked neatly in Drew's room when we got there. His bed had my pillow in the middle and my dreamcatcher hanging overhead.

"This is your room now," he said.

"Where will you sleep?"

"Dad's old room. He hasn't slept in the house since mom died. It's fine."

"Thank you," I said quietly.

Maddy started to unpack one of the boxes, but I stopped her. "I don't want to do that right now," I said. "I think I'll go for a run."

"A run?" Drew said, a hint of laughter in his voice. "Since when do you run?"

I elbowed him playfully in the side. "Started a few weeks ago. I normally run at night. It helps clear my head."

His smile faded pretty quickly, and he nodded. "Did you want one of us to go with you?"

I shook my head. "I'd prefer to be alone right now."

I reached into my duffel bag next to my bed and retrieved my bow and satchel of arrows. Neither asked any questions as I left the room and departed through the front door.

The wind whipped through my hair, invigorating me with a euphoric sense of freedom as I ran from my struggles and worries, leaving them far behind. This was how I coped with Luke's abandonment. This was how I coped with my foster parents telling me they didn't want me anymore. This was how I coped with Drew no longer loving me. My mother abandoning me. Lucia's death.

Before long I was crying, and my tears were drying on my face as fast as they came. As I neared the meadow, the branches whipping at my face, I forced my energy down through my legs and leaped into the air, bending gravity so that I could soar higher and higher. There was a freedom that came with gravitybending, and I liked the feeling of it. It was probably the craft I enjoyed the most. Drew was impressed with how fast I was learning the craft, but always encouraged me to practice the others, too.

When I landed in the meadow, I pitched a ball of water toward the apple tree. It narrowly missed, so I hurled another and another until they were hitting the exact places I had intended. Then I threw my hands upward, sending a stream of water into the sky, and then spread my arms apart and watched as the water rained down on everything in the meadow.

But this exhausted me. Harnessing the crafts was tiring, which was why Drew insisted that I practice and build up my tolerance and endurance.

Firebending came easiest for me. I didn't like to think of the reason why—I was more like a dark lord than a light lord—but I felt it was obvious, despite Drew's insistence that it wasn't.

Fire always seemed to linger at my fingertips. It was actually more difficult to contain the fire than it was to let it loose. And even at that moment, my fingertips were being licked by flames. I moved them around in circles, mesmerized by the flickering light that played so innocently. Suddenly, a vision of Luke entered my head, and I threw my hand toward the grass, letting the flame spread to the ground. Of course a stream of water was right behind it, but it did feel good to let the fire out. Even if just for a second.

The beating beneath my soles was elevated now, and I felt the Earth's disapproval. She didn't like that I had recklessly set her on fire. I kicked off my shoes and let my feet sink into the cold, brittle grass. Beneath that frosty exterior, though, lay a hot molten core that beat with an intense energy—Earth's heartbeat. I loved feeling her beating against my skin.

I loved feeling Luke against my skin too.

I shook my head, mad at myself for letting him slip into my mind again. I pulled an arrow from my satchel and fired it into the tree's trunk.

An arrow for Luke.

An arrow for my foster parents.

One for Drew.

Another for Lucia.

One for my mother.

Before long, my satchel was empty. I extended my arm and, bending air, pulled each arrow out of the trunk one by one. As each arrow let go, I felt the losses of love even more.

Feeling utterly defeated, I collapsed on the ground at the base of the tree. And there, I rested my eyes and let the stress of the day carry me away to a dreamless sleep.

THE GROUND WAS cool and hard, and as my awareness came back to reality, I realized I had been sleeping. I sat up suddenly and grabbed my bow. How had I fallen asleep? And was that morning dew on the grass? Had I slept all night?

"You slept well," Drew said, and he jumped down from the branch above, landing next to me.

I clutched my chest, then smacked him. "You scared the hell out of me!"

"If it were only that easy," he teased.

"I fell asleep." I let him gather me into his arms. "I'm sorry. I hope I didn't scare you."

"I knew where you were going," he said, nudging my bow. "I brought you a blanket so you wouldn't freeze, although you didn't need it, so I used it." He grinned.

The coldness suddenly swept over my body. "How did I not freeze?"

"I guess that fur coat really does keep you warm." He winked.

"Fur coat?" I looked down at my sweater and jeans. What was he talking about?

He looked at me strangely. "You bent," he said. "You slept as a tiger all night."

"What? Are you sure?" *A tiger?* I ran my hand down my arm as if expecting to find some evidence of my transition.

"You didn't mean to?" Drew was just as confused as

I was.

"No," I said. "I didn't practice shapebending at all." It wasn't a secret that shapebending was my least favourite craft to practice. Shapebending was Ella Ingram's craft, and Ella was my least favourite person. I wondered if she and Luke had gotten back together since his enchantment broke. It had been two months. She had plenty of time to sink her claws back into him.

"Don't let your mind go there," Drew said.

I nodded.

"You must've changed while you were sleeping. Your body needed more warmth, so you just morphed into a tiger."

"That's weird, though, right?"

"Normally, yes, but after all the things I've seen you do these last few weeks, nothing surprises me anymore."

"I didn't hear or feel you at all," I said, panic rising a little. "How did I not hear you?"

"You were tired. How much sleep have you been getting?"

I turned away from him, avoiding his eyes. "Not much."

"Sarah?"

"I can't sleep, Drew. It's so hard to close my eyes because every time I do, I see him. I keep seeing his face after his enchantment lifted. He was . . ." my voice trailed off in an effort to stop the cry that wanted to escape with my next words.

Drew pulled me back into his chest.

"He left me," I cried. "I knew it could happen, but I thought he really loved me. I thought we were different."

Drew didn't have the words for me, but his warm embrace and strong caressing hands were enough. At least Drew hadn't abandoned me.

WHEN WE ARRIVED back at the house, Drew insisted that I lie down and try to get some more sleep, so that was where I spent most of the day. I still saw Luke when I closed my eyes, but it wasn't sadness I felt anymore. I was done feeling sorry for myself. I was angry now. Angry that he did this to me. Angry that he didn't follow through with his promise to fake it until he fell in love with me again. Not that I wanted him to do that. I had warned him not to, but would it have hurt less?

# CHAPTER 2

# *The Surprise*

## ~ SARAH ~

**DINNER WAS READY** by the time I emerged from Drew's room feeling well-rested and much better. Maddy had made spaghetti and meatballs, and they were just about to sit down, so I grabbed a plate and joined them.

"Feeling better?" Drew asked as I shoved a forkful of pasta into my mouth.

"Much. Thank you," I said.

"You *sound* better." Maddy smiled and gave Drew a promising look.

"Been thinking a lot," I said. "I've felt sorry for myself for far too long. I think it's time to get on with life."

Drew nodded slowly. "And . . . go to Yelram?"

"I don't know if I'm ready for that yet." I spun my fork around, trapping a strand of spaghetti. "I just . . . what if I fail?"

"What do you mean what if you fail?" Maddy said with a chuckle. "Fear of failing has never stopped you before. What's so different about this?"

"Because maybe now I know what failure feels like." I ignored the squeezing in my heart.

"You haven't failed," Drew said, pointing his fork at my chest, which was undoubtedly meant as a reference to my key necklace. "Somehow, and don't ask me how, you manage to get everything you set your mind to."

"Not everything," I muttered begrudgingly, although I regretted it instantly. It sounded childish.

Drew dropped his eyes to his plate. "Listen, Luke has some things he has to deal with too, and—"

"Two months," I said, cutting him off. "It's been two months, Drew. I haven't seen him. I haven't heard from him. But I know he's alive and well because Maddy at least got to see him."

"Sarah, he has a lot going on," Drew said.

I shook my head. "I don't know why you defend him. He hurt me, Drew."

"I know, Sarah. And I wish that he hadn't, but . . ." He struggled to find the right way to say something he knew I wouldn't like. "I mean, it's not a *huge* surprise that he was enchanted, and I just think . . . he's been a big help.

He's a good ally. He's proven himself trustworthy . . . and I'm sure he'll come around."

"I don't want him to *come around*. I just want to forget about him."

Maddy inhaled deeply, and she and Drew exchanged an awkward look.

"What?" I snapped. "If you have something to say, by all means, say it."

"Nothing," Maddy said.

"I think you two should go see a movie," Drew suggested.

"That's a great idea," Maddy piped up.

"Oh, I don't know," I started, "I don't really feeling much like—"

"Aw, come on, Sarah. It's been so long since we've done anything fun together. Let's go. Just you and me."

"Okay," I conceded. "But the early show. I don't want to be up too late."

"You're starting to sound old," Drew teased.

"I'll be eighteen tomorrow," I reminded him. "I *am* old."

I HAD FORGOTTEN what it felt like to laugh. Maddy and I had had so many good times together over the years, and I had almost let myself forget them all in exchange for the drama and heartache of the last six months.

After the movie, we went for ice-cream and

reminisced about our first sleepover, our grade seven science fair project that we did together (well, the one we *threw* together an hour before school because we stayed up and giggled all night and didn't manage to get anything done), our first crushes, and our more recent, serious relationships—Caleb and Luke. The conversation died a little at this topic. Maddy was mad at herself for ever trusting Caleb enough to give a piece of herself to him, and I wasn't particularly in the mood to ever remember Luke again. I had resolved to put him out of my mind and accept the loss.

Maddy texted Drew before we left the ice-cream shop and told him we were on our way back. She was going to stay and have a sleepover with me, like old times. We drove slowly up Drew's street, and when we got close to his house, I noticed cars parked along the side of the road.

Maddy pulled into Drew's driveway, parking behind a car that I didn't recognize.

"Who's that?" I wondered.

Maddy shut off the car and mumbled, "Don't know," then opened her door and got out. "Come on," she called before slamming her door.

An uncomfortable feeling sat in my stomach, so I scanned the cars on the side of the street and noticed Nicole Filmore's little white Volkswagon Golf . . . and Joel Trider's pick-up truck. . . and Kate MacDonald's black Civic. Where was everyone? I hadn't heard of any parties happening in our neighbourhood. The only birthday I knew of was mine, but . . .

I grabbed Maddy's arm before her fingers touched the front door. "Maddy," I said slowly, my heart racing, "is this a surprise party?"

"What?" Maddy had a look of intense excitement all over her face.

"Are you kidding me right now?" I threw my hands into the air and sat down on the step. "Tell me you're kidding me. You did not just invite a bunch of random people here tonight."

"I can honestly say that no, we did not *just* invite a bunch of random people here tonight."

"What's your play on words here?"

"We didn't *just* do it. . . . It's been planned for a few weeks."

I inhaled deeply. "I am so mad at you right now."

"Aw, come on, Sarah, it'll be fun." She extended the last word so that it was drawn out and annoyingly cute.

I sighed. "Who's all in there?"

"I don't know for sure, but I know Nicole, Mikayla, Kate, Jessica, Emily . . ." she continued rhyming off names from our graduating class. "Austin, Andre, Morgan, Jake, Brody, Tyler . . ." and then a bunch of Drew's friends that Maddy and I hung out with on occasion too. "Joel, Keagan—"

"Wait!" I interrupted. "Keagan who?"

"The only Keagan we know."

"Holly's boyfriend?"

"They're not together anymore. And that only lasted for like a minute."

After Drew dumped Holly for me, she had set her sights on Keagan Wild, the most sociable, outgoing guy in school. Every girl had a thing for him at least once throughout their high school experience, and if I was being honest with myself—even I did. And the fact that he was at my party made my stomach twist into knots.

"Are you okay?" Maddy asked.

I took a deep breath. "I hate surprises."

"Well, it's not really a surprise anymore, is it?"

I rolled my eyes.

"But can you do me a favour and at least *act* surprised? Drew put a lot of work into it, and he'd be so disappointed if he knew you knew."

I fake-smiled. "Sure, I'll pretend to be surprised."

Maddy pushed open the door, and I looked down at her feet as I followed her in. I kept my eyes low until everyone had a chance to coordinate their simultaneous "SURPRISE!" and then I gasped and threw my hands over my mouth. It only took a few seconds and then everyone was back to laughing, chatting, hugging me, hugging Maddy, and then the music was cranked up and the party was in full swing.

Maddy leaned into me as she took my coat. "Well

done."

I was greeting a group of friends when Keagan and Joel approached.

"Eighteen, huh?" Joel said as he took my hand and twirled me around as if inspecting me.

I pulled my hand from his. "And still human," I added, much to the delight of the girls, and Keagan.

"Still single?" Joel asked.

I blushed, and I wished all eyes weren't on me.

"If she was, do you think she'd want you?" Keagan teased his friend.

I was glad to have the distraction, and when more friends came over to join the banter with Keagan and Joel, I slipped away and into the kitchen to grab a drink.

"Hey, birthday girl," Drew said as he opened a bag of chips and poured the contents into a bowl. "Were you surprised?"

"First of all, it's not my birthday until tomorrow," I reminded him.

"I know, but I figured we had a better chance of surprising you *before* your actual birthday."

I grinned, and he smiled too, but then his faded as he studied my face. "You knew, didn't you?"

"No, not at all!" I assured him, although his eyes were narrowed and I knew he wasn't buying it. "Well, not until I saw the cars anyway," I added.

"I knew I should've gotten them to park around the

corner. I just figured most people would walk." He crouched lower so his mouth was at my ear. "Do me a favour and don't tell Maddy that you knew? She's been planning this for weeks."

I chuckled at their communal concern for each other, then pulled an invisible zipper across my lips and winked.

Keagan came into the kitchen and grabbed a bottle from the box on the floor next to the fridge.

"You look good, Sarah," he said as he popped his bottle cap and tossed it back into the box. "I remember when we were in grade nine together."

I smiled and nodded. I remembered it too, although I was sure my memory was much different than his—mine would have been of me drooling over the cutest, blonde-haired kid in art class who was able to burp the alphabet, and his memory was undoubtedly of the awkward red-head who painted the same thing over and over again every class—a tiger wearing rainbow stripes.

"Will you save me a dance later?" he asked, and his eyes were softer than they were a minute ago.

Drew cleared his throat, reminding me that we weren't alone.

"Yeah, maybe later," I said.

Keagan smiled, nodded at Drew, and returned to the back deck where the party had migrated.

"What was that all about?" Drew casually asked

when we were alone again.

"He's got potential," I said, grinning at the idea of it, although my stomach still twisted and turned as if I was betraying my heart.

"Nah," Drew said. "He's no good for you."

I shrugged. "He's a good distraction."

AS THE NIGHT went on, I loosened up and began enjoying the fact that this was my night. My chance to unwind and let go. Surrounded by friends and good music, a bonfire, and unlimited snacks, I wasn't tired anymore. I was happy. Alive. And I was ready for that dance with Keagan.

I found him standing near the fire talking to Nicole and Mikayla. When he saw me coming, he reached for me and I took his hand, letting him pull me toward them as if this was natural and we had done it a hundred times before. And I supposed that it was natural given our free-spirited demeanors at the moment, with far too many empty bottles as evidence that our characters were being altered.

"I was thinking I'd see if you were still available for that dance," I said, leaning on him more than I had intended.

Nicole laughed and then took my bottle. "How about I hold this while you go dance."

I heard the sizzling of the liquid on the fire as Keagan

took me in his arms for a slow dance to Sweet Home Alabama.

"You're feeling good," he said as he spun me around and caught me in his arms again.

"Yup. Decided it's time to put aside the shit that makes me sad, and surround myself with the things that make me happy."

"Well, I hope I can be one of those things," he said, watching my eyes as I tried to focus on his. His were glassy, but not nearly as unfocused as I knew mine were. He was better at managing his bottles than I was.

As we danced, with his arms on my waist and my arms draped over his shoulders, thoughts of Luke floated into my head. I tried to push him from my mind, but it was difficult not to think of him when he was the only other person I was ever this close to. Other than Drew, but we had already established that relationship was a result of our mutual enchantments.

But Luke was real. What I felt for him was real, and he just disappeared from my life. He just left me. My eyes prickled and I caught myself before it went any further.

"Wow, you feel like you're on fire," Keagan said.

Instinctively, I pulled away, willing the heat in my hands to resign. "I'm sorry," I said. "It's the fire."

It was true—it was the fire, but not the one blazing behind us; it was the one raging inside my body, begging to be let out.

"It's okay," Keagan said. "It was nice, actually."

Suddenly, Nicole gasped as Mikayla said something about the patio. I followed their eyes to a crowd up on the deck. Most people were turning now, watching a tall figure standing near the patio door. I couldn't make him out as it was too dark and the ground was swaying too much, but Nicole looked at me strangely and an uncomfortable feeling swept over me.

"You okay?" Keagan asked as he pushed a strand of hair from my face.

"I . . . may need to sit down. I'll be back." I left him by the fire and, focusing on each step and the ground just ahead, slowly made my way toward the house.

I was only a few feet from the patio when I saw him. He had been watching me, too, and his face was a mask of displeasure. He stood taller than most of the others on the deck, and wore dark blue jeans and a fitted white t-shirt. He was well-defined, even more so than when I saw him last. His hair was dark and messy, and I tried not to remember how I loved to run my fingers through it.

"Luke," I said, his name slipping too easily from my lips.

# CHAPTER 3

# The Real Surprise

## ~ SARAH ~

"CAN WE TALK?" he said, but he made no gesture to reach for me or embrace me like every other person had done when they greeted me that night.

"Aren't you even going to say happy birthday?" I said, feigning playfulness at the pleasure of the drink that had intoxicated me.

"I will," he said. "Tomorrow."

"Oh, you plan on talking to me tomorrow, do you?"

"Maybe," he said, and his eyes narrowed on mine.

I stumbled up the couple of steps so that I was only a foot from him now. Most of our audience had reconvened their conversations.

"Why did you come here?" I asked, my heart beating faster now.

"To see you."

"Miss me, do you?" It wasn't as clear and precise as I had meant. My eyes wandered around the floor and the backs of some of my friends, and then fell onto his chest.

"Can we go inside?" he asked. "You need some water and you should really sit down."

He reached for me, but the thought of our hands touching scared the hell out of me. I pulled back and nearly fell down the steps. His hands were on me anyway, regardless of how confident my efforts were, and with one hand on my lower back and one hand on my arm, he led me inside.

We passed the kitchen where Maddy was busying herself with mixing more punch, and Drew had his head down, reorganizing the contents of the fridge. There were two other couples in the living room and Luke was annoyed by this, but as he tried to steer me to the front door, I pulled away.

"What do you think you're doing?" I shouted.

"I want to talk to you. In private."

"You don't get that luxury, Luke! You're not my boyfriend anymore."

"Sarah, please don't push me away."

"What do you want from me, Luke? You want me to tell you I still need you? Well, I did. I needed you, but you abandoned me. You left me like you promised you never would. And that's okay, you know why? Because you were just doing what I told you to do. Not faking it. So in the end, it's not your fault. It's mine. You don't love me anymore, and I don't need you anymore."

"Sarah, I wasn't enchanted."

I had been turning away from him, prepared to go back to Keagan by the fire, but these last words stunned me. They slapped me so hard that I almost felt sober.

I stared at the door—my intended destination. "What did you say?"

"I mean, I *was*, but not the way you think."

"What are you saying, Luke?" I wanted so badly for his words to make sense and for the room to stop spinning.

"I was only enchanted to protect you from the beast. I wasn't enchanted to love you. That part happened all on its own."

I slowly turned back to face him, apparently needing his arm for stability. "So when the enchantment broke, your love didn't? You still felt the same toward me?"

"Yes." His eyes lit up as if this was what he had been dying to tell me.

"Great," I said, stepping away from him. "You loved me and you *still* left me. . . . I think I liked it better the other way." I wanted to make more sense, but my mind and mouth weren't connecting well.

"I didn't want to leave you, Sarah."

"But guess what, Luke? You did."

"I had stuff to deal with."

"Like what? What was more important than telling me you still loved me?"

"You wouldn't have believed me," he said. "And I didn't have the energy to try to convince you. I was . . . I was hurt too."

"*You* were hurt."

"Yes, Sarah, you kissed Drew, do you remember? Do you know how much that hurt? And when the enchantment was broken and my darkness returned, that kiss became the centre of my thoughts all of the freaking time. . . . Okay? I've been trying to get past it, Sarah, because I don't want to lose you, but it's hard. And I don't want my darkness bringing you down further."

"I know how you feel," I said. "It still burns when I think about you and Ella."

"Don't bring that into this, Sarah. You know it's not the same thing. You and I weren't together when I was with her."

"If you still loved me like you said you did, then you shouldn't have done it."

"Did you not love me when you kissed Drew?"

"Damnit Luke, that was different!"

"Why? Because you loved Drew, too?"

"Yes!"

He froze, a mixed look of hurt and anger on his face. "You see how it's different now?" he said, his voice low and pleading. "You kissed someone you loved. I kissed someone I hated because it made me feel closer to you."

I didn't know what to say. Was he right? My thoughts were too fuzzy to be sure, and I was having a harder time coming up with a rebuttal. But I still couldn't forgive or forget the pain I felt whenever I thought about him with Ella. Or worse, him leaving me.

"You left me." My voice was weak and frail and I didn't like it.

"I'm sorry."

I shook my head, hoping the tears that were threatening to appear would go away. "I can't go through that again."

"Sarah, I won't . . . I—"

"Don't touch me." I pulled away from him again, and stepped into Keagan, who was now standing next to me. How long had he been there?

"Is everything okay here?" Keagan asked. He glared at Luke, clearly siding with me on whatever disagreement he imagined we were having.

"There's no problem," Luke said calmly, but his jaw clenched, and I recognized the glint in his eye meaning he welcomed the challenge.

"That's not the way I see it," Keagan said. "Looks to me like you're harassing the birthday girl." Keagan stepped forward, positioning himself between me and Luke, and only leaving a chest-width between them.

"You're going to want to back the fuck up," Luke growled.

"And who's gonna make me?" Keagan laughed. "You think you can beat me?" At Luke's grin, Keagan added, "In your dreams, man."

"How about in *your* dreams?" Luke said, but it was said so low that I wasn't sure if Keagan had even heard.

Maddy appeared suddenly between the two, but they didn't take their eyes from each other. I knew Luke wouldn't swing first; he was stronger than that, so I slid my hand around Keagan's, hoping it would relax his fist.

"What the hell is going on here?" Maddy said, shoving her hand into Keagan's chest. "Luke is Drew's best friend, and you need to get out of his face right now."

"Chill, pipsqueak," Keagan laughed, messing up Maddy's hair. Maddy inhaled slowly and deeply, and then it was Luke's turn to come to her aid.

"Maddy," he said as he took her right arm which was tense and sporting a clenched fist, "he's not worth it."

"You're right," Maddy snarled.

Keagan turned to me. "What's your deal? You staying here with this guy?"

Luke's eyes fell to mine, and I felt, for one second, his regret and misery. But I wanted him to know that I had control over who I chose to love. And I didn't choose to be loved by someone who could abandon me in my weakest hour.

"Yeah, I'm done here," I said, and Luke's eyebrows darted up.

"Sarah," Maddy tried, but I left her standing there with Luke as I took Keagan's hand and pulled him toward the side door.

We passed Drew in the kitchen on our way out. He was talking to a group of friends, but when he saw me, he grabbed my arm. "Where are you going?" His eyes fell to my hand holding Keagan's. "Luke's here," he added quieter.

"I know," I said, smiling sarcastically. "Would've been nice to know he was coming."

"What's this?" Drew asked, motioning toward Keagan, who wasn't paying attention to our exchange, and instead engaging in another friendly discussion with the other guys in the kitchen.

"It's a distraction," I said.

"You don't need this, Sarah."

"How do you know what I need anymore, Drew?"

He opened his mouth, but then closed it.

Luke came into the kitchen, followed by Maddy. "Sarah," he said.

I only glanced at Luke before turning to Keagan, and taking his face in my hands, I pulled Keagan's mouth to mine. He reacted by sliding his hand around my waist and drawing me closer, but I was being pulled away at the same time.

"Keagan, get out, man," Drew said through gritted teeth.

"What? I thought you two were done?"

"We are," he said, glaring at me, "but she's drunk and you need to go."

Keagan raised his hands, a sign of respect in Drew's house. "Sarah, give me a call sometime," he said before taking his leave.

I slowly turned back to Drew and raised my chin in defiance. He just shook his head.

"You done now?" Luke said, a look of interest on his face.

"Done what?"

"Done proving your point. I get it, but whether you like it or not, Sarah, you still need me."

"I do not," I said firmly.

"You do." He took a step forward so that we were closer than I was comfortable with. "You need me to help get your world back. I know those monsters in there. I know how to defeat them."

Drew was clearing everyone out of the kitchen and into the backyard toward the bonfire. Soon, we were alone.

"I don't love you," I said, swallowing the lump in my throat while keeping my mind strong, not letting anything leak.

He watched me for a few long seconds. "That's fine."

I tried to keep my face void of emotion, but it hurt. "Good then. So we agree that you helping me is just a business arrangement."

"Just business," he repeated, keeping his eyes locked on mine.

"Then I'll have Drew let you know when we plan to go."

"About that," he started. "When will that be?"

"I don't know," I snapped. "That's why I said Drew would let you know."

"Sarah, you've had the key for two months."

"Don't judge me!" I shouted.

"And you'll be eighteen tomorrow."

"You can go now."

"I'm just saying I think it's time."

"Well, thank you for your input. I'll take it into consideration when I'm planning the biggest, most dangerous challenge of my life."

He shook his head and bit his lower lip. "We need to find that third ingredient before you push away everyone who cares about you."

"I'm not pushing anyone away."

"No? Sure feels like it."

"How would you know what it's like to feel anything?"

"Okay," Luke said, stepping back. "I'm leaving now. Nice to see you, Sarah."

"Wish I could say the same."

He shook his head, took his key, and left me standing alone, broken into a million pieces. But what choice did I have? I needed to build a fortress around my heart. It was the only way to protect it from my darkness. I wouldn't let the promise of love get in the way of my purpose. I wouldn't let my feelings for someone else dictate my goals. I needed to do this for me.

# CHAPTER 4

## *Ready*

### ~ SARAH ~

MY PHONE VIBRATED against my bedside table, startling me from a deep sleep. I had gone to bed shortly after Luke left, my appetite for fun and excitement having been flushed away with his departure. Why had he come? Did he really want to help me find the cure? Why suddenly *now* did he care? And was his enchantment really just to protect me from the beast—not fall in love with me? If that was true, then what we had was real. So how could he have left me? I sighed heavily and rubbed my head, which hurt more than I hoped.

My phone vibrated again, reminding me that someone was texting. Groaning, I rolled over, plucked my phone from the charger, and curled up with it under the covers.

## KEAGAN

**Today at 8:04am**
*Hey Sarah. Can't stop thinking*
*about that kiss last night. Can I*
*see you today?*

Keagan! My heart pounded with the memory of kissing him. In front of Luke. Of course I had only done it to prove a point, but Keagan liked it. And if I had to be honest, it wasn't that bad. Last year, if I had kissed Keagan Wild, and then he texted the next morning to say he couldn't stop thinking about it, I would've melted with pleasure. Any girl would have. He was insanely cute with wavy blonde hair, and dreamy blue eyes. He could also be easily described as funny, smart, and liked by all.

But he wasn't Luke.

I shook my head. I was being crazy. Keagan made sense. Keagan hadn't abandoned me. Keagan was from *Earth*. Keagan was *normal*. Maybe he wasn't such a bad option after all.

My phone lit up in my hands. This time Keagan was calling.

"Hey," I answered.

"Did I wake you?" His voice was low, seductive, and a little needy.

"Not really," I said. "Well, a little, I guess."

"Shoot. Sorry."

"S'okay."

"So last night . . . I can't stop thinking about that kiss."

"Yeah, I just saw your text."

"I was thinking maybe you and me could . . . you know . . . hang out sometime."

Dating was the furthest thing from my mind, and I wanted to be straight up and tell him that, but he *was* a good distraction. He was my only real connection to Earth and to a normal life.

"Sarah?" he said, reminding me that I had hesitated, busy trying to block images of Luke rolling into my thoughts. *Would I like to hang out with him sometime?*

"Sure," I said, and I felt an odd mixture of guilt and excitement.

"So . . . you're not seeing anyone right now?"

"No," I confirmed.

He was quiet for a few seconds, then asked, "Who was that guy last night? The one you were arguing with?"

"That was nothing," I said.

"Didn't seem like nothing."

My heart squeezed with the agony of trying to define who he was. An ex-boyfriend? Was it really over? I had spent the last two months convincing myself that he would come back for me. And now that he had, my heart was so cold and resistant to letting him back in. I couldn't go through that again. I had lost too much in my life already. It was the loneliest feeling in the world—abandonment.

"He's not an issue," I said. "But it's not like I'm looking for a boyfriend, Keagan. I just agreed to go out sometime. I don't know when, I'm just saying I'm not opposed to the idea."

Keagan was quiet for a minute. "I had a dream about you last night."

"About me?" My senses heightened. Had Luke lured him to Etak? "What was I doing?"

"I don't know," he said. "I never found you. I was looking for you everywhere. Then that *guy* showed up."

"Luke," I said, but it wasn't a question; I knew it was him.

"Yeah. The guy from last night."

"Go on."

"It was weird. He was all like giving me his blessing to be with you and stuff. He was telling me you like sushi and daisies and that you love tigers."

"He said all that?" I was sitting up now, a panic in my voice.

"Yeah," he chuckled. "Dreams can be so weird. I'm sure those things aren't even true."

But they were true. And Luke knew it. Why was he

doing this? Why was he encouraging Keagan and telling him things that I liked?

"Sarah?"

"What?" I brought myself out of my mixed up thoughts. "Sorry, I almost fell asleep there," I lied.

"I should let you go."

"Yeah. I'll call you later?"

"Okay. And . . . thanks for last night."

I was relieved that he couldn't see my face, distorted with amusement. "For . . . kissing you?"

"Yeah," he said quickly. "I mean, it was nice."

"Good-bye, Keagan," I laughed.

"Bye, Sarah. Call me later."

I ended the call and dropped my phone onto my blankets. Did that really just happen? What the hell was Luke trying to prove? This could only mean one thing— Luke was definitely over me. He went so far as to giving Keagan personal info on me. Did he *want* me with someone else?

AN HOUR LATER Drew knocked lightly on my bedroom door, then pushed it open a crack. "You awake?"

"Yeah," I admitted. I hadn't been able to get back to sleep after Keagan's call. I couldn't stop thinking about why Luke would've encouraged him to go for me. As many scenarios as I tried to play, the only one that made sense was that he was over me now and he wanted me to move on too. My chest squeezed with this thought.

"Did you sleep well?"

"Drew," I said, ignoring his question, "I'm ready."

"Ready for what?"

"To take back Yelram."

Drew came in and took a seat next to me. I sat up against the headboard and pulled my knees to my chest.

"Are you sure?"

"Hundred percent."

"What's changed?"

"Taking back Yelram has always been about more than just fighting monsters and reclaiming what's mine. It's been about discovering who I am and fulfilling my purpose." I fought back a sob that crept up my airways. "I never thought I could do it alone, and when Luke left me, I was sure I couldn't."

He squeezed my knee, a sign that he saw my tears.

"I'm ready now. It's time for me to accept my fate and get on with life." A tear slipped out and ran down my cheek, hitting my shirt with a soft sound.

"Come here." Drew pulled me into him and as soon as his big, warm arms were around me, I cried. I cried for Luke. I cried for the empty hole he drilled into my heart when he left. I cried for my mother, and the empty hole she left too. And for Lucia, the fresh memory of her death crippling me with pain. All three had left me. All three had abandoned me. And my heart was full of holes.

I didn't know how long it had been, but I was subdued and resting across his lap when Maddy came to the door.

"Knock knock," she said softly, and then a second later she was sitting on the bed too, caressing my back.

"Is she okay?" I heard her whisper.

He must have nodded as he didn't say any words.

"What's wrong?" Maddy asked quietly, her question directed at Drew.

"She's ready," he answered, his whisper louder and huskier than hers.

I wiped my face with my sleeve, preparing for the inevitable—the follow through.

"When?" Maddy asked, and this time her question was for me.

"Today," I answered.

"Did you get a good sleep?" she asked.

I nodded, and then slowly pushed myself out of bed. I pulled back the curtains and closed my eyes as the sun bathed my face in its warm light.

"Why don't you get ready," Drew said. "I'll call on Luke." He waited for my reaction, but when I didn't give one, he said, "Is that okay with you?"

I rolled my eyes to myself. "I don't care."

BY THE TIME I emerged from the washroom, showered and dressed, Luke was in the living room, standing over

Drew and Maddy while they studied a map spread out on the coffee table. He was wearing a blue t-shirt that hugged his arms and chest just right. My eyes followed it down to where it tucked neatly and seductively behind his belt buckle that topped a pair of dark jeans that also fit perfectly to his body. I wondered how long I had been staring, and I felt my face flush as my eyes slowly raised to meet his. He smiled, hesitantly, which made my chest squeeze. His mind was a fortress. He was blocking me from it. Hiding things from me. My own walls of defense shot up and my body stiffened in response.

"Happy birthday," he said, a playful grin at the corner of his mouth.

"Oh yeah," Maddy piped up. "Happy birthday! I completely forgot!"

"Happy birthday, Princess Sarah," Drew added, exaggerating his words with a bow.

But I ignored them all. My eyes were still glued to Luke's. "So, what? You're a matchmaker now?"

"What are you talking about?"

"Keagan told me about his *dream*. I thought when you said you would see him in his dreams that you meant you would fight him."

"That'd be unfair."

"So you just decided to set us up instead? Tell him all the secrets to my happiness?"

Luke shrugged. "Someone should get to make you

happy."

"That's not up to you," I snapped.

"Apparently."

*You left me!* I thought, directing this shrapnel right into his own thoughts.

For a second, his mind was open and I saw a flash of agony, anger, and resentment. The same feelings I felt. Was I portraying my worst feelings onto him? I tightened up the fortress even more and cleared my face.

"I'm sorry," he said, and I knew this was in response to the thought I hurled at him. Maddy's eyes flashed to mine for a second, then returned to the map.

"Why?" I asked. "Why did you tell him those things?"

"He likes you."

"So?"

"You deserve to be happy."

"I should be the one to decide who I get to be happy with, Luke. Not you."

"Wait," Maddy said, turning to Luke. "What did you do?"

When Luke didn't answer, his regret showed, but I wasn't about to let him get away with it so easily.

"He told Keagan he should go for me, and told him how I like daisies, and sushi, and tigers."

Maddy gasped, her mouth agape as her eyes mirrored her shock.

Luke nodded. "I didn't think he would run back and tell her."

"No," Maddy said, "you just figured he'd use that knowledge to win her over." She pushed her way past him, seemingly unable to stand near him. "Why would you do that?"

"Because he doesn't care about me, Maddy," I said, my eyes staying on Luke's. "If he did, he would know that something like that would really hurt me."

"Sarah—" Luke began, but Drew cut him off.

"Guys, daylight's burning. Let's get this plan in place, okay? There'll be plenty of opportunity to get your anger out on the battlefield."

I turned my eyes away from Luke's and made my way to the chair across the table from him.

"Is this Yelram?" I asked, touching the map that showed a large tract of land laden with ancient lines representing mountains, hills, and rivers, all bordered by ocean.

"It's an old map my father had," Drew answered. "Yelram is a small world, mostly ocean." He pointed to a green area in the Southwest region. Small blue lines ran through this section of the map and I imagined lazy rivers meandering through quiet valleys and picturesque mountains.

"Your palace is in this quadrant." Drew touched a mountainous area near the bottom of the map. "There's a village here too . . . well, more like a town or small city."

"There are towns and cities all throughout Yelram," Luke continued.

"Where's the portal?" I asked.

"In the centre of the four quadrants," Drew explained.

"Here?" I pointed to a place roughly in the middle of the map, appearing to be a circular area, surrounded by mountains.

Drew nodded. "The portal's protected by mountains on all sides, and each mountain range has a pass through it, leading to one of the four quadrants. Each quadrant has its own season."

"Season?" I asked, confused.

"It's always winter in the Northwest," Drew began, "and spring in the Northeast, summer in the Southeast and autumn in the Southwest."

I touched the place where my palace was marked, deep in the Southwest, and I imagined it surrounded by towering trees with the brightest and most beautiful colours of fall.

"Just be prepared for the fact that there won't likely be any survivors," Drew said matter-of-factly.

"But there might be," Maddy offered. "Maybe they had a chance to hide when the monsters came through."

Luke shook his head. "Even if they did, it's been seventeen years. There won't be much left anywhere in the world now."

My heart sank. I had hoped there would be survivors. I had hoped the people would've been able to defend themselves against the monsters. Would they have had time to run? To hide? Would they have known what was about to happen to them?

"The monsters aren't smart," Drew explained. "They're just ferocious and blood-thirsty. The people could've hidden. Found shelter. But after this many years, there's not likely to be any survivors."

I hated the straightforward tone he used to speak about Yelram and my people. I hated that, to him, this was not a rescue mission.

"So what's our plan then?" I asked.

"We kill the monsters while trying to find the last ingredient needed for the cure," Luke said. "The apple was in Nevaeh's Garden of Love, and the honey came from Lorendale's Garden of Faith, so it only makes sense that the third ingredient would also be in Yelram's sacred garden."

"Do we know what the ingredient is that we're looking for?"

"According to the History of the Worlds book," Drew began, "the Garden of Hope is known for its daisies."

An image floated through my mind. I was walking through a field of knee-high daisies, my hand stretched high to hold onto my mother's. Was it a memory? Or just a picture I remembered seeing at one point? Or simply a make-believe memory I concocted on my own?

"Do you remember something?" Maddy asked.

"I may remember the garden," I said, trying desperately to recall the feeling of peace that it brought in the few seconds it was there.

"What do you remember of it?"

"I was with my mother," I told them. "It was a beautiful place. But that's all I remember." I looked up at my friends, my eyes pinballing between theirs. "You don't think the monsters have destroyed it, do you?"

"They couldn't have," Luke said assuredly.

"How do you know?" Maddy pressed.

"Dark souls aren't able to get near the gardens. They're well protected. Full of light."

"Does that mean you won't be able to go in?" Maddy asked, quieter now.

Luke nodded. I considered for a moment that this could mean I, too, would be refused entry. The darkness was slowly infiltrating my soul, I could feel it, but would I still be able to get in? I was the keeper of the world. I was the keeper of the garden.

"Where is this Garden of Hope?" I asked.

The three looked down at the map, but didn't answer.

"You don't know where it is?"

"It's sacred and protected," Drew said. "Only the world's keeper knows where it is." They all turned their eyes to mine.

"Wait," I said, standing up, "are you saying I should know where this garden is?"

"We were hoping," Drew answered.

I hesitantly looked at the map, hoping the secret location would suddenly unveil itself to me. My eyes wandered from the Northwest Quadrant, to the Northeast, to the Southeast, and then finally to the Southwest. Nothing appeared. No magical memory occurred.

"It's okay," Luke said. "I want to take you to your palace first. Maybe something there will jog your memory. We'll be busy killing monsters anyway, and we may come across the garden on our way." He pulled the map from the coffee table and began folding it up. "Here," he said, giving the map to Drew. "Keep this on you. We'll need it in there."

My heart started racing. This was it. This was the moment we all suited up and held hands and I ported them into Yelram, opening my world up to dreamers, subjecting everyone to the dangers and nightmares of what my world had become. This was the moment where I faced my biggest fear—what if I couldn't do it? What if I wasn't cut out to be a Dream Warrior Princess? What if I couldn't take back my world? Where would I belong? Who would I be?

"Sarah?" Luke said, his hand on my arm. I pulled

away.

"I'm fine," I said. "I want to go for a run before we go. Can we leave after lunch?"

"A run? Now?" Maddy laughed. "Why don't you save your energy for Yelram?"

Luke shook his head. "No, she should clear her head. She should go. But not alone. Can I go with you?"

"No," I said, turning away from him. I couldn't let him near me. I couldn't let him hurt me again.

"I'll go," Drew said, and he went to the door and pulled on a pair of running sneakers. I didn't argue with him. I would've preferred to be alone, but at least I knew Drew wouldn't try to talk to me. He'd let me run in peace while he trailed quietly behind.

# CHAPTER 5

# *Confronting Luke*

## ~ MADDY ~

THE MINUTE THE door closed behind Sarah and Drew, I turned on Luke. "What game are you playing?"

He sat down on the sofa, feigning innocence. "What are you talking about?"

"What's your deal with Keagan? Why'd you tell him all that stuff about Sarah? And don't give me the same story about you wanting Sarah to be happy."

"I lured him to Etak."

"That part was obvious."

"I wanted to scare him into leaving Sarah alone."

I nodded. "He's definitely not what she needs right now."

"That's what I thought at first too, but after seeing him in a dream world, I had second thoughts."

"What do you mean?"

"He could be an asset," Luke explained. "He's very confident and strong, which makes him a powerful dreamer. I haven't seen many like him."

"How does that make him good for Sarah?"

"If they get . . . closer . . . then he could help protect her in Yelram."

I shook my head. "I'm lost. How?"

"He's a good fighter," Luke admitted. "Not much scares him, and I think—"

I gasped, cutting him off. "You think he could be a dream warrior and fight with us."

Luke nodded. "Imagine what we could do with him."

"And as a dreamer, he'd be capable of doing much more than even you and Drew," I added. "Luke, this is brilliant!"

"The only one who has real control over a dreamer is the keeper of that world. So as long as Sarah doesn't interfere, we're all good."

"But wait—how do we ensure he goes there when he falls asleep?"

"I may need you for that part. Only Sarah can lure him there, which I don't think she will do. I don't even want to tell her about this."

"I agree."

"But once Sarah crosses the threshold to Yelram, she reopens the world to dreamers, so it's fair game. We just have to convince Keagan that he wants to see Sarah when he goes to sleep, and he should be drawn to her."

"You think that will work?"

He shrugged. "Sarah always came to me when she dreamed. All she had to do was think of me. I never lured her."

"Okay, I'm in. I think it's a great idea. Sarah would hate it, but she hates everything nowadays anyway."

Luke tried to keep the hurt from reaching his face, but I noticed and I softened because of it. "This must be hard for you."

He shook his head. "Nah, I'm fine."

"She still loves you, you know."

His eyes narrowed on mine. "Why do you think that?"

I hesitated because I felt like I was somehow betraying Sarah. "I think . . . it's been really hard on her."

"She was enchanted. She told me."

"Yes, but her enchantment didn't change the way she felt about you. It changed the way she felt about Drew, but not you."

"You think?"

"I know."

"But she said—"

"She said what she had to say to convince herself that

she doesn't need you in her life. The darkness makes it easier for her to shut you out."

He watched my lips as if hoping I'd tell him more about how much she missed him, but I had already said too much.

"And your enchantment didn't change your feelings either," I redirected.

The lines around his lips tightened, impersonating a smile. "Not really."

"What were your terms?"

"To protect her from the beast while she was in Etak."

"Wow. It must have been agonizing for you to watch her fight the beast the first time."

"It nearly killed me. Literally. If I had failed to protect her, the enchantment would have killed me."

"Why did you leave her then? Why didn't you tell her how you felt?"

"Once the enchantment lifted, all the darkness returned to me. I remembered her kiss with Drew, and I was filled with so much jealousy and anger that I couldn't see anything else. I knew I wasn't good for her anymore. Not while she still had to fight off the darkness in her own body." He clenched his jaw. Then he drew in a long, deep breath. "Do you know that every single day—No. Every single *minute* I was away from her, I thought of nothing else? It physically hurt to breathe. I wanted to come back, but I couldn't."

"Why'd you come back now?" I asked.

"After you came to see me, I wondered if maybe I was the reason she hadn't gone. I thought by staying away I was doing her a favour, as much as it killed me. I thought maybe she just needed time to prepare herself. The Sarah I knew would've already been there. . . . I guess I just needed to come back and see what was keeping her from going. I needed to know that it wasn't me."

"What do you think it was?"

"I think she's scared. Finally." He chuckled to himself as if this was the most ironic thing ever, which, in a sense, it was.

"She was always so fearless," I recalled. "But *now* she hesitates. She has a key to heal her body, and she's gifted with seven crafts, but yet she hesitates." I laughed too.

"But her world needs her," Luke went on. "And although sometimes I can't tell if my thoughts are being controlled by my inner demons or my love for her, I need to help her find that cure and take back her world. Even if it means watching her move on with another guy in the meantime."

I reached out and touched his hand. "I'm sorry." I looked down so he couldn't see the pity in my eyes. "Thank you for coming back, even if she doesn't want you here. . . . It must suck."

"That it does." He sighed heavily and gave a fake smile. "What about Drew?" he asked.

64

"What about him?"

"What do you think he'll say about this plan?"

"Why do we have to tell him?" I winked.

Luke nodded. "I guess we don't."

"I'll go talk to Keagan now," I offered, "and plant a couple seeds of wonder and desire."

He nodded and smirked, and although I knew he saw this as an opportunity and advantage for Sarah, he also worried that Sarah might actually end up falling for Keagan.

## CHAPTER 6

# Take Us to Yelram

## ~ SARAH ~

**ALTHOUGH IT WAS** freeing to feel the cool November air at my face, and the hard, almost frozen ground beneath my feet, I felt tethered knowing Drew was keeping pace only a few steps behind. We hadn't said two words to each other, but he left his mind open for me, and I explored it with curiosity. He was revved up over our impending adventure into Yelram. He was proud of me for finally being able to face my fears, and he was confident that we would be successful in our mission and that the people of Yelram (if there were any left) would welcome me back with open arms.

Maybe he left his mind open on purpose. Maybe he

was trying to flood me with these thoughts, hoping I would adopt them as my own. But I wasn't as naïve. This wasn't going to be an easy adventure. If we were somehow able to destroy all the monsters that had likely multiplied over the past seventeen years, we still had to find the cure for my darkening soul, and then win the trust and respect of my people.

MADDY HAD GONE home to take care of some things before we left, so when we got back to the house from our run, Drew made lunch and the three of us ate in silence. When Maddy finally returned, she grabbed a quick bite to eat while Drew packed some food and supplies to last a few days before we'd have to return to Earth for more.

And then it was time to go. Ignoring the chaos of anxiety floating around inside my chest, I took my key in one hand, held Drew's hand with the other (while he held Maddy's, and she held Luke's), and closed my eyes. After taking a deep, shaky breath, I said, "Take us to Yelram."

The key trembled, and then an electrifying pulse ran through my body as we were swept away from Earth and through a deserted portal that had been untouched for far too long.

WHEN MY FEET touched ground again, my eyes were wide, but I saw nothing. I was still holding Drew's hand, though, and he led me through the darkness into the light. I turned around and saw that we had just walked through the face of a mountain. The field in front of us was larger than several football fields and was bordered by enormous mountains on every side. Just as Drew had said, there was a pass through the mountains at each of the four sides.

"We're at the portal," I realized. I wasn't sure why it surprised me, but I had hoped that we would appear on the front steps of my home.

"We'll get you home," Luke said, as if in answer to my disappointment.

An ear-piercing screech split the air. While the others covered their ears, I opened my mind to capture the sound—a monster calling to another. Movement caught my eye from across the field, and I turned in time to see an enormous black figure emerge from the hole in the mountain across from us. It hadn't yet seen us as we crouched lower in the tall grass, but I wondered if it had caught our scent.

"You okay?" Drew said, and I realized I was gripping his hand rather firmly. Luke had his sword drawn and was kneeling close to my right, while Maddy was holding her bow up, an arrow perched and ready to fly.

As my heart beat wildly, I slowly let go of Drew's hand, tucked my key into my shirt so that I could feel its warmth and security against my skin, and pulled my own sword. I was afraid to take a step, as if the whole field was a landmine and would destroy us at my first move.

"Look over there," Luke said, pointing to the right. Cresting over the distant mountaintops, a large, dark circle was emerging in the sky. Although similar to a moon rising, it was much darker and larger.

"What is it?" Drew asked.

"It looks like a moon," Maddy said.

"I've read about this before." A look of concern crossed Drew's face. His eyes moved back and forth across the sky as if he were reading something. "It's a keeper prophecy of some sort."

"It has something to do with me?" I asked.

He nodded. "I think so. We should go see Trinity."

"I agree," Luke said, and he went for my hand. I pulled it away.

"You think we should leave? Just like that? We just got here!"

Maddy's eyes were fixated on the large mass, which was rising quickly and had completed its task of surpassing the mountain's peak. "Sarah, this means something. We need to know what."

"Maybe it's just Yelram's moon," I suggested.

"No," Drew shook his head. "I can feel the darkness in it."

"And I can feel the power from it," Luke added.

Drew grabbed my arm before I could protest. "Take

us to Nevaeh," he said, and we were gone.

WE LANDED IN Nevaeh's garden outside of the golden gates, and it took everything in me not to hit Drew.

"Why did you take me from Yelram?" I demanded.

"Sarah, I don't feel right about that moon. We need to know what it means."

Luke and Maddy appeared a few seconds later. Luke sat down on the nearest bench and put his head in his hands.

"What's wrong with you?" I scoffed.

He didn't answer, but Drew did. "Being in a light world will be physically agonizing for him. . . . Now that his full darkness is restored."

I looked at Luke who wouldn't make eye contact with me. "Why don't you go home?"

"No," he said between gritted teeth.

The gates clanged and then loudly creaked as they slowly opened. Trinity appeared between the gap with a bright light behind her so that we weren't able to see beyond where she was coming from.

"What is it? What is wrong?" she urged, ushering us further into the garden.

"Trinity," Drew began, "we opened Yelram."

Trinity nodded. "It's about time, isn't it?"

"But," Drew continued, "as soon as we got there, a big black moon began rising in the sky." Drew waited for her to respond, but then said, "It means something. It must mean *something*."

"It does," Trinity finally confirmed. She turned to me and took my hands in hers. "How are you feeling, Sarah?"

"I'm fine," I answered.

"Good," she said, "because that black object is not a moon. It is the Eye of Darkness."

Luke stood up as soon as the words left her lips. "No," he said, but it wasn't an objection, it was a plea.

"What does this mean?" I asked her.

Trinity's face was blank as her lips moved in rhyme. "The eye will rise each night and day, three times each then take its prey. When all is gone from this world's light, the keeper's soul turns black as night."

A silence followed. Drew now took a place on the ground with his head in his hands, and Luke was pacing back and forth. Maddy's jaw was slack as the words floated around in her head.

"But . . ." Maddy began, "but why?"

"Sarah's soul has darkness in it," Trinity began to explain, "and because Yelram is connected to her through the keeper key, the moment she crossed into Yelram, the clock began ticking. She now has three days to find the cure and heal her soul before she and Yelram are both taken by darkness."

"But that's impossible," I said. "We can't even begin

to look for the cure until we kill all the monsters, but they're everywhere. It'll take days . . . no, *weeks* . . . just to do that part!"

Luke was standing behind me now, and I felt his hands on my shoulders. "Trinity," he began, "there's got to be a way to stop this."

"I'm sorry, Luke. You should know as well as anyone that once a soul starts darkening, there isn't anything else that can be done to reverse it. She'll need the cure."

"Okay," Drew said, standing up, "so we change our plans. We look for the cure first."

"In a world full of monsters—"

"We don't have a choice, Sarah!" he snapped. "We're not letting this . . . *sickness* take you."

Luke's grip tightened.

"What do I do when I find the third ingredient?" I asked.

"You still have the drink that I gave you?"

"The . . . apple juice?"

Trinity smiled, amused by my innocence. "It is the juice from an apple from the Garden of Love," she explained. "And you have the honey from Lorendale's Garden of Faith?"

"Yes," I answered.

"Then you will find the third ingredient—a plant—in Yelram's Garden of Hope. You will mix these three together and drink them. . . . Before the Eye of Darkness overtakes the sun."

"In three days," I repeated, hoping I had heard wrong.

"We'll need an army," Drew decided.

Luke nodded. "I'll bring forces from Etak."

"Wait," I said, holding my hands up to the both of them. "I don't want to be responsible for any more deaths. It's bad enough that you three are involved. If we bring more people, then there's bound to be fatalities and I—"

"Sarah," Drew cut me off, "we only have three days to find the cure while fighting off a world taken over by monsters. This isn't just about you. It's about the balance of the worlds. We need more men."

"And women," Maddy quickly added, not looking up from her sword, which she was casually inspecting.

"I will also send an army," Trinity added. "The balance of the worlds is an important mission, and I would be remiss if I didn't help in every way that I could."

"I'm sure I can persuade Eli to send some men," Drew said.

"Or women," Maddy added quietly.

Drew ignored her, but a smile was forming at the corner of his mouth. "I'll go see Eli now."

"Good," Luke added, "and I'll go home to round up some men"—he grinned at Maddy—"and women."

Drew nodded, and he was gone with the words, "Take me to Lorendale," Luke following closely behind with his own, "Take me home."

I felt the lump in my throat and could only nod my thanks to Trinity as she turned to leave Maddy and me alone. "Stay as long as you need," she said. "I have an army to prepare. I will send them through your portal when they are ready."

DREW RETURNED WITHIN a half an hour with news that Eli would send re-enforcements straight away. Luke took longer, but when he finally arrived, he had a powerful look of excitement about him.

"Let's go," he said. "My army's already there."

"You sent them in without us?" I nearly shouted.

"That's the whole idea, Sarah. They clear the way for us while we look for the cure."

I didn't like the way it sounded, but we had no other choice. Still, it sickened me to know that hundreds of innocent people would be going to my world to help clean up a mess that was left for me.

I reached for Drew's hand, and when everyone was linked, I led us back to Yelram once more.

# CHAPTER 7

# The Portal

## ~ SARAH ~

IT SHOULDN'T HAVE thrown me back in surprise to
witness it for myself, but it did. The once lonely field was
now crowded with hundreds of blue-clad soldiers on
wolves the size of horses, and it took every effort not to
collapse from the sight of it. These were Luke's soldiers,
evidenced by the way they carried themselves fearlessly,
holding tight with one hand to the mane of their
oversized wolves while wielding their mighty swords
with their other. Together, they fought off one, two, three,
. . . *six* ferocious creatures that were much stronger and
larger. My stomach turned as I witnessed the sea of
soldiers fighting for their lives, some being thrown

hundreds of yards to their deaths, others being ripped in two before they knew what was happening.

But they soon had help, and it filled me with joy to see the men and women in white—Nevaeh's army— emerge through the mountainside, their stunning white-winged unicorns carrying them gracefully to fight alongside their dark world allies on the battlefield.

The contrast in fighting styles was stark—the warriors in white were fluid, precise, and elegant in their movements, while the fighters in blue were aggressively merciless, although each style seemed to bring about the same results—blood and death.

A minute later the portal opened again, and another group of eager warriors came thundering onto the field— Lorendale's army. Their purple uniforms were almost lost in the thick, black—or was it purple?—fur of the large animals that they rode. *Gorillas?* The animals' heavy bodies pounded across the field toward the fight, their riders releasing arrows at the monsters whenever they had a clear shot.

Soon the battle slowed, leaving a wake of fallen warriors and defeated monsters. I tried to see this as a small victory, but the lost lives was no reason to celebrate. Panic churned in my chest when I realized that this was just the beginning. There would be more battles. More challenges. More sacrifices.

The armies organized themselves in groups around

the edges of the field, and their dispersal revealed four leaders remaining in the centre of the field—a purple soldier from Lorendale sat high on his enormous gorilla, while a petite, blonde warrior sat elegantly atop her horned pegasus, and a rugged-looking blue soldier, who was in need of a good shave, rested across a fierce, dark grey wolf. In the middle was a tall officer giving instructions. A tall officer with messy, dark brown hair, a perfectly fitted blue t-shirt and . . .

I spun around when I realized his familiarity. "Where's Luke?" I demanded.

"He joined the fight the moment we got here," Drew answered, nodding toward the centre of the field.

"Why would he do that?" I demanded. As if my thoughts controlled my powers, a second later I was standing next to Luke and the other three warriors.

I looked around, confused for a moment, but I didn't care how I managed to teleport myself, I only cared to hurl my question at Luke. "What were you thinking? You could've been killed!"

"What did you expect me to do, Sarah?" he said as he wiped the blood from his blade and then pushed it back into its holster. "I couldn't just stand back and watch my men get defeated when I knew my presence would bring them strength."

"But—"

"We came here to fight," he said, but then his face

softened, showing that he liked my concern for him. "Don't worry."

"What are our orders?" the man in need of a razor asked Luke. I couldn't help but notice that the other two warriors only watched me. They wanted my orders, not Luke's.

"Sarah," Luke began, "this is Devon, my second-in-command."

"We've met," Devon said mirthlessly. "You're the one who keeps trying to get our keeper killed."

"Devon," Luke warned.

I looked down, embarrassed at his lack of respect.

The other two riders had dismounted the moment Luke addressed me. The purple-clad man took my hand and kissed the top of it. "My Lady," he said, and there was a congenial tone to his voice that I liked very much. "I am Paul, Lorendale's second-in-command, and I am at your service."

I smiled, appreciative of the distraction from Devon whose gaze I felt burning into me. "Thank you, Paul."

The petite woman in white removed her helmet and bowed low, her blonde hair spilling around her face. "It's a pleasure to meet you, Sarah," she said. "I am Hannah, Nevaeh's second-in-command. We are honoured to be helping you in this mission."

"Thank you," I said, feeling my face flush. "Thank you all for coming. I am really grateful."

"How would you like us to proceed?" Hannah asked.

I looked to Luke, as I wasn't sure how to respond. What did I need them to do?

"Hannah," Luke began, "take Nevaeh's army to the Northwest Quadrant. It's winter there. Your white uniforms will blend in well. Paul, lead your army to the Southwest, and Devon, bring our boys through the Southeast Quadrant. We will follow Lorendale's army through the Southwest. Send word if you find the Garden of Hope."

Paul and Hannah stepped forward, producing their keys and laying them on their palms in front of me.

"What . . .? What are they doing?" I said, looking from Luke back to their keys.

"You'll need to touch their keys so that they can port to you if they find the garden."

I touched Hannah's key first, which glowed a bright white. I pulled my hand back a bit too quickly, but recovered my alarm with Paul's key, which I touched without hesitation and didn't pull back when it shone purple.

Devon whipped his key off over his head and held it out for me, but before I could touch it, Luke took it. "You'll report to me," he said, his voice darker than I liked.

"Got it," Devon said as he took his key back, threw it hastily around his neck, then twisted his fingers through the mane of his wolf. I could've imagined it, but it looked as though the wolf narrowed its eyes at me before it turned, taking Devon back toward the army of blue soldiers awaiting their orders.

Paul and Hannah mounted their animals once again. "Is this your wish, princess?" Paul asked, his eyes avoiding Luke's, but I knew this was necessary. He had to receive his orders from me, the world's keeper; not from Luke, a dark lord.

"Yes," I said, a shyness to my voice that I tried to dismiss with my next words. "Please be careful."

Paul nodded and smiled before giving his gorilla a pat on the back so that the animal took him speedily to his waiting army.

Hannah's voice softened. "Be careful too, Sarah. If we find the garden, I will come to you straight away."

"Thank you," I said, and she was gone, departing toward her own army of white.

I watched Luke's army disappear into the mountain's Southeast entrance, then turned to Luke. "Why didn't you want me to touch Devon's key?"

His eyes narrowed, and the muscles in his jaw tightened. "I don't want him near you."

"But he's your second," I said. "What are you afraid of?"

"Let's just say I trust very few people anymore." His mind flashed to his brother, Riley, and then to Ella. Both people he had once trusted but had recently tried to kill me.

"So we have three quadrants covered. What about the Northeast?" Maddy asked, breaking the quiet stare between Luke and me. I hadn't noticed her approach.

"We only have three armies," Luke answered simply. "If we have time, we'll search there after the other three quadrants have been secured. But it's the least likely place for a garden. It's mostly just mountains."

"Why are we going to the Southwest first?" I asked, wondering what our special stopover was for.

"I thought you should see where you were born," Luke said, a softness to his face that was new since arriving here. Being around his army brought darkness out of him. A darkness I didn't like. "And it's more likely that the garden will be near where you lived," he finished.

He turned away and whistled to a nearby wolf. The large black creature came immediately and stood protectively by Luke's side. He whistled to another and it came too. Although a bit smaller and lighter in colour, it was still sturdy and strong.

Luke motioned to the grey wolf. "You and Maddy take that one. Sarah and I will take this one." The black wolf raised its head as if proud to belong to Luke.

My stomach lurched. I didn't know if I could be that close to Luke without losing myself. I needed to stay focused and being near him was difficult. He was a reminder of love lost.

Drew was helping Maddy up onto the grey wolf when he caught me watching. "Are you okay?"

"Can I go with you?" I asked timidly.

"Sarah," Luke started, and I heard the hurt in his voice.

I kept my eyes on Drew as I answered his unspoken question. "I can't, Luke," I said. My eyes watered. "I can't forget."

Luke took my hand and it felt so warm and soft and I wanted him to hold it. I wanted to rewind time and be where we once were . . . before he promised he would never leave me, and then he did. I pulled away.

Drew's answer was delayed and I sensed that he didn't know what he should do. He wanted to ride with Maddy. He wanted to ensure her protection and he wasn't sure Luke would be focused enough on her to be the best man for the job. And he also didn't want to take an opportunity for reconciliation away from Luke. He thought I should forgive him.

"You know what? I'll get my own ride," I decided. I whistled into the field, hoping that somewhere out there in the dreary silence of an abandoned battlefield a warrior animal would hear me and come to my rescue. Preferably one of Nevaeh's beautiful white-winged unicorns. I preferred not to ride one of Luke's scary wolves if I had a choice in the matter.

"Your world doesn't listen to you yet," Drew said softly. "You'll have to earn the respect of its energy before you can command things from it."

"What are you talking about?" I snapped.

Drew was quiet. Everything was quiet. And no animals were coming.

"Why?" I asked.

"You're still forging a bond with it. Yelram doesn't recognize or . . . respect you yet. But when it does, you'll be much more powerful and have things under your control."

Maddy slid off the back of Drew's wolf and went to Luke. He reluctantly stretched his arm down and pulled her up. I pretended not to notice as she held onto him. Drew pulled me atop the grey wolf, and I wrapped my arms tight around his waist.

And we were off. The wind ripped through my hair as we charged across the field toward the hole in the mountain that Lorendale's army had disappeared through only moments before. The herd of gorillas and purple soldiers were far ahead, but their thundering footfalls told us we were heading in the right direction.

The forest was thick on this side of the mountain. The leaves were bright hues of orange, red, yellow, and brown, and I was stunned by their beauty. I loved autumn. It was my favourite time of year for this very reason—the striking colours and crisp, clean air. But then a thought occurred to me—did I love autumn because of the colours? Or did I love autumn because it felt like home? If I was born in Yelram's Southwest Quadrant, and I all I had known were these beautiful colours, then no wonder Earth seemed so bleak eleven months of the year.

It wasn't long before the air was filled with a steady rumble, drowning out the sounds we made by storming through the bushes. We were nearing Lorendale's army, evidenced by the roars from the gorillas and hollers from the warriors. They had found more monsters, and we were about to witness another bloodbath.

# CHAPTER 8

# *Dreamers and Dragons*

## ~ SARAH ~

THE FOREST THINNED as we rode into a clearing that revealed most of the purple warriors at the other end, fighting a pod of at least three enormous, winged monsters, with a clear resemblance to dragons. But then out of the woods from the opposite side, another dragon stormed into the clearing. It let out a stream of fire from his mouth and then bellowed, announcing his presence. Several warriors turned and raged toward it.

"Go, Drew!" I yelled. "Help them!" I kicked at the wolf, but it didn't move.

"No," Drew said, shaking his head and holding tight to the wolf's mane. "They don't need us, Sarah. We have a mission."

"We can't stand back and watch!" I shouted. But he wasn't moving, so I jumped off the wolf and ran, ignoring their yells for me to come back. Within seconds, I was in the midst of the chaos, having ported myself there with just my desire and my key.

It took me a few seconds to gather my bearings, but then I pulled my sword from its sheath as two purple warriors flew through the air and landed not far from me. I tried not to notice the odd angles at which their bodies fell.

Several more warriors were thrown, and three more burned from the fire that left the creature's mouth. Furious, I let out a roar of my own and threw my hand toward the monster as I closed the gap between us. A ball of fire left my fingertips and soared toward the dragon, striking him in the side of the head.

Then Drew flew overhead and released an arrow into the beast's eye, blinding it momentarily, long enough for Luke to throw it back a few feet with a force of wind. The monster was quick to recover, though, and as Maddy rocked the ground with a tremor, a newcomer joined the fight.

He wasn't dressed in purple like the rest of the warriors. He wore jeans and a t-shirt and had wavy blonde hair and bright blue eyes and . . . it was a mistake letting my guard down for that split second. The monster whipped its tail around and I only saw it out of the corner of my eye, about to smash into me, when Luke dove toward me and pushed me out of the way.

I fell back, but someone caught me, his gentle voice reassuring me not to worry because he had me. Luke glanced over his shoulder to make sure I was okay, but when he saw who was holding me, he muttered, "You gotta be kidding me." He returned to the fight and left me wondering whose arms I was in.

I slowly turned, everything inside me telling me that I didn't want to know. And when I saw his blonde hair, blue eyes, and winning smile, I regretted looking.

"Keagan," I said. "What are you doing here?"

"Looking for you," he answered, a playful grin on his lips.

The ground rumbled again, reminding me that we were in the middle of a deadly situation. I pushed Keagan aside and readied my bow, but before I could release any arrows, Keagan said, "I got this one," and he jumped over my head, soared through the air, and punched the monster right in the nose, stunning it for a second. Then he mounted the beast, called to a warrior for his sword, and when he had the hilt in his hand, Keagan drove the sword into the beast's skull.

As the creature fell, Keagan effortlessly jumped off and onto the ground next to me, tossing the sword back to the impressed warrior.

He reached for my hands, but I stepped back. "Why are you here?" I asked, my face hot with an anger I couldn't explain.

"I wanted to see you."

"But *why*!?" I said. "You shouldn't be here. You . . . it's not safe here. Why did you come here?"

"Because I like you, Sarah. Our kiss . . . I . . . I wanted to see you." He stepped closer again, and I backed away, this time looking to Maddy and Drew for help.

"Wave your hand in front of his face," Drew instructed, "and think about him leaving Yelram, through the memory fogger."

"W-what?" I stammered.

"That's how you wake him. That's how you get him out of here."

I followed Drew's instructions and Keagan began to fade. He reached for me. "Sarah?" he said, confusion all around him. I couldn't answer him. I could only stand there and watch him evaporate into the air.

"Come on!" Drew said as he ran toward his wolf. I was still standing, watching the place where Keagan disappeared and wondering how it happened. How he found me. Why was he here? Did Luke have anything to do with this?

A thick arm reached down, and I instinctively grabbed it with my left. He hauled me up behind him onto the dark wolf and we took off through the field.

I was holding onto Luke, barely aware of what was going on around me. All I could see was Keagan's face, and his fast, precise, fearless movements as he attacked the monster.

Drew and Maddy were riding alongside us now as we neared the edge of the forest. I glanced behind us and saw a large black mass following, gaining speed. It was like a dragon, but its head was larger and I could see its daggered teeth from fifty yards away. But it had wings, and as it ran, it would flap them, pushing itself off the ground and landing closer to us. It roared and thick reams of saliva strung from its top teeth to its lower teeth. My mind, thick with frustration and concern over Keagan's arrival, gripped the mind of the creature and I let it come closer and closer, feeling its elation as it neared its prey—us.

I slowly pried my right arm from Luke's body and threw it back toward the monster, imagining that I was holding it by its throat. The beast threw its head up, an uncomfortable movement suggesting he felt my hand. I tried it again, this time remembering Keagan and my anger that came when I thought about Luke meddling in my relationships. Keagan could've been killed. But if I had to be honest with myself, it wasn't all Luke's fault. I had kissed Keagan. I had made him want me. And if he had died today, it would've been my fault.

My hand was squeezing the air, tighter and tighter. I

felt the thick, cold, leathery skin of the monster against my fingertips, but there was nothing there. I could see Drew and Maddy now as their wolf had slowed and was now behind us. They were both watching the monster. We slowed too, and the creature, which was no longer advancing toward us, collapsed to the ground, the weight of his death pulling my arm down with it.

"How . . . did you do that?" Maddy asked as Drew brought their wolf next to ours.

"I *hate* what these monsters have done to my world. I *hate* that they are killing innocent people." There was a casual coldness to my voice that caused a shiver to run up my spine.

Maddy propped her eyebrows up and chuckled. "Cool. I wish I could do that."

Drew gave her a bothered look. "It's not a *good* feeling, Maddy."

"Sure it is," I said, dismissing his dig at me.

Luke said nothing, and instead held onto my one arm that was still wrapped around him, then grunted to the wolf who took us into the forest.

WE RODE HARD for an hour, burying ourselves deeper and deeper into the thick forest until we reached a wide stream.

"The wolves need a break," Luke said as he slowed near the river.

I slid off as soon as it was safe and walked away from him. Still angry and confused about Keagan's appearance, I pulled a dagger from my boot and threw it toward a tree near the water. It skimmed the tree, but missed. I pulled my other and threw it, too, and this time it stuck. Lower than I had intended, but it was still pleasing to hear the thud of the blade in the tree. I retrieved an arrow and my bow from my back and pulled the arrow taut. A hand came to mine, preventing me from releasing the arrow.

"What are you doing?" It was Drew and his voice was low in my ear. "I know you're upset, but wasting your energy on a tree isn't the answer."

"You're right," I said, letting the bow fall to my side. Drew went to retrieve my daggers and I rounded on Luke. "What the hell was that?"

Luke looked up as he finished washing his face in the river. He stood and took a few steps toward me as he dried his hands on his pants. "He's a good fighter, Sarah—"

"You lured him here!"

"I didn't lure him," he corrected. "It was more . . . suggestive coercion."

"You had *no* right, Luke!" My rage took over. How could he go and make that type of decision without me? How could he continue to interfere with my life when he had already chosen to have nothing to do with me? "You put his life in danger, and for what? Just so he could help fight?"

"So he could help *protect* you!" he shouted back, matching my temper.

"No! You risked his life and put me in danger. You didn't even tell me! How did you think this was going to play out?! Did you think I wouldn't notice him there? What the hell is going on with you?!"

"It was my fault," Maddy jumped in, silencing my attack on Luke. She was pale and nervous and took a tentative step back. "It was my idea," she said. "Don't be mad at him. It was all my idea."

"*You* brought him here?" I asked, my voice a lot quieter than it had been when directed at Luke.

She nodded. "I wanted to help, and I knew . . . I mean, I *thought* he'd be a good dream warrior." Her face lit up a little. "And I was right, Sarah. Did you see him? He was amazing!"

"It wasn't her idea. It was mine," Luke interrupted.

"But I was the one who went to Keagan and told him you liked him so he'd want to see you," Maddy added.

My mouth fell slack as I tried to formulate a response. Luke and Maddy planned this together? They lied to Keagan so that he would come help us? They put his life in danger on *purpose*?

A coldness swept the riverbank and I felt the presence of Keagan again. I turned around to find him standing only feet from me. He came to me and took me in his arms, and in true fairytale fashion, tried to kiss me. I pushed away and held him at arm's length while I watched Luke struggle with this.

"You're beautiful," Keagan said, ignoring the fact that we weren't alone. I remembered the days when dreaming gave you confidence, and I envied him for being able to dream so freely. He was so innocent to the workings and realisms of the dream worlds.

"Sarah, get him out of here," Drew growled, his eyes flashing to Luke.

I turned to Luke. "Do you see what you've done? Yelram is supposed to be a good world. He's supposed to have good dreams here. I won't be responsible for him having nightmares. Not when he shouldn't even be here."

I took Keagan's hands and pulled him into me where I pressed my lips to his and felt his body wrap around mine. I had to give him a kiss to remember. I had to make this a good dream for him. I had to help bring back the balance of the dream worlds, even if it meant kissing Keagan and giving him false hope.

I waved my hand and Keagan slowly disappeared, a thick fog enveloping him as he vanished. Luke was sitting at the river now, his back to me.

Drew handed my daggers to me, pressing the handles into my chest and giving me a look of sympathy. He knew my pain because he felt it too. Maddy had gone behind his back, the same as Luke had gone behind mine, and this bothered him.

I shoved the knives back into my boots and approached the grey wolf, petting its wild coat as I waited for Drew.

"Let's go," I said, keeping my eyes ahead. Drew climbed onto the wolf and pulled me up to sit behind him. Maddy looked as though she wanted to cry, but I couldn't care. They had both betrayed us and I wasn't ready to forgive either one of them.

We rode for several hours, stopping only to allow the wolves a drink or bite to eat. It was late when Luke slowed his animal near the base of a mountain.

"There's a cave up there," he said, pointing to a crevice in the mountainside. "And a river over there. We should camp here tonight."

My head was spinning. It had been a long day and my body hurt with exhaustion, my muscles already seizing with the agony of the day's battles.

Drew brought his wolf next to Luke's, and I slid off the moment I could. I headed for the mountainside and found footholds to help my way up. Luke climbed up past me and entered the cave first, pulling his sword and checking the dark corners. I didn't, though. I was still too mad to care if something was lurking in the shadows. Besides, my adrenalin was too high to entertain any fear.

The next hour passed without a word spoken. Maddy sat at the back of the cave holding her knees to her chest while Drew stood leaning against the edge of the cave, busying himself with watching the forest below. Luke wouldn't look at me, and as angry as I was at him for bringing Keagan here (it didn't matter that Maddy confessed; it was all his idea), it didn't take long for me to feel his pain. He hadn't meant to hurt me. He was only trying to help. Seeing me with Keagan felt like a fire-hot iron scalding his skin. He let me feel his pain, making me wish that I hadn't tried to get into his head.

"We need wood," Luke mumbled before jumping off the ledge down to the ground below.

"Where are you going?" I demanded. "It's not safe out there."

He pulled his daggers from his boots and flashed one in the air, signaling his competence and freewill.

"I'll go with him," Maddy said as she hurried in his direction. She kept her head low, but raised her eyes to mine as she passed. "I'm sorry," she whispered.

*It's not me you need to apologize to*, I thought to her. Her eyes flickered to Drew, but she kept moving in Luke's direction.

Once they were gone, Drew joined me inside the cave. "How are you holding up?" he asked as he took a seat next to me.

"I'm okay," I admitted. "Bit pissed off, but I'll get over

it." He was watching me, so I gave him a lopsided smile. "And you?"

"Why wouldn't she tell me? Or ask me? Include me?" I shrugged.

"I guess I thought, you know . . . we were friends."

"You are."

"But obviously she trusts Luke more. She conspired with him to lure Keagan here. She obviously didn't think I would approve."

"You're right—she knew you wouldn't have approved. Because she knows you're a decent person. Unlike Luke."

"He loves you, Sarah."

"Actions speak louder than words."

"He's here now, isn't he?"

"If he really loved me, Drew, do you think he could so easily abandon me?"

"You keep saying he abandoned you."

"That's kind of the definition of someone leaving you."

"Actually abandon means to give up completely. He didn't give up."

"Then what do you call it?"

"Protecting you. Staying would've been easy, but he knew that wasn't the best thing for you. But Sarah, you need to stop using that word. I know you're marred by your past, and then Lucia's death, and then Luke leaving you, but your mother didn't *abandon* you. She didn't give up. She chose her path because she wanted to protect you. Lucia didn't abandon you—she protected you too. Can you maybe give pause for thought on the matter with Luke? Perhaps he didn't abandon you, either. Perhaps it was to protect you."

I nodded, but let several minutes pass before I spoke again. "I'm just . . . so scared."

"Of what?"

"Losing him, too." An image of Luke dying flashed through my mind and I let Drew see it.

He put his arm around me and pulled me closer to him. "I get it."

"I mean if him leaving me hurts this bad, then what would it feel like if I let him back in and he . . . died?"

Drew nodded, and if I wasn't mistaken, brought his hand to his face to remove a rebel tear.

"My father was devastated when my mother died," he said. "I remember it as if it were yesterday. He almost gave up completely." He chuckled as if there was irony in his statement. "He almost *abandoned* life."

I squeezed his leg and kept my hand there for comfort.

"That's why it was always hard for me to show my feelings with you," he admitted. "Why I always kept my distance. I did love you, Sarah. I really did."

"I know," I said.

97

"I hate the enchantment for what it did to me. It tricked me. It fooled me into thinking that you could be mine. That we could be happy together. Everything I felt for you was taken away when that enchantment broke. No matter how much I tried to convince myself that it wasn't gone, I couldn't. I had to admit it. I loved you like a sister, but no more. And Maddy . . . suddenly she replaced those feelings that I felt for you, and sometimes I wonder if it's just another trick, you know? Like, maybe it's just another stupid enchantment."

"It's not," I said. "You started having feelings for Maddy long before the enchantment with me broke. If that was even possible, then your feelings are definitely real."

"I'm scared to lose her, Sarah. I'm scared to fall in love and then have it be fake . . . or worse, she dies like my mother."

Both of us were chasing rebel tears now. I wiped my sleeve across my face at the same time he sniffled.

"We're a sad case, you and I," I laughed. "Maybe we can both learn to love again."

"Sometimes I think if there's hope for you and Luke then maybe there'll be hope for me and Maddy."

Suddenly, Maddy's voice and the cracking of sticks could be heard from below.

"They're coming back," Drew said, a sigh of relief in his voice. He stood up, his face hardening again and returned to his perch where he could pretend that he wasn't hurting.

"Drew," I said, putting my hand on his shoulder. "Don't hold a grudge. Let her in. You need to trust your heart."

He sighed and turned around just as Luke was helping Maddy up over the ledge.

"How'd it go?" I asked, hoping they would see my interest as a gesture of forgiveness.

"Great!" Maddy exclaimed. "Lots of firewood. No monsters. Win-win."

Luke handed bundles of wood up to Maddy and she tossed them into the cave. Then he hoisted himself back up onto the ledge and my heart beat wildly at his presence. He smiled at me, but I looked away. Why was it so easy to give advice to Drew on love and trust, but it was so hard to do it myself?

Maddy busied herself with a fire, and Drew went to help her. I saw them exchange a few looks, and I was pleased with the progress they were making. But Luke was in front of me now and I couldn't pretend not to notice.

"I'm sorry," he said.

I smiled meekly. "Me too."

"I brought him here because I want to help."

I nodded. "I know."

"But that's not the only reason."

I looked at him, unsure whether I wanted to know the real reason.

"He's not your type, Sarah. . . . And I thought that if you were forced to spend time with him, you'd see that." He looked down and I knew he wanted to take my hands in his.

I folded my arms and bit my lip, compelling myself not to lash out at him for trying to control my feelings. "I had no interest in Keagan," I finally answered. "But you've forced me now to get to know him. And you better hope for your sake that he doesn't end up being someone I can trust more than you."

His heart squeezed in pain and I felt it in my own.

"When will you forgive me?" he asked, his voice low and pleading. "Sarah, it's complete agony having you shut me out like this. I said I am sorry that I left you. I'm sorry that I hurt you. I promise I will never leave you again."

I wished he hadn't said those last words: *I promise I will never leave you again.* It was such an impossible promise that it fictionalized the rest of his apology. But looking into his deep blue, pleading eyes, I saw his sorrow. I felt his pain. He believed what he was saying.

"I'll try," I said, my voice weak and frail. "I'll try to forgive you."

"Thank you." He smiled and stepped forward. His fingers gently brushed a strand of hair from my face and then lingered near my chin. His eyes were on my lips now and my heart beat wildly as he slowly closed the gap between us.

"Luke," I said, putting my hands on his chest. "I said I will try to forgive you, but it's going to take time, and I need you to give me space until then, okay?"

"Okay," he said, quickly taking a step back. "That's fair. I'll give you all the time you need."

"I . . . I'm going to go warm up." I left him standing by the ledge as I joined Drew and Maddy by the fire.

Maddy was watching me carefully as I sat down next to them. "All okay?"

I nodded as I stole a glance in Luke's direction. He was still standing where I left him, but a few seconds later he announced that he was going to check on the wolves and he disappeared off the ledge.

"Wanna talk about it?" Drew offered.

"To be honest, I'd really just like to get some rest."

I pulled a knapsack in for a pillow and curled up near the fire. A few minutes later, Luke came back and sat against the cave wall opposite me, his eyes heavy and sad, and I watched him until my own eyes closed with the weight of my exhaustion.

# CHAPTER 9

# *Wolf Talk*

## ~ SARAH ~

BY THE TIME I woke early the next morning, Drew and Luke had already mapped out and planned where we were heading next, the fire was snuffed out, and the wolves were ready.

"What's the plan?" I asked once I had eaten the plate of sausages left next to me.

Drew quickly laid out the map on the ground. "We're here. Lorendale's army went in this direction. We're going to follow them for a bit, but then we're taking a detour"—he pointed to a valley on the map—"to here. This is where your palace is."

"Wait—how long is this going to take us?" I was no

map expert, but this didn't look like a few hours' journey.

"There's a good chance the garden will be near the palace," Drew said. "It's the heaviest protected place in the world. We should be there by noon if we leave now and ride fast. Eli's army would've drawn the monsters further west, so we shouldn't have much resistance from here to there."

"Okay, so I hate to have to be the one to state the obvious here," I started, "but what happens if we search all three quadrants, and don't find the garden? What if it's in the fourth quadrant and we run out of time?"

Drew was by my side and had his hand on my shoulder. "Don't worry," he said. "We'll find the cure."

SOON WE WERE racing through the forest, Drew and Maddy leading us, and Luke taking up the rear. Maddy had her arms wrapped tight around Drew, and I envied their untainted, new love. I hadn't felt the transition, but my face was now set in a firm scowl as I squeezed my legs around Luke's wolf, trying hard not to need Luke for stability.

Two hours into the ride, a steady buzz of battle cries grew in the distance. We were catching up to Lorendale's army, who had seemingly run into another pod of monsters.

"Go around!" I heard Luke shout.

Drew and Maddy veered left, but through the trees, I

could see the ocean of purple fighters battling the large, grotesque creatures. My eyes stung with the air that rushed them, but I refused to blink. These courageous men (and women) were fighting for me. For the cure. For Yelram, and for the balance of the worlds. I owed them, and I wouldn't let their fight be in vain. I had to find the cure.

But suddenly a new warrior, dressed in blue jeans and a white t-shirt, entered the battle. His wavy blonde hair laid perfectly in place while he flew through the air and then landed on the monster's back.

*Keagan!*

He called down to a purple warrior who only hesitated briefly before tossing his sword up to Keagan. Keagan thrust the blade into the monster, finishing him off. Keagan turned to the last blood-hungry creature and, throwing his head toward it, caused the monster to stumble back into a dozen swords at the ready. The warriors all cheered as they hoisted Keagan onto their shoulders.

We were at the edge of the valley, stopped and watching the unbelievable fight. How was I supposed to ban him from coming back when he was coming on his own free will and he was actually saving lives?

"He's amazing," Maddy said.

"He is," I admitted.

"Sarah," Drew began, "maybe it isn't such a bad thing

if he sticks around for a bit."

I hated that I was considering it. He was fearless and remarkable and he saved lives. How could I *not* let him stay?

I hadn't realized I had ordered Luke's wolf to move forward, but we were now racing down the hill into the valley toward Keagan.

Keagan raised his hands and the sea of soldiers parted immediately, making way for me to ride directly to him.

"There you are," he said when he saw me. "I've been killing monsters all day looking for you."

I smiled. "Have you now?" I slid off the wolf and went to him.

"Well, not really, but it sounded good." He flashed his perfect white teeth.

Keagan looked up at Luke still sitting atop the animal. "What's he doing here?"

I shrugged. "It's your dream. Perhaps you two could be good friends."

Keagan considered this with amusement, then laughed. "Maybe so!" He turned to Luke. "A wolf!" he said. "I need to get me one of those." He scanned his surroundings as if searching for a wolf. Luke groaned, then whispered something into the ear of his wolf. A minute later, a brown wolf came sprinting through the valley toward us.

While Keagan effortlessly mounted this new wolf, I

wondered if Luke had somehow ordered the wolf to come. Or was Keagan really that strong of a dreamer? Whatever it was, I was just pleased that this wasn't a nightmare for him. He hadn't seen the monsters as a fear. It was all a fun obstacle for him on his way to find me.

Luke addressed Eli's army now: "Keep going. We'll need you to head west and try to draw the monsters with you. We'll be continuing south. You're doing a great job. Eli would be proud."

Keagan let out a loud laugh and pointed his thumb toward Luke. "This guy!" he laughed. Then he donned a cartoon expression of Luke, sat up straight, and repeated in a stiff voice, "You're doing a great job. Eli would be proud."

He found himself quite funny, although he was the only one laughing. Drew was shaking his head, Maddy was apologizing with her eyes as she still took responsibility for his presence, and Luke was holding his gaze on Eli's army, pretending not to have heard, but his jaw throbbed, and he was too close to losing his cool.

"Come, My Lady," Keagan said, extending a hand down to me. I couldn't help but glance quickly at Luke, who was *not* comfortable with the situation, but he didn't protest.

Reluctantly, I took Keagan's hand. "But I drive," I said, and Keagan looked delighted by this as he pulled me onto the wolf to sit in front of him. He sat closely behind, leaning over me so that he could hold onto the wolf's mane too.

"Let's go," I said. "Maybe we can find you some more monsters to slay."

"Awesome," Keagan laughed.

WE RODE FOR several hours without sign of any monsters—Eli's army was doing their job well. The sun was high in the sky now, and my legs and back were stiff and sore. I wondered how long it would be before Keagan woke on his own. I had no way of telling what time it was on Earth as the dream worlds kept their own measure of time, but if I had to guess by the way he seemed to be nodding off, it was getting time for him to wake.

We stopped for a drink by a river and when the wolves were refueling, Drew and Luke kept their distance while they studied the map in private.

"What are they doing?" Keagan asked, nodding toward the two.

"I don't know," I lied, realizing it was best to keep Keagan on a need-to-know basis.

"Sarah," he said, taking my hands, and I held my breath, hoping he wasn't going to prod on the subject of the map, "I think I love you."

I choked on a breath of air and coughed to try to cover my alarm. "I'm sorry," I said quickly.

"I'm serious," he said with his famous smile.

*You're not serious,* I thought, bending his mind slightly.

His eyebrows puckered in the middle as he contemplated this contradiction. "I know it sounds crazy," he said, justifying the conflict going on in his mind. "I mean, I hardly know you, but—"

"It's been nice having you here," I interrupted.

"Wherever *here* is," he laughed, his eyes resting on the oversized wolves next to us. "I only wish you would have me in real life."

"This isn't real?" I asked, intrigued by his wisdom.

"I know it's only a dream, but I'll take what I can get."

I carefully took my hands from his on the ruse that I had to fill up my canteen again. I knelt by the river, taking my time emptying and re-filling the canteen, my stomach and mind both churning with what was happening with Keagan.

When I stood up, Keagan was there. He took me into his arms and kissed me. I was too shocked to do anything about it and when he released me, he said, "I can't get you out of my mind. I need to have you."

"Settle down, Romeo," Luke said as he suddenly appeared next to us. He was taller than Keagan, although Keagan was the same width.

Keagan glared at him, then took me in his arms again and pulled me against him. "My dream, my Juliette." He tried to kiss me again, but a powerful wind tore us apart, sending him into the river.

"Luke!" I shouted.

"What?" Luke held up his hands. "It's his dream." Luke went to walk away, but as soon as his back was turned, he too was hit with a wind that nearly knocked him over.

"He didn't just do that," Luke chuckled, amused.

"Keagan," I warned, but it didn't matter. He was wet from the river, and worse—his pride had been hurt.

"Let's see what you're made of then," Keagan taunted as he raised his hands and the dirt beneath him raised too.

"What the hell is he doing?" Maddy demanded.

"He's a dreamer," Drew explained. "He can do whatever he wants."

Instead of anger, Luke's face reflected anticipation of a challenge he looked forward to.

"Luke," I tried, "please don't—"

"I want to see what he's capable of, Sarah." Luke waved a hand across his front and the dirt that Keagan had summoned flew into his own face. Then Keagan's eyes fell on Luke's sword at his waist. Luke saw this, but didn't make a move to protect it. Keagan summoned it, and the sword was in his hands the next second.

"Nice," Luke said with an eager smile. "What else you got?"

Keagan roared and ran at Luke with his sword pointed straight for his chest. Luke dove out of the way, summoned my sword from my belt, then got to his feet, a laugh at his lips. "Don't rush your attack," he said.

"Don't assume the attack is always in front of your face," Keagan retorted.

Luke only had a chance to hesitate before he was whacked from behind by a log that only seconds before had been soaking in the river. Keagan used the opportunity to run at him, sword blazing. Panicked, I waved my hands and sent him out of his dream before he could do more damage than he could be responsible for.

I stared at the place where Keagan just disappeared. My heart was racing, and my breath was quick and anxious. Maddy was at Luke's side ensuring he was okay, while Drew was pacing with his sword waiting for Keagan to come back so he could give him a taste of his own medicine.

"What the *hell* was that?" I finally shouted at Luke.

He slowly stood up, arching his sore back, but he was still wildly amused. "What?" he laughed, and when I didn't reciprocate in his idea of fun, he said, "Seriously, Sarah, he needed to be brought down a peg or two. The guy's way too sure of himself."

"The *guy* happens to be a dreamer in *my* world. A world that is supposed to give only *good* dreams, and you just . . . you just—"

"Gave him a good dream," Drew finished.

I turned on him, my face set to a firm scowl.

"Think about it, Sarah," Drew continued. "He beat Luke. He's probably wanted to do that since he met him."

"But he also learned he can't go around treating you like a piece of meat," Maddy added.

"He thinks he's just dreaming," I said. "Do any of you know what that's like?" When the only response I got was Maddy nodding slightly, I continued, "You feel safe, like it's your own space. It's the only place you can just let go and be free. He would never treat me like this on Earth, or if he thought for a second that any of this was real."

Luke and Drew were quiet, no doubt reminiscing about when I first started dreaming. I had fallen in love with Luke and for the first time in my life, I felt love and loved freely.

"He shouldn't be denied that opportunity," I finished.

Luke looked down. "I'm sorry. I guess I was just . . . maybe a little jealous."

"*He* is not the enemy," I said as I went to Luke and lifted his shirt to check his injury. "Save your anger for the monsters."

The air started to swirl gently around us, and I knew Keagan was coming back. I glared at Luke and Drew. "*Don't* say a word!"

When he appeared, I took his face in my hands. "You're my hero," I said, and I planted my lips on his. He slipped in his tongue and I let him as this had to be a good dream. He brought his hands to my waist and moaned as he pulled me closer to him. When the kiss was finished, I said, "but I'd prefer if you save your energy for the monsters."

"Whatever you say," he said, kissing me again.

I heard a crack behind us and knew it was Luke's fist breaking a tree. I curled my left hand around the back of Keagan's neck while I kept my lips to his, and then waved my right hand and sent him out of sleep for good.

"What the hell was *that*?" Luke shouted the second he was gone.

"A good dream," I said, dismissing the kiss and hoping he didn't care enough to push the matter.

"It was clearly more than a good dream."

"We still need him," I said, "so I gave him a reason to come back."

"So now you want his help?"

"Look around us, Luke," I said, referring to the destruction and devastation that we were currently in refuge from. "We are losing, and he is one of the only reasons we haven't lost yet." Luke was hurt by this, but it was the truth and he needed to come to terms with it. "Besides," I added, "he's not so bad after all. He's the closest thing to normal that I have right now."

Luke let out what sounded like a groan mixed with a growl and turned away.

"You caused this," I reminded him. "You were the one to bring him here."

"I honestly didn't think you'd fall for him."

"I'm *not*!"

His face distorted with some sort of agonizing thought, but before I could read it, he slammed his fist into another tree, toppling it over, and then left me standing there, my own mind reeling.

"Be easy on him, Sarah," Drew said gently after Luke was gone.

"I'm trying," I grumbled as I filled my canteen with water once more.

"I know he messed up," Maddy said, "but look at what he's done to show you how sorry he is. He's left his world to come on a death mission for you, he's brought three hundred of his own people to help, and now he has to watch you make out with another guy because that guy's better at protecting you than he is. That's gotta suck."

I grunted, because I wanted to have the last word, but I had no words to say. I was frustrated. Confused. Angry. Hurt. And I *hated* everything that was happening to me. To us.

Keagan's brown wolf came to my side and nudged me. I leaned against him, thankful for the distraction.

Drew nodded toward the wolf. "He likes you."

"What's not to like?" I muttered.

Maddy laughed. "I didn't think they had feelings."

"The wolves?" I asked.

"Yeah. I mean, they're like programmed soldiers. They don't even hesitate to kill." She shuddered. "It's kind of creepy, actually."

I took a position in front of the brown wolf and placed both hands on either side of its head. "He may be bred to kill, but only to protect. Luke told them to protect me at all costs." I looked deeper into the dark eyes of the wolf. "He loves to feel the wind in his face. He loves to play chase with other wolves." The wolf's eyes softened. "His pack calls him Malyn."

"Malyn?" Maddy whispered.

I smiled. "It means little warrior."

"Cool," Maddy exclaimed. "What's this wolf's name?" She motioned toward the grey wolf that she and Drew had been riding. He was resting on the ground near the river, listening to our conversation, but keeping quiet up until this point. When I approached him, he got up, surprising me with his size. Compared to Luke's wolf, this one had seemed small, but standing next to him now, with nothing to denounce his size, I could appreciate how enormous he really was. Easily the size of a horse, his stature was slightly more confident than Malyn's.

"What's your name?" I asked him as I ran a hand over his coarse coat. Reluctantly he told me, although he knew that I could see into his mind and there was no sense in lying.

"Angus," I announced. "It means unnaturally strong." The grey wolf straightened, showing off his strong body.

A low growl came from Luke's wolf, who was standing guard a little further into the woods. Malyn and Angus both lowered their heads. Drew pulled his sword, uncomfortable with the black wolf's threat.

"You're the alpha, aren't you?" I said, making my way to the big wolf.

"Sarah, keep your distance," Drew warned.

"He won't hurt me," I assured him. "Luke's orders."

The wolf bared his teeth, a hardness in his eyes that would've scared me had I not sensed the loyalty inside.

"He doesn't like how I can read their minds. It's how the pack communicates and he doesn't like an outsider knowing what they're thinking."

"Sarah, get back!" Drew hissed. Maddy raised her bow and pulled an arrow taut, aiming it at the wolf.

I lowered my eyes to the ground, slowly got down on one knee, then bowed my head, showing complete respect for this great animal that had been entrusted to protect me.

The guttural growl subsided and when I looked up, the wolf's features had softened. I slowly stood and reached my hand toward his face. When my fingers touched his fur, he didn't flinch. He liked it. I had earned his trust by showing my respect, and in return, he showed me his name.

"Gideon." I smiled. "You're a good leader. Thank you for protecting us."

"Get away from her!" Luke shouted, his voice coming from the distance. Gideon swiftly backed away and lowered his eyes to Luke. "Never show a wolf your weakness," Luke warned.

"He's fine," I snapped. "You should have more faith in him."

Gideon's eyes flashed to mine, and I saw for a half second a look of surprise.

Luke narrowed his eyes on me. "Were you trying to communicate with him?"

I shrugged. "I *was* communicating with him."

Luke shook his head. "I suppose you trust him now?"

"I do," I said, smiling at Gideon. He kept his head held high, but eyes averted.

"You should trust him too. He's a good leader. The others look up to him."

Luke considered the wolf. "The others look up to him," he repeated, mockingly.

"He leads them, even from here. He can communicate with them through their thoughts. Even when they're not close."

Luke considered me for a minute. "How about we stop making friends with the wolves and just get going."

"How's your back?" I asked, ignoring his insolence.

"I'll be fine," he mumbled, keeping his hands busy packing his canteen away.

I went to him and gently lifted his shirt. A purple bruise covered the lower right side of his ribs. I gently touched it and he sucked in some air when I did.

"Does that hurt?" I asked.

"I'm okay," he said.

"I . . . I don't know how to heal yet. But I could try."

"Don't worry about it. I'll be fine," he assured me, but I knew he was only protecting me from another disappointment.

"Drew?" I asked.

He shrugged apologetically. "I can only heal him if we go back to Earth."

"We should go then," I said. Even though Luke was pretending as though it was fine, his stiff movements and shallow breaths told me otherwise. My guess was that he had broken ribs.

"If we leave," Luke said, "we may not be able to come back to this place. We won't know where we are. We could lose all the progress we've made."

"He's fine," Drew said, nodding to Luke. "He's tough. He can handle it."

Gideon lowered himself so that Luke could climb on easier.

"I'll ride with you," I said, hesitating slightly. He was

mad at me, I knew, but this was my attempt at saying I was sorry for kissing Keagan. I also hoped that if I could ride with him, I could try healing him without having to endure the looks of sympathy if it didn't work. His eyes met mine for a second as if to check whether I was serious, then he slid forward so I could climb up behind him.

"We may find a doctor or healer when we get to your kingdom," Maddy said as she mounted Malyn.

My kingdom. That sounded so odd. Would there be anyone left? Would they recognize me? Accept me?

# CHAPTER 10

# *The Forgotten Home*

## ~ SARAH ~

SEVERAL HOURS PASSED, and every muscle in my body ached from the effort it took to hold onto Luke while keeping my thighs pressed against Gideon. The woods were thinning, and the colours of the trees were becoming more impressive. Up ahead we could see a clearing with tall grass, daisies, and massive oak trees with vibrant red and yellow colours. As if admiring the scenery too, Gideon slowed to a restless jog.

"What's wrong?" I asked as Luke struggled to control Gideon.

"We'll have to stop here," he said. "Drew, come help Sarah down."

Drew was at my side a few seconds later, but I didn't need his help. I slid off Gideon, avoiding his large body that was moving agitatedly from side to side. Drew pulled me away. The other two wolves were wary too, and kept their distance from their leader.

"We're almost there," Drew explained. "The wolves can feel it."

"Feel what?" I asked, disappointed that I hadn't felt it too.

"The kingdom would've been the most heavily guarded place in Yelram."

"You mean, you think it's still guarded?" I asked, hopeful.

"No," he answered quickly. "I mean, it would've had the most protection and enchantments surrounding it."

I cringed at the word enchantments. I didn't need any reminders of the magic that had ruined my happiness.

"We'll leave the wolves here," Luke decided. "They won't be any good to us in there."

"Should this be concerning at all?" Maddy questioned, eying the restless wolves suspiciously.

"No," Luke answered, "I feel it too. It's draining."

"It's making you weaker?" I asked.

He nodded.

"Then don't go in," I said, shaking my head. "We don't have to do this."

"You have to do this," he said, "and I want to be there

when you do."

I tried not to love that he wanted to be there with me when I saw my home for the first time. Because as much as I tried to convince myself that I didn't, I wanted him there too.

We left the wolves and walked into the clearing without them. Luke gave them orders to stay close and come immediately if he called for them, but judging by their nervous nature, I doubted they'd be any good to us even if we did need them.

My heart raced with anticipation as the four of us crossed the field of daisies that brought us to the bridge ahead. The old stone path led across a small river and then separated into three directions. We chose the middle path that took us down a cobblestone street with small, but impressive, stone buildings with thatched roofs, crumbling chimneys, and a lingering smell of death.

As we walked slowly and cautiously through the deserted streets, Luke approached a nearby home. He wiped the soot from the window and peered inside. It was clear when he found what he was looking for, as he pulled back, took a few seconds to process what he saw, then hung his head. When he came back to us, he put his arm around me, and we continued walking. He didn't need to say anything. I knew he saw death.

Drew and Maddy both had their bows aimed as though they were expecting an ambush, but I didn't have the strength in me to expect it also. I was saving all of my energy for the feat that was ahead of me—the quaint but impressive palace with its modest turrets and arched windows, which I imagined once contained beautiful stained glass. Underneath the scorched black exterior, you could still see that the facade had once been a remarkable white marble stone.

I studied every detail, hoping something would jog my memory, but as desperate as I searched, nothing was familiar.

"You were just a baby," Maddy said, understanding my frustration.

"But shouldn't I still remember *something*?"

No one replied. They all wondered the same, but admitting that I was too young to remember would be like admitting that our chances of finding the Garden of Hope were slim to none.

The entrance was before us now. Remnants of large wooden doors were scattered in the foyer beyond. I pulled my sword now too.

It was dark inside and eerily quiet. Drew entered first, Maddy right behind him, covering his blind spots. They made a good team, and I was so thankful to have them with me. Luke's hand was on my back and, without pre-thought, I took his hand with mine and held it firmly. For strength. Once Drew gave a nod, we walked through the doorway and into . . . my home.

Overhead, a massive chandelier hung lopsided from the mosaic tiled ceiling. It didn't matter that the tiles were crumbling or the chandelier was coated in dust and grime—the foyer was majestic and beautiful and I loved it immediately. A grand staircase ascended along either side of us onto a landing above that overlooked its marble railing to below. The stairs were carpeted in what was surely once a bright, beautiful yellow. On the main floor, surrounding the staircases, more rooms, concealed by impressive, double wooden doors promised secrets and treasures tucked inside. It struck me odd that these doors were closed as it was clear that the palace had been overtaken at one point, but my curiosity for what the upper floor held drew me toward the staircase. I wanted the yellow carpet beneath my feet, the smooth marble railing under my fingers as I imagined my mother carrying herself up the same staircase, and feeling the same coolness under her own hand. I ignored Drew and Maddy who hurried up past me to ensure my safety once I arrived at the top, and I was only mildly aware of Luke trailing close behind me.

At the top, I stood in the middle of the landing and looked down over the foyer below, the open doors, and the cathedral window above. This was where I would have grown up had things been different. Not in an unloving foster home, but here, in a palace fit for royalty. Because that's what I was here. Royalty. A princess. No matter how many times I told myself that, it still felt impossible.

The yellow carpet on the upstairs landing was only soiled where it led from one staircase to the other, as if the intruders never bothered to explore any of the three hallways that branched off, leading to the other ends of the palace. I headed toward the middle passage, which was the shortest and had a window at the end, but was stopped by Luke who took my hand.

"Ready to go?" he said. Drew was already on his way back down the opposite staircase.

"I want to see more," I said, feeling as though these hallways could hold a key to unlocking my memory.

Luke looked at me, puzzled. "There's nothing more to see up here."

I considered the three hallways. "There are rooms down there," I said. "Could be my bedroom. Luke, I need to see it."

He glanced at Drew. Drew shook his head.

"We don't see it," Maddy admitted.

I approached the middle hallway and stepped into it. It was definitely there.

"Sarah!" Luke shouted and he reached for me, but stopped as if there was a glass wall between us.

I stepped back out of the hallway and he enveloped me immediately. "You scared me. Where did you go?"

"There's a hallway down there. And two more on

either side."

"They must be protected," Drew said. "Must be their bedrooms."

Luke tried to put his arm through, but he couldn't. Drew and Maddy both tried too, but even they couldn't get through.

"Sarah, you can't go in there without us," Luke said.

"I'm sorry," I said, "but I have to."

He reached for me, but I stepped back into the hallway, regretting the panic on his face.

"It's probably the safest place for her right now," I heard Drew say.

Luke slammed his fist against the invisible barrier and then shouted down the hallway, far past where I was standing just on the other side.

"Be careful! Don't be long!" He pressed his forehead against the barrier, and I stood on my tiptoes and kissed his lips softly. He felt it, and it startled him, but then I saw a smile play at his mouth and he relaxed.

I didn't feel a need for my sword here, but I thought I'd be a fool not to at least hold it by my side as I studied the gold carved frames adorning the walls. There were only two doors in this corridor, across the hall from each other, half way down the hall. The doors were all intact here. The marble walls were pristine and white. Elaborate gold rectangles framed an array of beautiful paintings that lined the corridor. They were full of life and colour and my eyes took extra time to study them as I slowly made my way closer to the door on the right.

The details on the door were striking, and I couldn't resist running my hands over the wooden carvings, and when I did, I saw the crest. I remembered seeing this before. Not on a door, or in a palace, but on paper that my mother was doodling on when we were colouring together one day. She was smiling and humming as she drew it, and I watched quietly from next to her. When she saw me watching her, she smiled, took my finger, and ran it over the Y in the centre, and then carefully held the paper to a flickering flame in the middle of the table and burnt it. It had been a curious moment, and I never understood why she would burn such a pretty picture that she took such care in creating. Now I understood it. It was home. She wanted me to know it, but couldn't leave evidence of it for anyone to find.

My hand was on the door handle now. I gave it a push and listened to the gentle creak as it slowly opened. The room was larger than the whole main floor of any house I had ever lived in. It had beautiful arched windows that gave way to the most colourful views. Far too classy to be a child's room, I allowed myself to believe that it was my parents' bedroom.

A large four-poster bed stood in the centre of the far wall, surrounded by drapes and unmade as if the invasion had happened in the middle of their sleep. I winced, and a taste of vengeance lingered on my lips as I slowly approached the bed, taking in the surroundings. To my left, next to a massive window with thick, pleated drapes, stood an old wooden chair and three easels, each one with a half-finished painting—one of a colourful striped animal, one of a field of wild daisies, and one of a small blonde child. I ran my fingers across the canvas of the girl and noticed the initials on the bottom right—LJ. Leah Jefferson. My mother was an artist. As I studied her work, I felt an odd connection to her. Although I had never tried painting, I loved to draw. Maybe I would've been good at painting too. My eagerness to learn more about my past took me out of the grand bedroom and across the hall to the only other door in the corridor.

It wasn't until my hand was on the brass handle that I noticed the large S carved into the centre of the door. My heart quickened, and I held my breath, knowing this was more than likely my bedroom.

Inside was a large room about the same size as the previous one, and in the middle of the room, a hand-carved white, round crib as a centerpiece. A beautiful yellow sheer canopy encircled the crib, and in the centre of the canopy hung a dreamcatcher—similar to the one that Drew had given me—but this one had more lace and feathers and the array of colours reminded me of a rainbow. I touched the feathers and ran my hand along the perimeter of the crib. This was my nursery.

The west wall was a floor to ceiling bookcase filled with bright, colourful children's books. A soft white rug laid in front of the bookcase, a cozy rocking chair and ottoman in one corner, and a soft yellow beanbag next to it. I pictured my mother sitting in the chair reading books to me before bedtime. I wasn't in the yellow beanbag chair, though; I was on her lap, cuddling in close to feel her warmth, soaking up every bit of love I could as surely I knew that one day it would be gone.

On the opposite wall was an enormous window, concealed by thick, velvet curtains. A large window seat, adorned with pillows of all shapes, sizes, and colours spanned the length of the window and I imagined myself sitting in that seat and overlooking whatever spectacular things there were to see on the outside. Next to the bench stood an antique dress-up rack adorned with tiny tiaras, dainty dresses, feather boas, fancy hats, and a wig of long, messy, red curls.

On the north wall, opposite the entrance to the room, seven large paintings hung in a row, spanning from one end of the room to the other. I recognized the style of painting at once, and knew these were the works of my mother. The collection reminded me of a rainbow—each its own distinct colour.

The first painting was on a stark white background with a burst of blue water protruding from the centre. The realism surprised me, and I reached my fingers out to feel the wetness, hoping that the peace I felt when I saw the painting would soak my inner being. I almost didn't want to look away—I liked this painting.

The second painting appeared to be on fire with red and orange flames licking the edges of the canvas and enveloping the fantastic image in the centre of a large, coiled, black snake, but at the top where you would expect the head of a cobra to emerge, a woman with sleek black hair surfaced instead. She was uncomfortably and seductively familiar, and I wondered if the resemblance to Ella was intentional.

The third painting was bright and cheerful with the colour yellow dominating the canvas. A field of daisies covered the background on this creation, while a large yellow tiger and small girl stood forehead to forehead in the centre of the frame. Suddenly, it was clear to me that each painting represented one of the worlds. This was Yelram's. The daisies were Yelram's flower, and the symbolism of the child standing with her forehead against an animal's must have represented the craft of mindbending. I looked back at the red canvas, now knowing that this was, indeed, a depiction of Nitsua's craft—shapebending. And the first painting represented Nevaeh, and its craft of waterbending.

The fourth painting, the one in the middle of the seven, was predominately green and had a beautiful heart-shaped emerald in the centre, with each facet reflecting the colours of the rainbow. Drew's school ring suddenly felt snug on my finger, the emerald centre reminding me that this was how he protected me from entering the dream worlds when I slept. He had told me that Earth was the heart of the dream worlds and green was the centre colour in the rainbow, and that was why the emerald protected dreamers.

I moved on to the next canvas—a brilliant mix of blue tones that came together in a wild centre that was a tornado. This painting represented Etak, I could tell by the brilliant blue that matched the uniforms of Luke's army, and by the swirling vortex of air that represented airbending. Although this piece felt violent and unpredictable, I loved it the most.

The sixth painting was of a gorgeous violet coloured mountain against an indigo blue sky. The mountain looked as though it protruded from the canvas and when I stepped forward to consider the details of the strokes she used, I was thrown back in surprise by how the image changed to that of a gaping hole in the ground. Purple was the colour of Lorendale, and groundbending was Lorendale's craft, so this painting shouldn't have surprised me as much as it did. I moved to the side, wondering if the mountain would reappear, but it didn't until I was standing in front of the last painting.

Like the first canvas, this one was different than all the rest. Void of colour, this painting was nearly all black, although the texture to it resembled scales, and one red eye in the centre that was so lifelike that I kept finding myself looking away. The reflection in the glassy eye showed red flames, not unlike the firebending Leviathan was known for. Why would my mother ever think such a painting would be fit for a nursery?

I stepped back from the paintings and scanned each of them. Separately, they were a rollercoaster of emotions—darkness and light, happiness and misery, but together, they were a beautiful work of harmony and balance. I loved that my mother had a vision for it. I loved that she saw the worlds as reliant on each other. She knew that the worlds needed each other to survive.

The sound of shuffling footsteps came from the hallway, and suddenly the door creaked, and a woman holding a duster in one hand and a cloth in the other entered the room. I froze against the wall with the paintings, blending into the shadows from the drawn drapes. The older woman with long, unkempt grey hair, made her way into the room and began muttering to herself as she dusted the bookshelves. She had a worried, set look to her face, and I watched curiously as she focused her attention and purpose on the detailing of each book, taking it out to wipe its top, and setting it back in place. When she was done the first row, I stepped out from the wall and, careful not to startle her, said softly, "Hello."

I supposed it wouldn't have mattered if I had whispered or yelled, my presence was not expected, and the woman jumped back and clutched her chest simultaneously. I took another step out of the shadows and apologized for startling her.

She froze, stared at me, then closed her eyes tightly, shook her head and opened them again, as if she refused to believe what her eyes were telling her. "My Lady Leah?" she asked, her voice shaky from the introduction.

I touched my hair and smiled, reveling in the misunderstanding, but before I could correct her, she was in front of me and touching my face, studying its detail.

"I'm Sarah," I said quietly.

The woman took a step back, appearing even more startled than when I first announced my presence.

"Leah was my mother," I added carefully.

She was speechless as she considered this. I pulled Yelram's key from my shirt and showed her.

"The resemblance is remarkable," the woman finally said, her eyes scanning my every detail. "I always said you would end up with her hair."

I felt myself blush. "Thank you. I . . . I don't remember much of her. She died when I was young."

The woman was still studying my features. "You were much smaller then. Your hair much lighter. My goodness . . ."

"Who are you?" I asked, taking a small step

132

backward.

"Oh, I am so sorry, My Lady," she said as she bowed low. "I am . . . I mean, I *was* your nanny. Miss Louisa. Back when your hair was still blonde and you resembled your father more than you did your mother. But look at you now!" She flung her frail arms around me.

"My hair was blonde?" I asked. I had always pictured myself as a child with a full head of wild red hair.

"Blonde as blonde can be," she laughed. Her eyes fell to the painting behind me where the blonde child rested her forehead against the yellow tiger. "But you wanted to be just like your mother." She motioned toward the dress-up rack near the window. "You found that wig at a store one day when you were out with your mother. She had to buy it for you—you wouldn't take it off." Louisa chuckled. "You wore it all the time."

"So I could look like her?"

She nodded, a look of pure joy on her face.

"And she loved to paint you."

I turned and saw the image of the girl and the tiger more clearly now. Now, I noticed her pale yellow dress with lace trimmed socks. I saw the ringlets at the bottom of her hair. I saw the daisy in her hand as she stroked the tiger's face.

"The gallery is full of paintings of you, My Lady. Your mother loved you very much."

"She did?"

"Oh yes," she said, with a twinkle in her eyes. "Both your parents loved you. Everything they did was for you."

My eyes glistened with this thought.

"I took care of you when you were just a little pumpkin," Louisa went on. "Now look at you. You're a full grown woman now. You would be how old . . . let me see . . ."

"Eighteen," we both said in unison.

I smiled, feeling the warmth of her love. "I just had my eighteenth birthday."

"You're all grown up."

I blushed again. "I guess so."

Tears sprung to her eyes. "Miss Sarah, I thought you were dead all these years. There has been no news of you. Nothing." She wiped her eyes on her sleeve. "I used to mind you when your parents had business to take care of, or when they would go away on holidays together. You took your first steps with me, you know. In this very room, in fact."

"I did?" I smiled as I looked around the room, imagining a small child with sweet blonde hair toddling around the grand furniture

"You most certainly did. Your mother never wanted to admit it. She said they were your *practice steps* and you took your real steps when she was there to see it." She laughed at the memory, and it was nice to see the wrinkles around her eyes. Her skin was so tight that I imagined she hadn't smiled in years.

"How did you get into the corridors?" I asked. "My friends weren't able to."

"I had been granted special access from your parents for the purpose of taking care of you," she said, somewhat sheepishly. "I sleep in your parents' bedroom, and I use the back staircase to get down to the kitchen."

Before I knew what I was doing, my arms were around her. I was so overcome with emotion over finding my caregiver. The woman who helped raise me. She knew my past. She could help me piece together my memories. Help me remember my parents. "I am so glad I found you," I said. "Thank you."

"I am not worthy of your thanks," she said as her eyes fell to the floor.

"Well, I may not remember all that you've done for me as a child, but if my parents trusted you with me, I am sure you deserve some credit."

"Perhaps at one point, Miss Sar—My *Lady*."

"What do you mean?"

"When the war started, I tried to help my friends and family. I knew I couldn't get them into the chamber halls, and I felt guilty hiding here alone while others had to bare the atrocities of the war, so I left the palace and stayed with my family. I tried to help them."

"That was noble of you."

She shook her head, silencing my gesture of kindness, and continued, "But it got worse. Every sunrise we would find more and more of our people . . . dead. It wasn't just the monsters killing them—there were viruses spreading too. A type of plague that wiped whole villages out." She turned away and sat down on the rocker chair as if to settle her shaking legs. "I got scared."

I touched her shoulder gently. "It sounds terrifying. I'm sure it was."

She clasped her hands to her mouth, and a sob escaped from her determined lips. "I was a coward," she cried. "I ran. I told them I would be back." Her sobs were louder now as she released the burden of the guilt she had been carrying for years. "I hid in here until . . . it was over." She cried in my arms as I tried to soothe her, but I had no words. I couldn't relate. I couldn't understand, but I tried to. As her leader, I tried to understand.

"There's nothing you could have done," I said. "And you would've had the same fate as them."

"My sister," she cried, "and her children. . . . I was so helpless. I would have traded places with them in a heartbeat. I would have given them the security of the chamber halls, and I would have endured the suffering . . . but I couldn't."

And suddenly I could relate. Because I felt the same as she once had. I would trade all the glory of life just to bring back my people. People I had never known, but still knew as loyal and caring.

"I'm sorry, My Lady," Louisa said as she wiped her face on her sleeve. "I shouldn't have burdened you with the details."

"Not at all, Louisa. I'm glad you shared it with me. We've all done things we aren't proud of. But dwelling on regrets and mistakes we've made won't change the past. All we can do is learn from them."

She smiled. "You are just like your mother, you know that?"

I smiled, but inside I hurt. I wished that I did know that. But I didn't. Because I didn't know my mother.

"You were lucky to find the chamber halls," Louisa said. "After the war that killed your father, took away your mother, and wiped out whole villages, things began to settle again. It's only been in the last few months that the monsters have either come back or woken up. And it's not safe out there anymore."

"I can't stay," I said.

"What? Why not? You can't go back out there."

"My friends are out there, Louisa. We are on a mission."

"Oh, you must bring them in!" she declared. Right away. It's not safe there. Come." She took my arm and hurried me out of the room. "We must go get them."

"But how do I let them in? You said yourself that no one can get in."

"You have the key, so you can bring them through. Just hold their hands."

We were at the corridor's end now. Luke was pacing restlessly across the entrance of the hall, while Drew and Maddy stood with their bows by their side, watching the foyer below.

When I came out of the chamber hall, Luke grabbed a hold of me and held me close to him. I coughed as he squeezed the air from my lungs.

"What took you so long!" he demanded.

"I found someone," I said. I turned back to the hallway, but Louisa wouldn't come forward. She took a step back. "Follow me," I said. "I can bring you in." I reached for Maddy's hand and took her and Luke across first, then went back for Drew. When we were all together in the safety of the chamber hall, I made the introductions.

"Miss Louisa was my nanny when I was little," I began. "She helped take care of me. Miss Louisa, these are my friends—Drew, keeper of Earth, Maddy, my best friend from Earth, and Luke, keeper of Etak."

With the last introduction, Louisa gasped and grabbed my arm, pulling me closer to her. Her narrowed eyes were on Luke as she bravely stood in front of me.

"You are not welcome here!" she hissed.

"It's okay, Louisa," I said, stepping away from her grasp. "Luke is on our side. He can be trusted."

Luke stepped forward, his hands in the air. "I promise you, Miss Louisa, I am not here to harm anyone. I am only here to help Sarah."

"It's a trap!" Louisa shouted. "Sarah, don't believe him. His father was responsible for Yelram's fall. His father killed the King! You mustn't trust him, Sarah. You mustn't!"

"Miss Louisa," Luke said, "I'm not going to hurt her. I . . . I love her."

My eyes darted to his, but I tried not to let him see my alarm.

Luke continued, but this time his eyes were on me, "I would marry her tomorrow if she would have me."

"Of course you would," Louisa spat. "Then you could take control of *this* world too."

"Miss Louisa," I started, ignoring the way my heart flittered at Luke's admission of love. "Luke has brought an army to help destroy the monsters. He's on our side."

"The same army that is killing your people right now?" she hissed.

"No," Luke said, "I've given them orders to—"

"Come, Sarah," Louisa said as she pulled my arm and led me to the end of the hallway where a large window overlooked the courtyard below. "Behold your kingdom's courtyard. Look who occupies it."

I followed her shaky finger to the garden below, which was filled with bright green trees, popping yellow flowers . . . and blue-clad soldiers.

# CHAPTER 11

## *Occupied*

### ~ SARAH ~

I HAD JUMPED back from the window the moment I saw them, even though Miss Louisa had assured me they couldn't see in. I couldn't bear to see them. Luke's army. Occupying my palace. Killing my people.

Luke and Drew were at the window now too. Drew didn't hesitate to draw his bow. "Will my arrows go through the barrier?" he asked.

"No," Miss Louisa replied. "The barriers overlooking the courtyard are secured. Presumably so Miss Sarah wouldn't accidentally toddle out of them when she was little."

"Luke?" I said softly.

"They're not my soldiers," he answered, his eyes fixated on one particular soldier that hovered underneath a canopy of leaves.

"Then who are they?" I asked, wanting desperately to believe him.

"Riley's." His jaw was set firm now. He reached for his blade but I held him back.

"We're outnumbered," I reminded him.

He threw his fist into the barrier, which barely made a sound.

"Easy," I said. "I can't heal broken bones yet." I took his hand in mine and brought his fingers to my lips, which I knew would bring his eyes back to mine. "I need you to stay focused."

"How did they get here?" Maddy asked. "Riley doesn't have a key."

"They must have snuck in when the portal was open," Luke growled.

Drew scowled at the soldiers below. "Let's find the damn cure so we can come back and kill these sons of bitches."

"Louisa, do you know where the Garden of Hope is?" I asked, remembering suddenly why we had come. My memory wasn't jarred as Luke had hoped, so perhaps Louisa could offer some help in my memory's absence.

Louisa shook her head reluctantly. "I'm sorry, My Lady," she said, "I was never privy to that information."

She looked distraught at not being able to provide us with more help.

"It's okay, Louisa. You've been a great help already. Thank you."

She lowered her eyes again, as she did the last time I thanked her, and I hoped I hadn't reminded her of the guilt she carried.

"We have to go," I said, "but I will come back for you. I promise."

"Where will you go? How will you avoid the enemy?" Louisa pleaded.

"We have wolves waiting in the forests nearby. We'll go back to them and head for the Northwest."

"Sarah," Louisa said, taking my hands, "if there are any survivors, they'll be in the mountains. It's the safest place from the enemy monsters."

"Which mountains?"

"I don't know," she admitted. "I just remember those that left the villages were heading for the mountains. They may not have made it, but if they did, you may find some of your people there."

"Thank you, Louisa." I kissed her cheek. "We will take back Yelram. We will."

Her gaze faltered on Luke, who was standing by the hall's end, ready to go with his sword in hand. "Be careful of him," Louisa said. "I know he says he loves you, but darkness runs deep."

This was like a stab in the heart as I didn't want to believe it, but I managed to force a smile and a quick hug, then turned to go.

We left the palace carefully and quietly, all of our bows aimed and ready as we covered each other's backs and walked down the centre of the street, headed for the bridge beyond.

We didn't see it coming, or hear it for that matter. I saw his blue uniform before I heard him, but by this time it was too late. He wasn't the only one with an arrow pointed at us. We were surrounded. They stepped out of the shadows, some with arrows, some with swords, others double-fisted with daggers.

"Well, well, well, if it isn't the Fantastic Four." Riley's grimace was not a welcoming one.

"Riley," Luke growled.

"It's about time you got here," Riley said. "I was about to think you hadn't made it, although we cleared half the monsters for you, so I couldn't imagine how you wouldn't have been able to do it—especially with Lorendale's army leading you."

"What are you doing, Riley?" Luke said, his arrow aimed for his brother's heart.

"I'm here to stop you from making a huge mistake. Let the bitch turn, brother. Yelram joins the dark worlds and you two, as sick as it makes me, can be together."

"Screw you, Riley," Luke spat.

"Before you think about releasing that arrow, brother, just remember that all of *my* arrows are on your girlfriend. You release that, and she's dead before I am."

Air left my lungs, and I tried not to let my trembling knees fail me.

Maddy spoke up, "So what is it you want from us? You want us to stop looking for the cure?"

"Well, that'd be a good start," Riley laughed. "I haven't decided whether to just kill Sarah now, which will secure my future, or let her live so my brother can have his piece when this is all over." Riley grinned as he looked Maddy up and down. "And maybe I'll keep you around too, so I can have myself a little piece."

I instinctively reached for Drew and steadied him at the same time Luke said, "Easy, Drew."

Riley laughed. "Okay, then, so Drew's got a thing for blondie. Can't blame him. But I guess if there's no chance of me getting a piece of that, then there's no sense in keeping her around." He nodded to the soldier on his left, then said, "Kill her. And then kill the rest."

The soldier pulled a long, bloodied blade from his holster and grinned as he slowly approached.

"Riley!" Luke roared. "You can't do this!" When Riley didn't answer, he turned to the soldier advancing on us, his blade shining in the late afternoon sun. "I forbid you to listen to him!"

But it was like the soldiers were under a spell. They

paid no mind to Luke's orders. It was like they didn't hear him at all.

"Riley," I tried, "it's me you want. Let them go, and I promise I'll stay and you can kill me however you like."

"No!" Luke shouted, but I pulled away from him and took a step toward the soldier.

"Please, Riley!" I begged.

"Now why would I do that, *princess*? Why would I settle for *one*, when I could have all four?"

My thoughts were desperate, but I couldn't reach any of their minds. *Please don't do this!* I screamed at them inside of my head. None of them so much as flinched. *You don't want to hurt us! Please don't hurt my friends!*

When the soldier was within reach, he thrust his sword into me, but when it should've penetrated, it didn't. Luke had thrown his sword with a blast of air, and when the metal hit the ground, it was the only sound to be heard. Then you could've heard a pin drop, save for Luke's wild breath.

"Riley," he growled, "you're a coward! Why don't you come fight me like a real man!"

Riley's eyes narrowed on his brother's. "You think I care about looking like a *real man*, brother? I only care about winning worlds, starting with this one, and when you're dead too, Etak will be all mine."

Luke threw his hands toward his brother, and another blast of wind whipped through the air, but Riley was ready for it and threw one back at him, only with Riley's wind came a dagger. A dagger that was aiming for Luke's chest. I shoved him out of the way, and took the dagger in my right arm.

"SARAH!" Maddy screamed as she dove on the ground next to me.

Luke hadn't yet realized what had happened, but it was clear the moment that he did. He pulled his sword from his belt and everything around him blew as if he were a category five hurricane. Maddy stood up and held onto Drew for support, and then they both began releasing arrows. The hurricane subsided, and Luke rushed for Riley as Drew and Maddy threw their bows aside in exchange for their swords now that the soldiers were too close for arrows, but all I could do was hold my shoulder where Riley's dagger still dug deep.

And then the ground began to rumble.

*Oh no,* I thought. At least we had a fighting chance against these soldiers, but a monster would be too much.

An angry roar split the air, its echo bouncing off the buildings surrounding us. The sound was coming from behind Riley. The dirt and dust in the air was still settling, but I could see the large mass bounding toward us.

Luke and Riley both stopped their fight, and Luke turned to run back for me. He scooped me up from the ground just as the beast set its sights on Riley. The creature picked Riley up in his large jowls and threw him against a building. Then he took one of his massive paws and swiped another soldier out of the way, but then the remaining soldiers were on him, and they were slashing the bright-coloured beast as it roared and fought back with every bit of fury it had.

Suddenly, we were being pulled away, out of the street, and into a dark alley. It was Louisa. She was cloaked in a black hooded garment that covered most of her face and body, and she was shushing us as we took cover in the darkness and watched the merciless attack unfold.

"What are you doing here?" I scolded. "Get back inside!"

She smiled, her eyes glistening. "I know how I can redeem myself now," she said as she yanked the dagger from my arm and quickly tied a cloth around my shoulder to stop the bleeding. The relief was immediate, but my movement was still limited. Then she untied her cloak and in one swift movement, draped it around me, tucking my hair into it, and that's when I noticed her own vibrant red hair . . . or wig.

I gasped, realizing her redemption plan. "No!" I said, shaking my head and reaching for her, but she pulled away, her face set in a determined look.

"My job was to keep you safe." Without another word, Louisa turned and ran back into the street, then ensuring that the soldiers heard her, she ran in the opposite direction.

As soon as he saw her red hair, Riley ordered his men after Louisa. We watched in horror as the soldiers chased her down a street. She was much more agile than I predicted. Skills learned, no doubt, from the years living with monsters.

When they were gone, I went back for the multi-coloured creature that they left for dead. It was breathing heavy, and as we got closer, I realized that it wasn't a beast. It was an oversized tiger. One that was covered in stripes—rainbow stripes. Just like the one my mother had painted. Like the one I had drawn again and again over the years. The tiger's eyes were deep brown and soulful. One had a little yellow ring around the iris, and it was familiar and comforting all at once. I knew this animal. This animal knew me.

"Lucia?" I said, touching the tiger's face.

*Sarah,* she thought.

"You're alive!" I nearly shouted. I threw myself into her gigantic body, reveling in her warmth and the rhythmic sound of her beating heart. I ignored everything around me—the screaming pain in my shoulder, Luke's attempt to restrain me, and the sound of Drew's arrow being stretched taut.

"Sarah, be careful," Maddy warned.

Lucia purred and groaned as I laughed and pressed my body into hers. My Lucia was alive. She was a beautiful rainbow tiger. She was powerful and ferocious and everything that she couldn't be on Earth. And we were together. But she was also dying. Her body was covered in blood and sweat. Her wounds were deep and painful, but she tried not to show it. She tried to only show me her joy of our reunion.

Luke was petting her, showing his respect and his own pleasure at her return. Maddy was watching in disbelief, but amusement at the same time. Drew smiled at Lucia, offering his hand for her to smell, as if she might not remember him.

The ground began to sway as if we were on a boat. I stumbled and someone caught me.

"We need to get her out of here," Luke said. "Both of them."

I wrapped my good arm around Lucia and held Luke's hand with my other. "Take us to Earth" he said, and I let myself fall into the swirl of the worlds.

# CHAPTER 12

# *Needing Space*

## ~ SARAH ~

DREW'S HEALING HANDS were on me the moment we landed in his backyard, but I pushed him away and ordered him to heal Lucia first. He didn't argue, as that would've wasted time. Instead, he turned his attention to Lucia.

"You shouldn't have done that," Luke said as he sat down next to me on the grass.

"She's in worse shape than I am."

"I meant what you did back there. You shouldn't have taken that blade for me. That was stupid. You could've been killed."

"You're welcome."

"Sarah, I'm serious."

"I'm sorry," I said, "but to be honest, it wasn't a conscious decision. I saw the dagger and I just reacted. I'm sorry, but I can't say I wouldn't do it again."

He was watching me, his eyes curious and caring. "Well, thank you anyway," he finally said. "You probably saved my life."

"What do you mean *probably*? I definitely did. I'm your hero right now. You should probably give me like a medal or something."

He chuckled. "You're definitely my hero."

"Can you believe it?" I said. "Can you believe we found Lucia?"

"I can," he said, matter-of-factly.

"What do you mean?"

"She never abandoned you. She did what she had to do to protect you. To ensure you moved forward. And I never believed that your parents would have killed her off for good. They knew where she was going once she died. Back to her home."

"Did you know that?"

He fixed his eyes on Lucia, slowly recovering with Drew's gentle touch. "I had a feeling, but I didn't know for sure, and I didn't want to give you false hope."

I smiled, my heart softening at his genuine thoughtfulness. "Thank you."

He moved his lips to my hand and closed his eyes,

reveling in the sensation that our flesh made when connected.

Drew returned. "She's all yours, Sarah."

I ran to Lucia, and she braced herself for my attack. I hurled myself at her gigantic neck, and she nuzzled me with her enormous head.

*I missed you so much,* I told her.

*I knew you could do it,* she replied. *I knew you could find the key and take back Yelram.*

*You knew all along, didn't you?*

*Yes. It was my mission from day one.*

*I thought you left me forever.*

*We never leave each other forever. There is always a tomorrow. It may be in another world, but there's always a tomorrow, Sarah.*

I squeezed her tighter. *I need to find the Garden of Hope, Lucia. Do you know where it is?*

*I do,* she replied.

*You do?* I hadn't expected her answer.

*In the mountains where it's protected.*

*How do we get there? Which mountains?* I released her, ran to Drew, pulled out the map from his backpack, and ran back to Lucia. I sprawled the map onto the ground. *Where is it, girl?*

She raised an enormous paw and set it down on the map in the location I most feared — the Northeast Quadrant.

"What is this?" Luke asked as he, Drew, and Maddy joined us. Drew was holding my arm as he finished healing me at the same time.

"Lucia says the Garden of Hope is in the mountains in the Northeast Quadrant."

Drew closed his eyes and groaned. "Go figure."

"It's okay," I said. "It's not too late. At least we know now."

Maddy picked up the map. "So we send word to the armies to head there now, and then we follow. This can work."

"We can't pull the armies from their quadrants," Drew said, his eyes focused on the map.

"Why not?" Maddy challenged.

"That many people heading in one direction will draw all the monsters. We're better off going in alone. Quietly. We need to keep clearing the other quadrants anyway."

"Okay," I said, taking a deep breath. "Look at the mountains. They seem to be much larger around the perimeter of the quadrant. I'll bet that was to protect the garden. We need to get right in the middle."

"We'll have to move fast," Luke said. "And we can't have any *hold-ups*."

"As in?"

"Keagan." No one said anything, but I waited for his explanation. "He's just slowing us down," Luke said, his face a contortion of frustration. And jealousy. "He's always fooling around . . . trying to *kiss* you."

"He thinks he's dreaming," I said. "If he knew how important the mission was—"

"We can't get rid of him now," Drew said. "As annoying as he is, he's been a good asset."

"He could get us killed," Luke argued.

"Fine," I said. "I'll consider blocking him. If that can be done."

"It can't," Drew said. "You'd just have to keep sending him out of sleep. Or make him a dreamcatcher with Yelram's stone in the web."

"We don't have time for that," Maddy said.

Suddenly, Lucia began to growl. She lowered her head low to the ground, her eyes locked on the patio door behind us. She walked slowly through the yard until she reached the bottom step of the back deck.

"What is it, girl?" I said, petting her nervously, but then a figure appeared in the patio door. The door slid open and there stood Ella, holding the arm of a very confused Keagan.

"I hope you don't mind I let myself in. I did knock, but no one came so . . ." She threw Keagan to the floor, Ella's strength much greater than his on Earth.

"What the hell is going on?" Keagan sputtered as he clambered to his feet.

Luke and Drew were standing in front of us now.

"What are you doing here, Ella?" Luke growled.

"Well, it's quite amazing what college students will tell a pretty face who just shows up and starts asking questions." She kicked Keagan's foot. "And once I found this love sick fool, he opened up and told me everything I needed to know."

"That's only because I thought you were Sarah!" Keagan shouted.

I glanced at Keagan, then Luke, who was vibrating with rage.

"Doesn't matter, you fool," Ella laughed. "One day you will realize that love is only a blindfold that lies and betrays."

"What do you want, Ella?" I asked, my voice calmer than the rest. She was here for a purpose, and I couldn't read her properly to be able to tell what it was. It wasn't vengeance, per se. Not now, anyway. She had an ulterior motive.

"I want in," she said matter-of-factly.

"No," Luke said before she could even explain.

"In on what?" I asked as I brought my hand to Luke's arm, refraining him from pulling his sword.

"I want to help find what you're looking for." She looked at Luke, then Drew, then me. "I mean, this guy doesn't seem to know every little detail, but I know he's dreaming of Sarah an awful lot."

"What's your point?"

"He tells me that he fights a lot of monsters, and that you guys are on a mission for something. I have to assume you're still looking for that cure."

"I told you, you crazy bitch," Keagan shouted, "it's just a *dream!*"

Ella laughed. "Isn't he adorable? *Just a dream.*"

Lucia jumped in front of me and let out of loud roar, a warning for Ella to back off.

"Easy, tiger," Ella said, her hands in the air. "I'm not looking for a fight."

Luke pulled his sword. "Leave, Ella, before I kill you myself."

A shrapnel of pain ejected from Ella and I felt it deep in my heart. Her eyes were only on his as she backed away. She took her key from her shirt and narrowed her eyes on Luke, although I saw the rejection in them. "Take me home." And she was gone.

"What . . . the *hell* . . . is going on here?" Keagan slowly stood up and went to the spot where Ella stood only seconds before. He pulled open the patio door and looked inside the house, then off the side of the deck, but he couldn't find her. She was gone with the wind that forced our eyes closed at the last second.

Keagan pushed his hands into his hair. "Am I dreaming right now?" He came to me and shook me. "Sarah, am I *dreaming?*"

Luke pulled Keagan's firm grip from my shoulders.

"You're not dreaming, man. Relax."

"Then what just happened? That . . . *girl* . . . just shows up, and she's Sarah, and then she's not. And then we come here. And there's . . . a *tiger*! A real, gigantic, living tiger with *rainbow* stripes! And then she talks about my dreams, and then she disappears into thin air!" He paced the deck, his eyes glued to mine. "Can someone please tell me what's going on?"

"Keagan," I started, "you're going to want to sit down for this."

Luke waved his hand and made a chair move from the corner of the deck to where Keagan was standing. Keagan looked at Luke, then at the chair, and, eyes wide with alarm, slowly sat down.

"There's Earth," I explained. "And then there are six other worlds. You can only visit them when you're dreaming." I waited for him to ask a question, but he just sat there, staring, waiting for more. "Three of them are light worlds—where you have good dreams. And three of them are dark worlds."

"Where you have nightmares," he finished. He was easier to convince than Maddy had been, no doubt due to the illogical events he had just witnessed.

"Each world has a keeper," I continued. "Drew is the keeper of Earth." Drew took out his key to show Keagan. "Luke is the keeper of Etak. And I'm the keeper of Yelram."

His eyebrows were pulled together now. He shook his head as if to shake out the things that didn't make sense. "Where have I been dreaming?"

"Yelram. My world," I answered. "It was overrun by monsters, and we're trying to reclaim it."

"Is it one of the good worlds?"

"It's supposed to be."

"What about *his* world?" Keagan nodded toward Luke, who was doing his best to keep his cool.

"Etak is a dark world," I said.

Keagan grinned. "Could've guessed."

"Doesn't mean Luke's a bad guy," I said. "He's helping us."

"No, for sure," Keagan said, but I knew he enjoyed this piece of information.

"Luke has sent an army to help fight the monsters," I added.

"Are those the guys in purple?" Keagan smirked.

"No, they're from another world. They're covering the Southwest Quadrant, where we have been. Luke's army is in the Southeast. And Nevaeh's army is in the Northwest Quadrant."

"What are you looking for?"

"A garden," I said. "There's a special garden somewhere, and it should be obvious when we find it."

"And why are you looking for a garden?"

"There's a cure in it," I said. "I . . . was poisoned by a

beast, and I only have forty-eight hours left to find this cure."

"Before you what—*die?*"

"Not exactly," I said. "If I don't find the cure, I'll become a dark lord, and my world will become a dark world."

Keagan glared at Luke. "So you might as well be dead is what you're saying."

Luke was at him in less than a second with his hand around his neck. He threw Keagan into the brick exterior of Drew's house. "Listen to me carefully, Keagan," he growled as I pulled at his arms. Drew didn't help. He was okay with whatever Luke saw fit. "Now that you know far more than you should, you either shut the hell up and follow directions, or I kill you."

For the first time since I met him, Keagan showed an angry side to him. He jabbed Luke in the side and when Luke let go, he tried to left-hook him in the jaw, but Luke was quick and blocked it. They had each other in a hold, ready to pound each other.

"That's enough!" I yelled, and I bent both of their minds so strongly that they both dropped to the ground and grabbed their heads.

When I released them, Luke gasped, "How did you do that?"

I, too, gasped, my heart racing. I had only meant to bend their minds to stop fighting, but it came out much stronger and fiercer than I had intended.

"I'm sorry," I said, crouching next to them. "Did I hurt you?"

"Yes!" Luke said, but he wasn't upset. "You need to practise that. That's awesome."

I frowned at him, remembering why I had felt the need to hurt him in the first place. "Do not touch Keagan again. Do you understand?"

He nodded reluctantly.

"So let me get this straight," Keagan said when I turned my attention back to him. "You're the one in charge here."

I shook my head. "No. We're all working together."

"Yeah, but you call the shots."

"It's not like that," I said.

"This mission is for Sarah," Luke said. "It's her life on the line, and it's her world. We treat her with respect and we listen to her."

Keagan nodded. "Well, I'm in. I'll fight with you. On one condition."

Luke let out a heavy, frustrated sigh.

"What is it?" I asked.

"I don't go as a dreamer. I want to be awake."

"No," Luke said.

"Why not?"

"Because Sarah won't have any control over you."

"You mean she won't be able to wake me up?"

"Exactly!"

"She won't need to," Keagan said, then he turned to me. "Sarah, I promise I will listen to every order you give. I'll stay by your side, I won't leave you, and I'll kill all the monsters in your way."

"That's my job," Luke said under his breath.

"Then there'll be two of us," Keagan added under *his* breath.

"It's dangerous," I said. "Keagan, it's not a game. You could die."

"I know," he said, "but so could you. And I want to be there to lessen the chances of that happening." He reached for my hands, and I let him have them. "Plus, I want to find that cure and keep you on the good side."

"You won't have the same skills you have while dreaming," I said. "You won't be invincible, either."

He seemed to think about this. "That's okay. I'd still rather be awake and with you than coming and going and not knowing what's happening to you."

"No," I said. "It's far too dangerous. He has absolutely no training, and I can't be responsible for—"

"Sarah," Drew began, "he already knows too much."

"You're not killing him, Drew."

"Geezus," Keagan said. "Can we just talk about this for a second?"

Drew came to me, ignoring Keagan. "Sarah, listen," he said, his voice low. "Keagan is clearly a good fighter.

He knows martial arts, and his confidence will take care of the rest. It can't hurt to have another person helping."

"And who knows," Maddy added, "maybe he'll get a craft when he crosses over."

"Or maybe not," I reminded her.

Luke was quiet, but his jaw clenched in a way that showed his frustration. "They're right," he grumbled. "And if anything happens to him, Drew can port him home."

"Nothing's going to happen to me," Keagan insisted.

"Fine," I resigned. "But Drew stays close so he can bring him back home and heal him."

"Awesome," Keagan said. "You won't regret it."

"Thank you," I said. "I appreciate it. It'll be easier with you there."

He smiled, keeping his eyes on mine.

"We should get something to eat," Maddy said, interrupting us. "And then pack some more food to go."

"Good idea." Drew followed her into the house.

"Can I talk to you alone for a minute?" Keagan asked as Maddy and Drew brushed past us.

I looked at Luke who had more than a small issue with this. *Just give us a minute. Please.*

He narrowed his eyes on Keagan before following Drew into the house. "You got sixty seconds," he said before the door closed.

"Sarah," Keagan said the moment Luke was gone. "I

can't stop thinking about you. All I can do is dream about you—although now I know why—and all of my daytime hours are consumed with thoughts of you."

Keagan was everything I would've wanted six months ago—sweet, smart, outgoing, good looking, athletic . . . but now my heart was torn. Torn between the guy who stood just on the other side of the patio door with his back to us, but his mind wide open for me to hear his menaced thoughts, and the guy in front of me who represented normalcy and stability. The guy who hadn't yet hurt me.

"Do you have feelings for Luke?" he asked.

"Luke and I have history," I reminded him. "It's complicated."

"But he's a dark world guy, right?"

"He's not one of the bad guys."

"He hurt you, though," he said, and there was a hardness to his jaw.

"Yes," I admitted, "which is why I . . . have a hard time trusting. I don't want to get hurt again."

"I won't hurt you, Sarah." He took my hands in his. "I can promise you that I will never hurt you. I will never leave you."

His words caused an eruption of frustration. They were too familiar. It didn't matter who said them, or how pure their intentions were, the reality was that I would be a fool to believe such promises.

"Sarah, I really like you. Please give me a chance."

I swallowed and looked down. "Keagan, I just can't commit to anything right now. I'm sorry."

"It's okay," he said. He pulled me into his arms. "I get it. Take your time."

"Thank you." I reciprocated the hug and patted his back gently. I didn't want to hurt him. I hadn't wanted him to be involved at all. But he was, and now I was stuck in this confusing relationship triangle.

"Can I ask you something?" he asked as he let me go. "When Luke and I were fighting just then, what did you do to break that up?"

He was referring to how I bent their minds to stop the fight, but I knew better than to explain it to him.

"Keepers have powers," I said, hoping he would just leave it at that.

"What kind of powers?" But he didn't.

"Luke is an airbender, Drew is a gravitybender, and there are other powers from each of the other worlds. Even Maddy is a groundbender when we're in the dream worlds."

"What about you?" He noticed that I was avoiding his question.

"Actually, I have all the crafts. I think it's because my mother was a dreamer, and my father was a keeper."

He was about to ask again about Yelram's craft.

"You should go get something to eat," I said. "I just

need a few minutes alone."

"Is everything okay?"

I nodded, but walked away from him as I didn't want him to see my eyes watering. I needed space. Mind space. "Tell them I'll be back in a few."

"Sure."

I heard the patio door open and then close, and I ran as fast as I could to the old apple tree. My quiet place. I could've ported myself there, but the wind felt exceptionally refreshing on my face, and the way my legs moved, hard and fast and with purpose, it released a lot of pent-up frustration.

Once there, I fell to the ground at the roots of the tree and cried in my hands. What was I doing? I was still madly in love with a dark world keeper while fighting for my own soul to get my world back to its former light glory. Could I do that with a dark lord? Was it counterproductive? And then there was Keagan. I didn't want to lead him on, but I also didn't want to turn him away. Why did I want to keep him close? What was my attraction to him?

I wasn't alone five minutes before Luke appeared in the middle of the portal.

"You okay?"

"I'm fine," I said, wiping my eyes quickly on my sleeve. I plucked some grass from the earth and played with it in my fingers. He was standing in front of me, so

I kept my eyes to the ground.

"Then why are you crying?"

"I'm allowed to cry," I said. "I've been through a lot today."

"You have," he agreed. He sat down in front of me, his legs on either side of mine. "Look at me."

My eyes found his and they locked. I loved his eyes. Sometimes they were dark and mysterious; other times, like right now, they were bright blue and full of hope.

"I miss you," I blurted.

His eyes closed, and his lips curled up in a smile. "You have no idea how happy that makes me to hear you say that."

"But I can't be with you," I said. "What good is all of this if I just go and throw it all away for a dark lord?"

"What are you talking about?"

"What happens after I find the cure and take back my world? What good is any of that if I just end up with you? My world doesn't accept you, and they'd probably never accept me if I was with you."

"Sarah, it's not like that. It doesn't matter what your people think. I love you, and I know you still love me. We could get married and Etak would be yours and —"

"Yelram would be yours," I finished for him.

"No," he said. "I was going to say we could be together forever. But yes, Etak and Yelram would be merged — we could rule them both together."

"I'm not even sure I can forgive you yet, much less marry you."

He was hurt by that. Very hurt, but he didn't challenge me. Because he knew it too. What would happen to me if I married a dark lord? What would happen to Yelram? My people? How could I ever earn their trust if I abandoned them for a dark lord? If Etak and Yelram merged at our marriage, my people would experience sadness and anger and jealousy and all the feelings of a dark world.

A tear slipped down my cheek at these thoughts, and Luke wiped it away.

"I love you," he said, and he leaned forward, resting his lips on my forehead.

I wanted to say it too, but I couldn't let him know how much of a hold he still had on me. "It hurts so bad to keep you away, but I need to find myself first. I need to figure out who I am and what I need to do for my world."

"I'll be here waiting. And I'll never stop loving you, Sarah. No matter what you choose. . . . Or *who* you choose."

"Luke, I don't feel nearly as much for him as I do for you."

"But you do feel something." It was a question. And a statement.

I nodded. "He's normal."

"But you're not normal, Sarah. You're a keeper. You

will never have a normal life."

"My father was a keeper. My mother was normal."

Luke didn't say anything to this. He couldn't. He had no argument.

"I'm sorry," I finally said. Because I was. I didn't want to hurt him. I wanted to touch him. To hold him. To kiss him. I wanted to stay in his arms forever. That's what my heart wanted, but my head wanted something different. My head wanted stability. Reassurance. Continuity. Control.

And because my head was in charge these days, I stood up and took one last look at the man that I loved with all my heart. "I'm sorry." The tears were out before I turned around, and my feet took me back to Drew's.

DREW AND MADDY were prepping Keagan when I returned to the house. He had daggers, a sword, bow and arrow, and new form-fitting clothing that would serve him better in battle than his sweatshirt and jeans.

"Where's Luke?" Maddy asked as Drew ran through some more drills with Keagan.

"I'm sure he'll be here soon," I answered, avoiding her eyes.

She didn't have to say it—I knew she was disappointed with me for not being able to let him back in.

"How's he doing?" I asked, nodding to Keagan.

"He's a natural," she said. "Turns out he has a couple of black belts. He's quite the ninja."

"Doesn't make him invincible."

"He's a good asset, Sarah."

I nodded as I watched Keagan stow his knives in his boots. I was more worried about him for some reason. I shouldn't have been. I should've been more worried about Maddy. But she knew what she was getting herself into; Keagan didn't. He was innocent. He trusted me. He was doing this because of me.

Luke arrived a few minutes later, and we ate some sandwiches and stocked up on supplies before I climbed on top of Lucia. Everyone held onto a part of me, and I ported us back to Yelram.

*Middle of the Northeast Quadrant.* "Take us home." *Middle of the Northeast Quadrant.*

# CHAPTER 13

# The Northeast Quadrant

## ~ SARAH ~

THE NORTHEAST QUADRANT looked an awful lot like the portal.

"Damnit!" I said when I recognized the field of fallen monsters and soldiers, surrounded by mountains on every side.

"What's wrong?" Luke released his hold on my leg and pulled his sword instead.

"I tried to port us into the middle of the Northeast Quadrant where the Garden of Hope should be."

"It's fine," Luke said. "We can go from here. It's not far, and we know where we're going this time."

"But why didn't it work?"

"You've never been there, Sarah," Drew said. "You'll need to develop a connection with your world first." Drew pulled out his compass and held it up, studying the arrow.

"But I did connect. When we were at my palace."

"And I'm sure if you tried to port back there, you could," he said as he pointed toward the mountain with the large opening, which presumably led us to the Northeast.

"That's how I was able to find you on Earth," Luke added. "I thought about you when I ported, and I was able to appear near you. Wherever you were."

Keagan looked away, trying to ignore how this sounded and what it would mean to me.

I pulled the map out of Drew's backpack and laid it on the ground. I shoved my finger into the middle of the map. "So we're here, and we want to get here." I pointed to the middle of the mountains in the Northeast. "We have these huge mountains to get through, which could take *forever*, not to mention the fact that we don't have any transportation—no offence, Lucia—and soon it will be dark, and—"

"Sarah," Maddy interrupted, "there's no point in getting frustrated. It won't do anyone any good."

I felt my face contort. "We need transportation."

"Well," Keagan started, "do you think Lucia here could round us up some more tigers?"

Lucia considered him for a minute, then looked at me as if asking for permission. She was eager to give it a try, and I could tell it woke an old energy inside her. Without any further direction from me, she sprinted into the middle of the field and let out three ferocious roars that shook the ground and echoed against the backdrop of the mountains.

Once the echoes dissipated, in the far off distance, a much fainter roar could be heard. And then another. Less than a minute later, one small, orange figure could be seen racing down the snowy mountainside that separated us from the Northwest Quadrant, and another striped orange animal bounded down the mountain bordering the Southeast.

"It worked!" I laughed. "Great idea, Keagan!"

Lucia gathered the two tigers, both larger than her and without the impressive array of colours in their stripes. Next to them, Lucia looked small, but knowing she was easily the size of a horse made me appreciate the sheer size of these two animals.

"Drew and I will ride together," Maddy announced. Her eyes didn't meet mine. She knew there were only three tigers, and five riders. Someone would have to ride with me.

Neither Luke nor Keagan made a move for the other tiger.

"You can have that one," Keagan offered to Luke.

"Nah, man, it's cool," Luke said. "You should take it."

I rolled my eyes. "Luke, you take it. Keagan will come with me." Keagan sniggered, enjoying his win. "Only because you know how to ride an animal. Keagan will probably break his neck if he tries."

Luke grinned as he mounted the enormous tiger, but before Keagan could join me atop Lucia, a collection of howls came from the Southeast tunnel.

"Go," Luke said, pointing us toward the Northeast. "I'll catch up."

"What is it?" I pressed, but he didn't have to answer as a storm of blue warriors on wolfback came thundering through the mountains into the circle.

"Go!" Luke shouted again before racing toward his army.

I squeezed my legs, signaling for Lucia to follow Luke.

"Sarah, wait!" Keagan called after me, but I couldn't take my eyes from Luke.

"Drew, stay with Keagan!" I yelled over my shoulder.

As Lucia raced toward Luke and his army, I was relieved to discover that it was Devon leading the pack, and not Riley.

"He was in the Southwest," Luke was saying when I was close enough to overhear. "With at least a dozen men, but no more. We took out a few, but—"

"You took out a few of our own men?" Devon cut him

off, displeased with the information.

"Devon, they're not *our* men. They're Riley's. He's not on our side anymore."

"And whose side are *you* on, Luke? I get that your brother's a piece of shit, but are you doing what's best for Etak? . . . Or Yelram?"

I was outraged at the way Devon spoke to Luke, accusing him of betraying his own world! I wanted to scream at him! I wanted to throw him to the ground and choke the disrespect right out of him! . . . But I didn't need to. He had fallen off his wolf, and was on his hands and knees, clutching his head.

"Make it stop!" he screamed as he rolled around on the ground.

Luke hesitated, but then he pulled me from Lucia, catching me in his arms. "Sarah!" he said, shaking me.

Reluctantly, I pulled my eyes from Devon's thrashing body, and the second I did, his screaming stopped, which was when I realized I had been the one torturing him. But instead of feeling regret like I did when I had done it to Luke and Keagan, a smile crept across my face.

"Next time, I won't stop," I heard myself say. "Don't ever speak to Luke that way again."

Devon, trembling, slowly stood up. "How did you do that?" he spluttered.

"She has powers stronger than you can imagine," Luke answered. "Which is why she needs the cure.

Imagine the pain she'll cause if she joins the dark side."

Devon climbed back onto his wolf. "So you want us to go find Riley."

"Yes, and then go to the Northwest and help Nevaeh clear that quadrant."

Devon nodded, then glanced nervously in my direction. He turned to leave, but Luke held his hand out and the wolf stopped. Luke took the wolf by the face and stared deep into his eyes. "Send Gideon to me," he said, his voice low, but firm.

Devon eyed him curiously, but instead of questioning his leader, he waited for his moment, then led the wolf back to where their army waited.

"What was that about?" I asked when we were alone.

"What?"

"You told the wolf to send Gideon."

"And?" He pretended that this wasn't a big thing, but I knew he wondered if I was right about the wolves being able to telepathically communicate over long distances.

"Why did you call for him?"

Luke shrugged. "To see if it'd work." He grabbed a hold of his tiger's coat and pulled himself up. "You said they can communicate with each other. If that's true, then maybe Gideon can find us, and since you trust him so much, I thought you might want to have him around. For protection."

Lucia crouched, and I mounted her. "So what you're

saying is that I was right," I teased.

"Let's just see if it works, shall we?" He grinned.

I smiled too as we turned our animals toward the Northeast.

"By the way," I said, "I'm sorry about what I did to Devon. I didn't realize I was doing it."

Luke chuckled. "Don't apologize. He'll have more respect for you now."

"Well, it felt awesome to put him in his place. He had no right to talk to you like that."

"Devon's an old friend. He's just concerned about me." He considered me for a moment. "Does it hurt you at all when you do that?"

"No," I laughed. "It actually feels *really* good."

Luke frowned. "I was afraid of that. We need to find that cure. Let's go."

He led me back to the others, and I wondered for a moment if he would still love me if I was always that evil.

THE SKY WAS darkening faster than I liked. Luke, who had once been the lead, fell back to ride alongside me. I knew the night sky concerned him, too.

Whether it was the darkness that kept the creatures away, or the draw of excitement from the other quadrants, we were able to ride for a couple of hours without encountering any monsters.

It was pitch black now, the sky thick with clouds that

shadowed the moon's light. At best guess, it was coming on to midnight. My body was tired and sore, even though Lucia was doing all of the work.

"We should stop soon," Drew called back over his shoulder. "Give the tigers a rest and get some sleep."

Keagan motioned ahead. "It looks like these mountains are coming together. I bet there's a passage through them. Might be a safe place to stop."

Suddenly, Drew stopped.

"What is it?" Maddy pressed.

"I don't know," he admitted. "Something's out there." He glanced at me over his shoulder. *Can you sense it?*

My eyes were already closed, searching the distance for another energy, thought, or emotion that wasn't one of ours. And then I found it.

It was angry and hungry and carried no fear. The thoughts were foreign, but I knew they belonged to a monster. The energy was massive and getting closer.

"It's a monster," I said. "Get ready."

"How many?" Luke asked.

"Just one," I confirmed.

"How do you *know* that?" Keagan asked, but we ignored him and readied our bows and swords.

"Get off the tigers," Drew whispered. "Sarah, send them to flank us."

Lucia nudged the other tigers and they parted,

reluctantly, to take positions where they could attack the monster before it attacked us.

My heart was beating through my chest. Keagan put his hand on my shoulder. "Stay here," he said as he slowly crept ahead.

Then a thundering roar filled the silence, followed by another and another. The first one had belonged to Lucia and it meant, "Charge!"

We still couldn't see the monster, but we heard it screeching as it felt the claws of the tigers digging into its flesh. I continued searching for the monster's mind, but it was angry and frantic and thrashing.

"Don't release any arrows," I ordered.

"I think I have a shot," Maddy said.

"Not yet!" I shouted. "You could hit Lucia."

Then I had an idea. I twisted my hands around until they formed a bright ball of fire, then I threw it into the air and lit up the sky.

"Brilliant," Drew said, then began advancing on the beast as he released arrow after arrow.

Keagan followed Drew, while Luke stayed back with me. It wasn't going to be a long fight, and I knew the others could handle it.

When the monster fell, the others retrieved their arrows and Lucia hurried back to me immediately. I assessed her for any injuries and was thankful she was only bruised.

"You're my hero," I told her as she purred happily.

"The monster came from that mountain pass," Drew said. "If we encounter another one inside the pass, we probably won't be so lucky."

"I'll send one of the tigers through and see if it's safe," I decided. I didn't like the idea, but it was better than going in blind.

I nodded to Lucia who made a small noise to the other tigers. They looked at each other, then decided which one would go—it was Luke's tiger.

"Be careful," I told her. I knew she was female. They all were. Female and fierce.

We waited for what seemed like thirty minutes. My bow was getting too heavy to hold, but I didn't dare let my guard down. Lucia paced restlessly, waiting for her friend to return.

Then we heard the heavy footfalls of the tiger as she bounded back through the mountain pass toward us. Lucia and the other tiger met her and they exchanged a series of grunts and growls. I knew what they were saying—the valley on the other side of the pass was filled with monsters even larger than the one that we had just killed. There was a man-made barricade at the end of the pass, which blocked the larger monsters from being able to get through.

"What's happening?" Keagan asked.

"It's too dangerous," I said. "There are too many

monsters on the other side."

Luke took my hand and squeezed it. *Watch what you say.*

"Maybe there's just a few," Keagan said, but I was shaking my head.

*Sarah*, Drew warned. They were worried I would reveal my craft to Keagan.

"Let's find a place to rest on this side," I suggested. "We'll check out the pass tomorrow in daylight."

As we headed back toward the steep climb up the mountainside, Drew, Luke, and Maddy left their minds open for me to show them images of what Lucia's friend had seen. Dozens of fierce, hungry monsters trapped inside a valley that we needed to clear before we could go any farther.

My hope was fading.

THE TIGERS EXPLORED the mountainside as we slowly followed. My legs were trembling from exhaustion, and when Lucia returned with news that they had found a safe place to rest, I mounted her once again and let her lead us to our destination.

There was a flat ledge large enough for the animals to rest and keep watch, and above the ledge was a steep climb to a deep crevice that we hoped would lead to a cave comfortable and safe enough for the five of us to sleep in.

At first the cave was dark and quiet, but as our eyes adjusted, I saw flickers of light from the darkest corners. I reached back and gripped the hand of the person closest. Luke. He had seen the light too, and his other hand slowly reached for his belt while Drew flicked on a flashlight and shone it into one of the corners.

Eyeballs. Faces. People.

They were huddled in the corners, terrified.

"Don't be afraid," I said as I grabbed Drew's flashlight and shone it on me. "We're not going to hurt you."

I heard a few gasps, and I wondered if the shadows on my face and my wild hair had scared them. I shone the light on Drew, Keagan, Maddy, and Luke, then to the floor.

"We just need a place to sleep tonight. We're fighting the monsters, trying to get rid of them. For you."

Luke took the flashlight from my hand and shone it back on me. "This is Princess Sarah, the daughter of Queen Leah and King Jefferson."

More gasps and murmurs filled the room, suggesting that this was the reason for their alarm earlier. Not my wild, unruly hair. Well, yes, my hair, but only because they had recognized it.

Slowly, one by one, the frightened people emerged from the corners. They ignited their lanterns and soon the room was well lit.

There were about ten of them in total, and each

carried a weapon of some sort, whether it was a club made from a tree branch, a makeshift knife, or a bow and arrow that looked as though it would require great skill to reach its target.

"What are you doing here?" I asked as a man approached me, raised his lantern next to my face, and studied my eyes.

"We're guarding the caves," he answered, as if this should have been obvious.

Past him, there was a smaller entrance leading deeper into the mountain.

"Are there more of you?" I asked.

He nodded. "We are only the night shift."

I couldn't help but study the club in his hand and wondered how effective it would be against a monster. I swallowed, feeling the weight of responsibility for these people.

"Are you really the princess?" the man asked as the others leaned in for my answer.

"Yes," I said, nodding.

The man smiled and turned to his fellow night crew members. "She's come to save us."

"She's come to find a cure," Luke corrected him. "And we don't have much time. The fate of Yelram depends on us finding that cure."

The survivors looked at each other. "Who pissed in your cornflakes?" one of them murmured.

I suppressed a grin. "I'm sorry," I said. "He didn't mean to make it sound so definitive. It is true that I've been poisoned from the beast that killed my parents, and I am looking for the cure, which we believe is in the Garden of Hope. But we are also killing the monsters and trying to restore the world."

"Who are you, anyway?" the guy with the makeshift knife asked Luke, shining the lantern in his eyes while twisting the knife menacingly in his other hand.

Luke pushed the lantern aside, annoyed by him. "Luke," he growled.

I took Luke's arm, squeezing it. "These are my friends," I said. "They've come to help." I pointed to Drew first. "Drew is Earth's keeper. He helped keep me safe over the years until I was ready to take back Yelram. This is my best friend, Maddy, she's a dreamer and a great warrior. My friend, Keagan, also a dreamer here to help us." I grinned and looked at Luke. "And you've met Luke. He's Etak's keeper, and he helped me find the key and—"

"Etak!" shouted the guy with the knife. "You brought a dark world keeper here?" This guy was more trouble than the rest. He was young, like us, and probably didn't remember a time when the world was a peaceful place. He had a fire in his eyes that seemed to always yearn for a fight.

"Yeah," Luke said. "And?"

"I think what Simon is trying to say," the man with the club began, "is that Yelram is a world in despair. We already have enough darkness in it."

Luke and Simon were glaring into each other's eyes. This was worse than when Luke and Drew went head to head over me. This was much worse. This was Luke—the guy I loved, and my people—the ones I belonged to.

"Your Highness, please," the man begged. "Please ask him to leave. He's upsetting your people."

My voice got caught in my throat. I looked to Luke who was angry, then to Maddy who was shocked, and Drew who didn't seem to have a thought on the matter. Keagan was pleased.

"I . . ." I began.

"Really?" Luke said, his eyes on me now.

"No, it's just—"

"Don't worry about it," he said. He handed me the flashlight and turned to leave.

"Luke," I tried. He stopped, but didn't turn around again. He waited, and I didn't have any words for him so he left.

Maddy and Drew hurried out after him, but Keagan stayed inside.

"Ugh," Keagan groaned. "That was rough."

His presence was comforting, and I suddenly wanted him to comfort me. He slipped his hand into mine, and I squeezed it.

"You did the right thing, Sarah," Simon said.

Keagan stiffened next to me. "Shouldn't you be calling her princess or something?"

Simon locked eyes with him for a few seconds too long and then said, "Of course."

"No," I said. "It's fine. Really. It sounds weird, especially coming from someone my own age."

Simon grinned, but I saw that it was meant for Keagan more than it was for me.

"Luke isn't a bad guy," I said, addressing the group of them now. "He helped me find the key. He came to help kill the monsters. He even—" I considered telling them about how Luke brought his own army to help, but I didn't know if this would frighten them more, so I left it out. "He's a good guy," I finished.

"Sarah, he's a dark lord," Simon said. "Being good isn't part of their genetics."

"He's different," I defended.

"I doubt it," Simon said.

Keagan had his arm around my waist, protectively now, as I knew he didn't like Simon. He squeezed my side and then finally said, "There's no point in dwelling on it, Simon. He's gone."

Simon watched Keagan for a second, then lifted his head higher. "Good then."

"Now," Keagan began, "about that mountain pass. What's on the other side?"

Simon snickered. "On the other side of *that* mountain pass?" His eyes lit up, then he shrugged. "Why don't you go find out?"

My jaw clenched, knowing that Simon knew that a pod of monsters lurked on the other side of the pass, and that a man-made barricade was the only thing stopping them from coming through.

I reached into his mind and softened it just a little. Enough for him to put his guard down and trust us a little more.

"It's a whole valley full of monsters," Simon said. We lured them in from the other side and then barricaded the tunnels."

Keagan shuffled uncomfortably. "How many?"

"Probably fifty?" Simon guessed. "Maybe less now. We pick off one or two every once in a while." He sounded proud of this, but I saw his fear, too. *Picking off* monsters wasn't as easy as he was trying to make it sound.

Fifty monsters. All in one confined valley. How were we ever going to get through?

"How do we get through?" Keagan asked, as if he had caught my thought.

Simon chuckled. "You don't. There's just more monsters on the other side anyway."

"We're looking for the Garden of Hope," I explained. "We need to get through."

Simon shrugged. "I hope you have more man power than what I've just seen. Even with that dark lord on your side, you don't stand a chance."

Keagan stiffened. "I don't like your tone or your attitude," he hissed. "Show some respect for your princess."

Simon narrowed his eyes on Keagan, then slowly blinked as he brought his eyes to mine. "My apologies, princess."

A woman, probably in her mid to late twenties, approached me next. She took my hand in hers and said, "You look just like her, you know."

"My mother?"

She nodded. "I was just young when I had the privilege of meeting her. She came to our house when my little brother was sick. She healed him."

"My mother healed him?"

"Yes," she said, the memory causing her eyes to blur.

"But how did she heal him? I thought only the keeper has the power to heal."

"Oh, no," she said, almost excited. "When your parents were married, his craft and powers passed on to her. She could use them in Yelram."

I smiled. "Really?"

"Yes." She looked down, and then her mind was flooded with grief over the memory of her queen fleeing Yelram. "Where did she take you? We all knew she left.

She didn't want to leave the king, but she had to protect you and hide the key."

My hand was squeezing hers. My mother loved my father enough that it killed her to have to leave him. "She took me to Earth," I said.

She smiled. "We thought so. That's where she was from. Nevaeh would've been safer, and a more obvious choice, but I think she felt more comfortable hiding you on Earth."

"What's your name?" I asked.

"Beth," she answered with a warm smile.

"Beth," I said tentatively, "do you believe what they said about Luke?" My voice was lower now, and although it wasn't the most opportune time to discuss it, Keagan was deep into a conversation with two men about their weapons and how they could make them better, so he wasn't listening.

"Oh, My Lady, I couldn't tell you for sure what the right thing to do is. I saw you holding his hand. I can tell he means something to you." She looked down. "But I don't think your people will accept him. I don't think it's what's right for us. We need too much healing."

I nodded, and the sting of tears erupted from my eyes. She took my hand again. "But this one seems nice," she said, motioning to Keagan. "He's kind, has genuine eyes, and he keeps looking over here to make sure you're okay."

I glanced over at Keagan and our eyes met. He smiled. "He is a good guy."

She squeezed my hand again.

"I have another question for you," I said. "I haven't been able to heal yet. Do you know why?"

Her eyes glazed over again as she thought hard about this. "Perhaps the world doesn't recognize you yet as its proper keeper?"

This was what Drew had said too, for why I couldn't call the tigers myself. The world hadn't recognized me yet.

"Once the people get to know you and learn to trust you, I'm sure your full powers as keeper will be restored."

*The people need to trust me. Want me. Respect me. And until I earn that, until I can show them that they can trust me, until they want me to be their keeper, I am not fully theirs yet.*

Maddy came back into the cave and my head jerked up to meet her eyes. *Is he okay?* I thought into her mind. She just nodded.

"We'll need to sleep for the night," Maddy announced to the man with the club. "Is that okay with you?"

"Of course," the man said. "You can come deeper into the caves if you want. It's warmer in there."

"No," Maddy said, her face cold as she unpacked her sleeping bag. "Here is fine. We don't need anything, and we'll leave at first light."

She caught eyes with me for a second, and I shot her a warning glance. Why was she being so cold to my people?

"Listen," I said to Beth, but loud enough for the others to hear. "We have proper weapons. Could we sleep here alone tonight?"

They looked at each other as if uneasy about this request.

"We have things to discuss," I said, "and I'd prefer it if we were alone."

"As long as you don't let the dark lord back in here," Simon muttered loud enough for everyone to hear.

Maddy ripped a dagger from her boot and crossed the cave in three strides. She had Simon pinned to the wall with the blade under his chin before he knew what she was doing. "That dark lord you're referring to happens to be the reason that your princess stands in front of you all right now. That dark lord saved her life more times than you can count. That dark lord has more courage and strength than you ever will." There was a quake to her voice, and I knew she was on the verge of crying.

"Maddy," I said softly, but she wouldn't look at me. "Okay," I said, directing this to the rest of the survivors, "so obviously we can take care of ourselves for the night. If you could all leave us alone, that would be great." No one moved as they all watched Maddy. "It's an order," I added, and slowly they all left us alone.

"Maddy," I began.

"I'm sorry," she said. "I know I shouldn't have done that—"

"No," I said, cutting her off. "I was going to say thank you. He annoyed the hell out of me."

She looked at me for a second, then we both started laughing. But then she got serious again and said, "Luke's sleeping outside."

"He can come in here," I said. "That's why I told everyone to leave."

"I don't think he wants to."

I closed my eyes, angry at myself for not sticking up for him when I had the chance. The approval of my people was just too important.

Drew came back in a few minutes later.

"Is he okay?" I asked.

He gave a sympathetic look. "He understands. Just leave him be and get some sleep."

I wasn't sure if this meant that Luke didn't want to see me, but I was too exhausted to go talk to him. Besides, Keagan was lying on his sleeping bag, watching me, and I thought it was best if he didn't know how much Luke's absence bothered me.

I found a dark corner and laid out my sleeping bag while Drew and Maddy curled up under a blanket together. We all said goodnight, then I watched as Keagan's eyelids got heavy and closed for good. But I couldn't sleep. I kept replaying in my mind how these survivors had rejected Luke. Louisa had rejected Luke. And I couldn't heal because my own people couldn't trust me. I remembered their makeshift weapons and thought about how they delegated ten people every night to go stand guard, protecting the rest of the villagers inside the mountain from the monsters that lurked outside. They didn't belong here. They deserved a fearless life under the sun, exploring their world. These children deserved a life of happiness and adventure. I needed to rid the world of monsters and bring it back to its former glory and place of protection and peace. And we couldn't do that without more help. Not with fifty monsters waiting for us on the other side of the pass, and even more monsters beyond that valley. We needed re-enforcements. . . . We needed Nitsua. We needed Ella.

Luke wouldn't like it, much less approve, so I couldn't tell him. Or anyone—not even Maddy. I would have to go alone, when everyone was sleeping, and if all went well, I'd be back before they woke in the morning. But how could I get back to this place? How could I ensure I wouldn't return to the portal and have to find my way back to this mountain? Drew had said I'd be able to port back to the palace because I had made a connection to it. Luke had said he was able to find me on Earth because he had made a connection with me. Would I be able to come back here because this was where my friends were?

Or would I have to make a more meaningful connection with the place first? If I had to make a connection, I knew the way I would want to make it. My mind wandered to Luke and our moments on the rocks at Peggy's Cove where he held me in his arms, and I felt like the safest girl in the world. I wanted to be in his arms again. To forget all about the madness and chaos going on in Yelram. I wanted to rewind time and be where we were so that I could appreciate it more than I did. Luke was my key to making a connection and being able to come back here. It was easy with him. I knew how to let him love me, I just had to let myself do it. Take my guard down just for the night and let him love me.

I waited nearly an hour, to be sure that everyone was in a deep asleep. Then I tiptoed past Keagan, around Maddy and Drew, and through the cave's exit. Luke wasn't there, so I turned right and climbed the slippery steps to a ledge that had a beautiful view of the evergreen forest below, although I knew Luke would see it as a vantage point for scouting.

"Why are you still up?" he said before I was able to find him sitting with his back against the mountainside.

"Can't sleep." I couldn't tell him about my plan. I wanted to, but I knew he would resist, or worse—follow me and ruin any chance of alliance that I might have with Ella.

I sat down next to him, as close as I could let myself.

There was still a half a foot between us, but it felt unnatural to bridge the gap anymore just yet.

"You okay?" he asked, watching me curiously.

"I'm fine," I lied. "I just . . . feel sick about how they treated you."

"It's fine," he said. "I didn't expect them to be excited to see me. They gave me the same welcome that my people would give you."

"I suppose," I said, thinking about Devon and his burning hatred for me.

"So what'd you think of them? The villagers." His voice was low and cracked a little as if he was maybe almost asleep before I arrived.

I wasn't sure how to answer that. I thought they were nice . . . to me, but they were unwelcoming and cold to him. They didn't trust him and they didn't want him there. I wished they knew him like I did. He had a soft side. He had a heart.

"I'm sorry they weren't nice to you," was all I could say.

He shook his head. "They've been through a lot, and they blame the dark worlds. Etak, especially. I can't blame them."

I wished I knew how he could be so understanding. I studied his features in the moonlight. They seemed softer in this light. Kinder.

"Will you kiss me?" I asked, and it sounded rushed,

because it was.

"What?" I had surprised him.

"Here on this ledge," I said, moving closer. "I . . . I really want to kiss you."

He smiled. "Why? . . . I mean, don't get me wrong, yes, I will definitely kiss you"—he reached over and took my face in his hand, caressing my cheek—"but why the change of heart?"

I closed my eyes as his lips moved closer to mine, and finally they were there, just lingering, but it still took my breath away to feel his skin on mine. Eventually, they moved, and he slowly kissed me. I didn't want to move, for fear his lips would leave. I wanted to stay like this forever. Just like this. Just me and him alone on a ledge with no one around. Just like it was supposed to be.

But then he moved his lips from mine. "Why?" he asked again, this time there was pressure for me to answer. He was on to me. He knew it was unlike me to do this without a reason.

"Luke, this isn't easy for me," I began. "There are few moments that pass in the day when I don't wish for your arms to be around me." My heart fluttered at this admission. "But my heart tells me one thing, and my head is leading me in a completely different direction."

"Away from me."

I nodded.

He scooped his hand around the back of my neck, his

fingers wrapping around my hair. "Then I guess I should make good use of the time when your heart's in charge." He brought his lips to mine again, and I was glad to be sitting as I was sure my knees would've failed me. He gently laid me down on the rock, his body hovering protectively above, and our lips still together. It was slow and perfect, and I hadn't noticed until the tear tricked down my temple to my ear that I was moved by it. His lips stopped, and I opened my eyes to find his. They were watching me, glistening with the same wetness that mine were.

"I've missed you so much," he breathed.

I ran the back of my fingers over his cheek, then closed my eyes and pulled him into me where we laid together on that lonely rock, him cradling me with his arm, and my head on his chest where I felt and heard his heart beating wildly. The same as mine.

"I wish it could always be like this," he said.

"Me too," I admitted. "You know if I don't find the cure, then we can be together."

He shook his head. "I don't want to think about that."

"Why? Are you afraid you won't be attracted to me if I'm as dark inside as Ella?"

He laughed. "No. No, that's not it at all. I'm sure I would be just as attracted to you, if not more."

"Why more?"

"It's just there's more temptation. That's all."

My throat burned with the memory of Ella tempting him . . . and me. But I wouldn't let it destroy this moment. We were lying together above a sweet-scented forest and beneath a star-filled sky, and I would not let a jealous thought ruin this moment.

"I forgive you for what you did. . . . For leaving me," I began. "I know that you thought you were helping me, and I believe you that it was just as hard for you as it was for me." His arms tightened around me. "And I want to thank you for it."

"Thank me?"

"It gave me time to realize that I expect too much from people. I expected my mother to raise me, and I was disappointed when she didn't. I expected Lucia to always be there, and I was devastated when she died. I expected you to love me and always be there for me, and I was angry when you weren't."

"And that's a good thing, why?"

"Because I realize now that I can't keep the key to my happiness in someone else's pocket."

He kissed the top of my head and pulled me in closer. "Don't hate me for asking this, but do you think the reason you keep Keagan close is because you're afraid to hurt him? You're afraid to put him through what you went through?"

I froze as I let this peculiar question penetrate. "No," I said. "He's a good fighter. I think we need him."

"Don't give me that, Sarah. You would never risk someone's life because it benefits you. You're doing this for him for some reason. Or . . . because there's a part of you that wonders if it could work with him."

"If I felt that way, why would I be out here with you right now?"

"Because no matter how curious you are about him, you still can't get enough of me."

I laughed into his chest. "Maybe."

"Just an FYI, you won't ever be able to get enough of me . . . because we're made for each other, Sarah. And when you accept that, you'll be much happier."

"Oh, is that so?"

"It is. And *that's* why you're out here with me right now. Because deep down you know that."

He was so sure of himself that it made me smile. I pushed the *real* reason for our ledge rendezvous out of my head, and instead kissed him again.

"Are you tired?" I asked, hoping that he was. I wanted him to fall asleep in my arms. I, of course, couldn't because I had more work to do, but I wanted to have this one last moment together before he woke up and realized I had deceived him.

He finished a yawn and then answered, "Getting there."

"Can I stay with you tonight?"

"Out here? Won't you be cold?"

"Not if I'm in your arms."

It took nearly an hour for him to fall asleep, but when his breaths were heavy and his arms were limp, I gently rolled out of his reach. I wanted to bend down and kiss him once more, for the last time, but I couldn't risk waking him, and the thought of it being our last kiss made my eyes warm with sadness. So I stole a moment to watch him sleep instead. He looked so peaceful—the lines of worry vanished as he recharged and prepared for another day. Tomorrow would be easier. Tomorrow we would have re-enforcements. Tomorrow we could find the cure and he could return to his world. Without me. I pinched my eyes closed and tried to rid that thought from my mind. Then I turned and quietly climbed down the slippery slope, until I was far enough away that the syphon of wind from my departure would go unnoticed.

# CHAPTER 14

# *Joining Forces*

## ~ SARAH ~

I HAD NEVER been at Nitsua's portal. On the two occasions that I had been to Nitsua, it was either through a dream, or with Luke, and Luke had made enough connections in this world that he didn't need to go through the portal. But I hadn't, so the portal was where I was entering. It wasn't a pretty meadow with a beautiful, large tree like Earth's portal. Or a daisy-filled field surrounded by picturesque mountains like Yelram's portal. Nitsua's portal was a huge stone on the top of a cliff. And when I came through it, taking in the dark surroundings, I wasn't alone.

The guard, donning a red cape over black tights,

stood immediately as if my sudden appearance was a complete surprise. And I supposed it had been. Not many keepers would visit Nitsua. Light world keepers were too wise, Luke was no longer an ally, and that only left Leviathan. And surely Victor would know his way around Nitsua by now.

"Wh-who are you?" the young guard asked as he pulled his sword from his belt.

"I'm Sarah of Yelram. I'm here to see Ella."

Another guard, much larger and confident than the first, rose to his feet out of the shadows. "She's been waiting for you." His voice was so deep and dark that it sent shivers up my spine. "Send word for Ella," he said to the junior guard. "Now."

The young guard ran, tripping over his own feet, and disappeared down over a bank. A few seconds later, he was soaring on the back of a dragon, heading in what I presumed to be the direction of Ella's castle.

The guard in charge slowly came to me, the earth shaking beneath his heavy footsteps. I held my head high, trying not to show my fear, as he circled slowly. When he was behind me, he quickly brought his hand to my neck, and I felt a sharp dagger tip at my throat.

My heart beat wildly. Had Ella told them that if I came, they had permission to kill me? My hand was still clutched tightly around my key, but I couldn't allow myself to leave just yet, besides, he could still kill me while we ported back to Yelram, and then I would die at Luke's feet.

"What do you want with Ella?" he said, his hot breath in my ear.

"I need her help," I told him.

"You want an alliance with Nitsua?" he asked, a laugh on his breath. "You bring her the greatest pain of her life and then you expect her to do you a favour?"

"I never meant to hurt her."

The dagger pierced my skin, and I felt warm blood run down my neck.

Ella appeared suddenly out of thin air. "Let her go now!" she shouted to her guard who hastily dropped me to the ground. I brought my hand to my neck and felt the blood run through my fingers.

Ella came to me and reached down. She grabbed me by my neck and pulled me up. I could hardly breathe as her hand clutched tighter around my airway. Then she dropped me to the ground again. "There," she said. "You're healed. No harm done."

"Thank you," I gasped.

She glared at her guard. "I said to let me know when she came, not to kill her before I got here."

"I only wanted to taste her blood," he said, as if this was an acceptable defense.

"Well, she's not yours to play with." Ella snapped her fingers and turned into Luke. "She's mine."

*No!* I thought desperately, putting up an internal wall of defense. I wouldn't be tempted by her this time. I wouldn't fall prey to her wicked ways.

But as quick as she changed into Luke, she changed back into herself. "Relax," she laughed. "Come with me."

She took my hand and her key, and a minute later we were standing in an elaborately decorated room inside her castle. There were four deep red sofas forming a perimeter around a dark brown coffee table. The walls of the room were lined with swords, spears, helmets, and shields. Ella motioned for me to sit down on a sofa and as I did, she took the opposite one.

"What brings you here, princess?" she said as a servant came into the room with two crystal glasses of a dark yellow liquid.

I took my glass and swirled the liquid around, with no intention of drinking it for fear I'd end up poisoned. "I would like to take you up on your offer for help," I announced.

Ella's eyes brightened. "You need my help."

"I do."

"Does Luke know you're here?"

"He does not."

She nodded slowly, took a drink and set her glass on the table. "What do you need me to do?"

"We need you to help clear the Northeast Quadrant of Yelram. We have Luke's army in the Southeast,

Lorendale's army in the Southwest, and Nevaeh's army in the Northwest."

"Wow," she said, seemingly impressed. "It's quite the operation you have going on there." She took another drink. "What are you looking for?"

"Well, right now we're trying to get rid of the monsters."

"What are you looking for?" she asked again, not buying this answer.

"The cure," I said. "We know it's in the Garden of Hope."

"Which is where?"

"We believe it's in the Northeast Quadrant, but haven't found it yet."

"And you want us to go in and clear out the monsters while you try to find it."

"Yes," I said.

"What happens if you don't find the cure?"

"I have just over thirty hours left, and if we don't find it by then, Yelram becomes a dark world. . . . And I become a dark lord . . . like you."

"And that's such a bad thing, why?"

"Well, for one, the balance of the worlds will be off, and Earth will plunge into darkness."

"Still not seeing why I should help. That would be a good thing for me as a dark lord."

"Yelram is supposed to be a light world, Ella. I owe it

to my people to restore it properly."

"But what about Luke? Won't you be leaving him behind if you restore your world? How will you be together then?"

I shook my head, the sting of tears threatening at the corner of my eyes. "I don't think we could be."

Her eyebrows raised slightly, but she tried not to show me her delight over this news.

"Will you help us?"

"I will help Luke," she said. "But your friends won't like it."

"It's my world, and my decision."

"They'll think I'm there to sabotage your efforts. Because obviously I have something to gain if you don't find the cure."

"But you also have something to gain if I do."

We both knew this. If I found the cure and restored Yelram, Luke would no longer be mine. She would once again have a chance at winning his heart. I kept my face impervious to this as I tried not to read her indecent thoughts.

"I'll help," she said.

"Thank you, Ella." I sighed with relief.

"On one condition." She leaned forward in her seat and held my stare with hers. "Luke comes with me."

"What?"

"We'll need someone to show us where to go, and all

I'm asking is that Luke be the one."

*No!* my heart screamed. *You can't let her do this. She'll tempt him. She'll take him. He'll fall in love with her.*

"Okay," I said, stabbing my own heart with my decision. This had to be done. It didn't matter if Luke fell to her wicked ways. It would be easier to cast him aside when this whole thing was done.

"Fabulous!" Ella said, clapping her hands together. She stood up and snapped her fingers. The door opened and a tall, fierce woman with long black hair braided around her head entered the room. "We will gather an army," Ella said, "and meet you at your portal at sunrise."

"Thank you, Ella."

The fierce woman growled and took several heady footsteps toward us. "What are you doing, Ella!" she roared. "She is the enemy! What have you promised her?"

"Dana!" Ella warned as she held her hand up. "You are not in command here. We are going to Yelram to help kill the monsters."

"In exchange for what? What is she giving us?" Dana demanded.

"She is giving us an alliance when her world turns dark."

Dana turned her steely eyes to mine as if to ask me if it were true, yet she dared not question her master.

"I'll see you at sunrise," I said before taking my key. I held it firmly and nervously in my hand, thinking ravenously of my time with Luke on the ledge and begging my key to not let me down. *Return me to the ledge.* "Take me home."

WHEN ALL THE particles of my body were present, and the hard mountain was beneath my feet, I quickly looked around, my eyes adjusting to the fading darkness. I was on the ledge, surrounded by peaks, valleys, and evergreens. I had done it. I had returned to the same spot.

"Where've you been?"

I spun around to find Luke standing behind me with Drew and Maddy next to him, hiding in the quiet shadows cast by the mountain wall.

"You scared me!" I said. "What are you all doing here?"

"Waiting for you," Luke answered, a hardness to his voice that was far from welcoming.

"How long have you been waiting?"

"Since Keagan realized you were gone," Drew said. "An hour maybe."

"Where is Keagan?"

"Out looking for you," Maddy said.

"Out *there*?" I motioned to the monster-ridden forest below. "How could you let him go by himself?"

"He couldn't be convinced to stay here and wait,"

Maddy answered.

"Wait—why are you guys here? Why didn't *you* go?"

"Why would we risk our lives?" Luke said, his face a mask of anger. "I knew we wouldn't find you in the mountains. I knew you weren't in Yelram at all."

I gulped. "How did you know?"

"I had a hard time believing your kiss was genuine. I couldn't figure out why you came to me, but I knew there was a reason. A motive. And I thought about it all night, until Keagan woke us up saying you were gone, and I realized you had disappeared from my side too. And then it made sense. The only reason you kissed me was so you could create a connection with me in this world, so when you left us in the middle of the night, you could be sure to come back." He was angry. Hurt. Disappointed. And he let me see it all.

"I wanted to kiss you," I said, trying to reconcile his hurt.

He just shook his head. "Maybe. But that's not why you did it."

It was true—I kissed him because I wanted to make a connection. If it weren't for that reason, I would've kept my distance and held onto my pride a little longer. But that didn't mean it wasn't genuine. That I didn't love it. That I didn't want it.

"So where were you?" Drew asked, and his tone was just as unpleasant as Luke's had been.

My eyes lingered on Luke's for a few seconds longer before I turned to Drew with my answer. "I went for help."

"Where?" Drew pressed, his tone firmer.

But we were interrupted. Keagan was climbing up onto the ledge, daggers in his hands.

"Sarah!" Keagan exclaimed when he saw me.

*You're alive!* I threw my arms around him as he picked me up and swung me in a circle.

"Where were you? Are you okay?" He set me down and then pulled me away so that he could search my body for injuries.

"She's fine," Drew said, "and she was just about to tell us where she went." Drew glared at my hand that Keagan was holding.

I slipped my hand from Keagan's and cleared my throat. "I went to Nitsua."

Maddy gasped while Luke turned and threw his fist into the mountain. I closed my eyes and tried to ignore it.

"We need help. There's a whole pod of monsters waiting beyond that pass and we couldn't get through it on our own. Ella agreed to send an army to help us clear the quadrant so we can find the cure."

"She agreed," Maddy said, reluctant to believe it was true.

"Yes," I said.

"What does she want in return?" Luke's voice was

deep and dark. The others were quiet, eager to hear my answer.

"Nothing in return." I looked away.

"Then what's her condition?" Luke said, narrowing his eyes on me. He knew I wasn't telling the whole truth. "Does she want an alliance with Yelram? Does she want part of your soul? Ella does nothing unless she gains something from it."

"Not everyone is evil, Luke," I said, which was really just my way of avoiding his question.

He scoffed. "Not everyone, but she's a dark lord, Sarah."

"And so are you," I spat. "So do you really want to sit here and tell me there's no good in her because of who she is? Because that's what everyone tries to tell me about you, but I choose not to believe it."

Luke pushed his hands through his hair and growled, turning away.

"Assuming we have no choice now, when is she coming?" Maddy asked.

"They'll be at the portal by sunrise."

Maddy looked up at the pink sky. "I guess we better go get ready then."

Drew led the way off the ledge, then helped Maddy down. Keagan waited for me, but Luke didn't look at me as he followed Maddy.

"Luke," I said, taking his arm as he passed. "I—"

"Please don't, Sarah," he said, but he didn't pull his arm from my grip. "Just do me a favour and figure out what you want. *Who* you want." He glanced at Keagan and then climbed down from the ledge.

Keagan waited for me to acknowledge him still standing there. It took me a few seconds to wipe the hurt from my face, and when I could smile weakly, I turned to him. "I'm sorry you went out looking for me. I would've told you but I couldn't risk you trying to stop me."

"I wouldn't have stopped you," he said. "I would've gone with you."

"Or that," I said, smirking.

"You don't think I could've held my own against Ella?"

"I wouldn't have wanted to find out."

"Sarah," he said, taking my hands, "I don't want you to worry about me. I'm here because I want to be."

"You're here because of me."

"It's not *just* that. I feel alive here. I love being with you, yes, but I also love fighting for something."

"Are you mad at me for bringing Ella and her army?"

"I trust you. I know you well enough to know you don't jump into things without thinking them through first."

"Thank you," I said.

"For believing in you?"

I laughed. "Yes, actually."

He hugged me and kissed my forehead. "I'll always believe in you."

I pinched my eyes closed, trying to block any of this from reaching my heart, but it was difficult. His lips were warm and tender on my head, and there was a questionable longing in my heart.

"We should go," he said, motioning for me to start down the ledge first. "We have an army to meet."

I PORTED US back to the field where we stood facing the portal entrance where we waited for Ella and her army to arrive. Within a few minutes, the mountainside lit up and the first soldier appeared. She was tall with long black hair and I recognized her at once—Dana, Ella's second-in-command. There was a darkness about her that I didn't like. She had her sword drawn and was eager to slay a monster. When she saw us, she held her head high and lowered her sword, calling for the rest to come through the portal.

Ella came out next. She was on foot and smaller than Dana.

"What's she doing here?" Luke shouted.

"What do you mean?" I asked. "I told you she was sending an army."

"You told me she was *sending* an army. You didn't tell me she was coming too."

"Sorry, I assumed you would know."

"Why would I know that? None of the other armies sent their keeper. The second-in-command comes for the keeper."

"It's fine," I assured him.

"She's not going near you," he said, "or the cure."

"Sarah puts a charm on Ella's key, blocking her from transporting in or out of Yelram," Drew decided. "That's the only way we do this. Otherwise, she could destroy the cure or kill us all, and just leave."

Luke nodded. "Good idea."

"But she can't just go unsupervised, either," Drew said.

"She'll be supervised," I confirmed.

"Not by you she won't," Luke challenged. "You're not going near her, Sarah."

"I'll go with Ella," Drew said. "Luke, you stay with Sarah, Maddy, and Keagan."

Luke nodded his thanks, and I regretted to have to tell them that the arrangements had already been made.

"Actually," I started, "she's agreed to help us under the condition that Luke be the one to go with her."

"What?" the three of them said at once.

"Those were her terms."

"And you were okay with that?" Maddy pressed.

"What choice did I have? We need her army to clear the quadrant for us." My eyes were on Luke's, and for some reason I couldn't look away. "I may not trust her, but I trust Luke. And I know he won't let her out of his sight."

"Sarah, don't do this," Luke said, his voice low and pleading and meant only for me.

"It's already been done." I broke connection with Luke and looked past him. Ella's army was pouring out of the portal now. Their mode of transportation was panthers. Large, black panthers. Their fierce red eyes matched the red uniforms of their riders, and although this should have scared me, I felt comforted by the sight.

Luke took my hand. "Touch my key." He placed my hand on his key and it burned for a second.

"What was that?"

"I blocked you," he said, his eyes watery.

"What does that mean?"

"It means you can't port to me."

"Why would you do that?" I said, my heart stinging with rejection.

"Because Ella isn't here to help because she likes you. If you show up, she won't hesitate to have you killed."

I closed my eyes, hoping I hadn't just made a colossal mistake. We needed her. I wanted to trust her. At least I knew he was safe. She loved him. I knew that.

"You held up your end of the bargain," Ella said, her eyes on Luke.

"Thank you for coming, Ella," I said, trying unsuccessfully to draw her attention back to me.

"Well, I suppose it's good to keep your enemies close." She grinned. "Who knows, maybe one day you and I will be allies." She winked, and I knew she predicted that I wouldn't find the cure.

Luke rolled his eyes. "Ella, I've agreed to be your *chauffeur* on the condition that Sarah charm your key so you can't transport in or out of this world without her approval."

Ella feigned surprise. "What are you afraid I'll do, Luke?"

"I don't know, maybe kill Sarah . . . maybe help destroy the world . . ."

"And why would I do that?"

"I don't know why you do the twisted things you do. Sarah might trust you, but I don't."

They watched each other for a few long seconds, before Ella said, "Fine. But how do I know you won't leave me in the middle of the night and go back to her? How do I know this isn't a trap and you won't be the one screwing me over?"

Luke scoffed, a look of disgust on his face as if he was supposed to care what she thought.

"He won't leave you," I assured her.

"That doesn't hold a lot of weight with me. Luke has a history of leaving me for you. If you expect me to give up my transporting powers, Luke has to, as well."

My heart hammered against my chest. If he wasn't

able to transport, then he couldn't escape her. What if . . . what if . . .

"I'll do it," Luke growled, and I instinctively grabbed his arm. "It's okay, Sarah," he said. "We'll draw the monsters into the valleys while you search the forests for the garden."

My eyes pinballed his, desperate for a way out of this. I was throwing him into a lion's den and taking his only lifeline. What if he needed help? What if . . .

"Here," Ella said as she took off her key. "Don't think about it, just do it. I'm not going to let him die, Sarah."

"What do I do?" I asked Luke, my voice trembling.

He removed his key too. "Take your key in one hand, and our keys in the other. Then say, 'Until my fate is sealed, you are forbidden to transport within or out of Yelram."

I repeated after him, and our three keys glowed. Ella took hers back and draped it around her neck. Luke did the same.

"Let's go then," Ella announced.

"Luke knows where to go," I began. "Good luck to you and your army, Ella."

She grinned, but her eyes stayed on Luke's. What had I done? She clearly had only one motive for being here, and I handed him to her on a silver platter. My heart was beating so loudly now that I wondered if anyone else could hear it too.

Luke pulled me into him with one arm so that he could still hold his sword at the ready with the other. My back was to Ella, and I knew this was so he could keep an eye on her. "Be careful," he whispered into my ear, the sensation sending a shiver up my spine.

My fists curled around his shirt, willing him to stay close for just a moment longer, before I had to watch him walk away with her, knowing that, until we found the cure (or for the next thirty hours, whichever came first), he belonged to her—the only other girl who was ever able to earn his affection. Thirty hours. Yesterday, forty-eight hours didn't seem like enough time; today, thirty hours seemed like a lifetime.

I swallowed hard. "You be careful too," I whispered back. "With her."

"Don't worry about me. Just focus on you and finding the cure."

"I will," I promised.

"And Sarah," he said, his voice firmer now, lacking tenderness. "Do what you need to do to survive."

I nodded, letting a small sob escape. "You too."

He hesitated, then his lips parted. "And . . . if Keagan makes you happy, then let him. You need all the light you can get right now."

I shook my head but no words came.

"And if you decide he's not the one, let me know." He made a noise as if he was going to say something else, but then thought better of it. He released me, turning away as he did.

My heart cried, shivering with his departure. I wanted his lips to stay near me for just a few more minutes. I wanted his strong arms around me. I didn't want to let him go with Ella. But I had to. I felt his agony, too, as he realized he was letting me go with Keagan right after he gave me permission to let Keagan make me happy. He knew I would be spending time alone with Keagan, and it killed him as much as this killed me.

*I love you,* he thought, but then I wondered if perhaps it was my own thought. He wasn't looking at me. He was walking away, his head held high, his sword at the ready.

Ella glanced at me over her shoulder, and I didn't like the look she gave. Smugness. Greed. Whatever it was, I chose to ignore it. Because I needed her more than I distrusted her. She would kill the monsters. She would have to for self-preservation, and when we found the cure, she could leave, and Luke . . . would leave too.

I watched them walk away together, through her army, and back to a pair of black panthers waiting for them, and hoped he wouldn't fall prey to her tempting ways.

# CHAPTER 15

# *Yelram's Keeper*

## ~ SARAH ~

**DREW, MADDY, KEAGAN,** and I ported back to the mountain ledge.

"You're getting good at that porting thing," Keagan noticed as I slipped my hand out of his.

"She's been practising," Drew muttered, and the salt in his words indicated he meant this only for me. He didn't like what I had done to Luke—leaving him in the middle of the night to make an alliance with Ella—even though he would've done the same thing for the sake of his world.

"Ella's army will clear the valleys," I reminded him. "We can follow behind and search the forests and mountains for the garden."

"Sounds like a good plan," Keagan said, giving me a reassuring smile.

My mind swirled with memories of being with Luke in the late hours of the night, and everywhere I looked— the rough mountain wall that was against our backs, the forest below that framed our romantic landscape, the sky above that watched my indiscretions—reminded me of him. But when I wasn't focusing on the things around me, I was picturing him riding alongside Ella, trying hard to resist her temptations. How could he not? I wasn't even able to resist her. She was a beautiful woman with fire and energy, and she could turn into any person that he most desired. I pinched my eyes closed and shook my head. I had betrayed him right before he left. He was angry and hurt and this would make resisting her temptations that much harder.

Drew's hand was on my shoulder. I knew it was his because it was firm and it squeezed tight; it wasn't kind and gentle like Keagan's would have been.

"You okay?" he asked, his voice a low whisper.

I nodded while keeping my eyes on the forest below.

"Don't worry about him," Drew said. "He'll be fine."

"Come on." Maddy took my hand and led me past Drew and Keagan, then I followed her down the slippery slope into the cave. "We have some time. Why don't we spend it getting to know your people?"

I liked this idea. I could pull strength from Yelram's people. I could remind myself why I was there—to help them. To take back their world. *My* world. To reunite them with family and friends and return Yelram to a world void of conflict, full of love and peace and kindness, laughter and games, and beautiful places to discover.

I already felt better by the time we entered the section of the cave they called The Gathering Place. A low fire that stretched at least ten feet wide was barely burning. The coals were red hot and there were sticks stretched across them, each donning a thick ball of white dough.

"Bread balls," a large woman to our right said as we approached. "Would you like to try one?" Her hair was tied back in a sloppy bun, and the heat from the fire caused strands to stick to her face.

"Sure," I said, without hesitation. Maddy and I both took a stick from her hand, then Maddy turned it on me and pretended it was a hammer, conking me on the head with it. I laughed, but the woman did not, so I gave Maddy a stern look, and she immediately put her head down, a grimace peeking out at the corner of her mouth.

"We survive on these and berries and the herbs and plants we can grow on the mountainside. It's too dangerous to go to the ground," the woman explained.

"Mmmm," Maddy said as she took a bite of her bread. "It's delicious."

"That one was an experiment. It has honey and thyme and oregano. A bit of rosemary, I think, too. Do you like it?"

I took a bite of mine and the bread melted in my mouth. The flavour surprised me, and my mouth woke in wonder to it.

The woman clasped her hands together with delight. "I'm so glad you like it, Your Highness."

My smile was weak, but full of gratitude and she saw it. She gave a small, awkward curtsy, but the biggest she could muster with a torso and legs as large as hers. "I'm Jocelyn," she said with a large grin.

"Thank you, Jocelyn." I extended my hand and she gladly took it. "And this is my best friend, Maddy," I introduced. Maddy shook Jocelyn's hand next, but her cheeks were full of bread so she just smiled.

"Where are the others you came with? The three men you were with last night?"

"Drew, Keagan, and Luke," I supplied.

"Yes. The two men and the dark lord." She shuddered, which made me feel sick to my stomach. I had sent that dark lord away.

"Drew and Keagan are outside with the animals," I said. "Luke is . . . gone." I wasn't sure how much I needed to tell her. Would they still trust me if I told them that I allowed a whole army of darkness into our world and that I had entrusted *him*, a dark lord keeper, to watch over them?

Jocelyn let out a heavy, exaggerated sigh. "Well, I must say, Your Highness, I think you've made a smart decision. It wasn't right having him here. He doesn't belong here, you know. Your mother would never have wanted that."

It felt like she had stabbed me. I nearly gasped, and was thankful for Maddy making a choking noise on her bread to cover up my alarm.

"He's not a bad guy," Maddy said, her mouth too full of food, but I knew she wanted to have the first word on the matter. Or the only word. Perhaps she knew I wouldn't defend him in front of the people I was still working for approval from.

"I don't mean to be frank," Jocelyn began, "but you don't know how these worlds work. You can't *choose* to be good or bad. It's just who you are."

I nodded, hoping to finish the conversation, but this seemed to frustrate Maddy. She stared at me for a second before muttering under her breath, "Maybe I shouldn't be here right now." She looked up at Jocelyn and smiled. "It was a pleasure to meet you. I should go check on the guys and make sure everything's still all *good*." This last word was added as a dig, but Jocelyn hadn't noticed it. Only *I* knew how sarcastic the sweet little blonde girl could be.

I watched Maddy leave, bothered that I didn't have

the strength to stick up for Luke myself, but knowing I didn't have a choice right now. I needed to earn the trust of these people, and I couldn't start by telling them how much I trusted the dark side.

Jocelyn was waving others over by the time I returned my attention to her.

"Doesn't she look just like her?" I heard one woman say as two others studied my features as if I were a statue on display.

"I think she looks like her father," another woman said. "Look at her nose. It's just like his."

"But her hair. Do you ever remember seeing hair like that before? Only the queen could pull off hair like that."

I was suddenly aware of how tangled my hair must have looked. When was the last time it saw a brush? I tucked a strand behind my ear and wished they would all stop staring at me.

"Your Highness?" said a small voice from behind me. I spun around to find a young girl, about the age of seven or eight, twisting her fingers nervously.

I squatted down, grateful for the distraction from all the prying eyes. "Yes, sweetheart?"

"Are you really the princess? Have you really come to rescue us?"

I smiled and took her hands in mine. "What is your name?"

"Rachel," she answered, her eyes shifting to the side

for just a second.

"Well, Rachel, this is all new to me, but I have some friends here helping too, and we are doing our very best to make this place safe for you."

"My mama tells me stories about how it used to be," she said. "It sounds like it was a much better place a long time ago."

"I hear that too," I said. "I don't remember it, but I intend to do everything I can to bring it back." I tapped her nose with my finger. "For you. Okay?"

She smiled large, but she still twisted her little fingers. There was another question weighing on her mind, so I waited for it.

"Can you . . . heal people?" she asked, her voice much smaller now that I doubted anyone else heard over their whispers. "My mama tells me that the keeper has the power to heal. She saw it before."

I pursed my lips, a feeling of disappointment rushing through me. "A keeper does," I said. "But I . . . I can't yet."

"Aren't you the keeper?"

I nodded, hoping for the interrogation to be over soon. I squeezed her hand. "I'm sort of sick right now," I told her. "And I'm looking for a cure. When I find it, I hope to be able to heal others."

I heard a mixture of murmurs in the crowd, and I wondered if suddenly I wasn't who they wanted me to be.

"You don't look sick," she said, and she raised her tiny hand to my face. "Not like my mama."

My breath caught in my throat. She had wanted me to heal her mother. What was she sick with? How many people were dying? I hung my head, ashamed and disappointed in myself. "As soon as I can heal, I will come back," I promised.

"Mama said she won't be here much longer," Rachel said, and a tear slipped down her cheek. She quickly wiped it away, embarrassed that she let it go in the first place.

"I'll hurry then," I told her.

The sudden hush of the crowd brought me to my feet again, and I saw the people parting to allow for an older man to gently push his way through, a heavy limp slowing him down. His grey hair was short and wiry, although it still stuck out over his ears. He had a bit of a beard, just as coarse as his hair, but his eyes were soft, old with lines and detail, and the deepest brown I had ever seen. Although not the same colour, they reminded me of Luke's, and I liked him at once.

I smiled as the man took my hand and kissed it gently. "You're just as beautiful as your mother."

I blushed. "Thank you."

"I lived in the village next to the palace. I was at your birthing ceremony." His voice was gentle and low, commanding the attention of everyone around. The room was silent.

"Birthing ceremony?" I asked, feeling my cheeks heat again. Was giving birth a public event here?

"Three days after a royal is born, it is customary to present the child to the people," he explained. "And the people hold their three fingers up like this"—he raised his right hand as if making an oath, and only his three fingers were raised—"and we make a promise to accept and protect the child."

"That's beautiful," I said. "Well, thank you."

"I am Joshua, and I am a man of my word," he said. He straightened tall, leaning heavily on his right leg to support his imbalance, then raised his right hand again, high above his head for the crowd to see his three crippled fingers. "I promise to accept and protect you, Princess Sarah."

I wasn't sure what came over me, but seeing this frail man declare his allegiance to me, even though the only proof he had of my legacy was my hair, brought an overwhelming feeling that flooded through my body. I flung my arms around him, careful not to knock him over, and as I held him, his left arm around me, but his right arm still high in the air, I noticed others raising their hands. I slowly pulled back and watched in amazement as the whole room raised their three fingers in my honour.

This was the moment I had only dreamed about. If I

never found the cure, I found my home. I belonged here. And although they thought they were there to protect me, I was there to protect them. I raised my right hand. "I promise to protect you. I promise to be the leader my mother once was."

My heart was so full of love that I felt it would burst. I clung to Joshua, the old man that helped bring me home. "Thank you," I cried into his shoulder.

Joshua straightened, bringing two arms around me now and held on tighter as if I was his new crutch. He trusted me to bare his weight. "Thank *you*, Your Majesty," he said. "You've healed me."

I pulled back to read his face. His eyes went to his legs and he stepped from side to side with ease.

"What do you mean?" I said, breathless.

"It looks as though you've earned that key." He hoisted his cane into the air and the crowd cheered.

I looked at my hands, wondering if it could be true. My heart was racing. Had Yelram finally recognized me as its rightful keeper? Had I earned the respect of the people enough to gain control of my healing power?

I spun around, searching the crowd for the young girl. "Where is she?" I asked desperately. "Where's Rachel, the girl that was just here?"

Jocelyn took my arm and led me through the crowd where we caught up with the girl on her way back through the caves.

"Rachel!" I called before she could disappear around the corner. "I want to see your mother."

Rachel's mother was in one of the farthest caves inside the mountain. We travelled through a tunnel that led outside and then walked through a treed part of the mountainside before reentering another tunnel. She was there alone, propped up with a few blankets behind her.

"Mama, it's her! It's the keeper!" Rachel shouted as she ran to her mother.

"Elizabeth," Jocelyn began, "this is Her Royal Highness, Princess Sarah."

I shook my head, dismissing the formal introduction. I was sure I would never get used to that. "It's just Sarah," I said as I took a seat next to the frail, sickly woman.

"Can you heal her?" Rachel asked.

I gave a weak smile, but couldn't answer. The fact was, I didn't know if I could heal her. I had only done it once before—five minutes ago—and wasn't sure at all how I managed to do it. All I had done was held him. I had been feeling an immense sense of gratitude and love, and that was the only thing I could think of that might be at all useful. I didn't even know what Elizabeth was sick with.

Elizabeth closed her eyes and laid her head back against the wall. At best guess, she was in her early forties, but her face was tired. She was losing the battle—

whatever the fight was.

My hands were on her the next second, and I only realized because I felt them burning. Was she feverish? But I was only touching her clothes. Her arms. I moved my hands to her face, willing for healing energy to leave my body and enter hers. Her face was hot too. Scorching hot. Why didn't anyone have a cold facecloth on her? I moved my hands to her chest, then stomach, then down her legs, removing the blankets as I went. She was shivering, which I couldn't explain since my hands felt like they had first degree burns on them. I pushed that thought out of my mind, though, and focused instead on the energy that was required to heal her.

A moment later, she moved her legs and bent them as if she were going to stand up. Her face was alight with wonder. She reached for the wall of the cave and took a deep breath, then pulled herself up. Then she let out a laugh that echoed around the cave walls.

"I'm better!" she cried. "Thank you, Your High—"

"Sarah. Please," I insisted.

"Thank you, Sarah." Elizabeth laughed as she threw her arms around me. Rachel did too, her head resting against my stomach. I smoothed her hair as her mother clung to me, and I absorbed every bit of happiness flooding the room.

Word of Elizabeth's healing spread quickly, and soon others joined us. Together, we celebrated Elizabeth's life, and my newly acquired healing abilities. Others brought their ailments—one child with a bad cut on his arm that looked infected (caused by a fall down the mountain over a month ago), a teenage girl with severe migraines (her healing felt similar to Elizabeth's, and I wondered if they had had the same condition), a man with regular chest pains (who was too proud to present himself, and had to be brought forward by his wife), and another child who had lost his vision years ago and wore a blindfold so others wouldn't be scared by the whiteness of his eyes.

It took what seemed like hours, but one by one, each of the injured and sick were healed. And with each new healing, I felt stronger and more alive!

Our moment of celebration was interrupted by Maddy bursting through the cave's entrance.

"Sarah!" she shouted as she searched the crowd. "It's time!" She considered the crowd before continuing in a more neutral voice, "We can leave now."

I knew this meant that Ella's army had passed through. I closed my eyes, a rush of worry for Luke clouding my senses. Was he okay? Did he make it through? Had Ella bewitched him yet? Should I even care? Maybe I wanted him to be happy so he could move on. Because my people needed me, and it was no secret that they were not fans of Luke.

# CHAPTER 16

# The Valley of Death

## ~ SARAH ~

"I CAN HEAL NOW," I gushed to Maddy as we hurried through the dark caves, meandering through the tunnels.

"Really? How?" Her breathing was less effort for her, and I wondered when she got fitter than me.

"I think it's because the people accepted me. They trust me now."

"That's awesome!" she exclaimed. "Hopefully we won't need it, but it's good to know we have it."

We burst through the main entrance where Keagan and Drew were waiting for us.

"Come on," Drew said, sheathing his sword. "We're wasting time. What the hell took you so long?"

"I couldn't find her," Maddy answered. "But good news—she can heal now."

"Great," Drew said, but I could tell the delay in our departure had more weight on him than the news of my increased power.

"That's fantastic," Keagan said, giving me a look of genuine celebration.

"Thank you, *Keagan*," I said, spitting the words in Drew's direction.

"Yeah, yeah, it's wonderful," Drew said as he led the way down the mountain. "Luke was here about an hour ago. They were heading into the valley down there to take out the monsters. It's safe to go now."

"Luke was here?" My stomach flipped at the mention of his name.

"Yeah, while you were off playing house," he added disrespectfully.

"Is he okay?"

"He's fine."

"Was Ella with him?" I tried to ignore the heartache that came with wishing I had been there to see him.

"Of course," he said, and I could hear a snarl at the corners of his words. "But just her. No one else."

"They were alone?"

Drew stopped his descent and turned to face me. "You sent him on that mission," he growled. "Remember that." He kept his eyes on mine for far too long, making me feel weak and nauseated.

"I did it for us," I finally said.

"You did it for *you*," he spat back.

"You think I *wanted* him gone?" I shouted, feeling my anger rise.

"I do," he said, his fury matching mine. "I think you were too weak to tell him you have feelings for Keagan, and you were tired of playing both sides."

I gasped. He had it completely wrong. How could he say such a hurtful thing? Was that really what he thought? That I sent Luke away with Ella because I wanted to be alone with Keagan? And if he thought that, did Luke think it too? Was that why he told me to figure out what I wanted? To decide if Keagan was the one who could make me happy? I couldn't breathe. My chest was caving in with the pressure of these agonizing thoughts.

"That's enough," Maddy said, and she passed me, giving me a sympathetic look as she did. She pushed Drew forward. "Leave her alone," she muttered. He just pulled his arm from her grip and continued down the mountain while I followed them, trying to catch my breath and avoid Keagan's eyes.

Lucia was pacing the ground when we reached the base of the mountain. When she saw me, she hurried to my side. I assured her that I was fine, but when I looked up, I realized the reason for her uneasiness—Gideon and Angus had joined us! The wolves stood on one side while the three tigers prowled restlessly opposite them.

"Oh yeah, and we have some more back-up," Drew said, nodding toward the wolves. "Lucia doesn't like it, though."

"It's okay, girl," I told her. "I trust them." Immediately, she and the other tigers relaxed. "When did they get here?"

"Luke brought them. They caught up with him on the way in."

I remembered back to when we were at the portal with Devon, and Luke had told Devon's wolf to send Gideon to him, not quite convinced that it would work. I wished I could've seen Luke's face when Gideon caught up to him in the forest.

"He kept one of them with him, and dropped these two off for protection," Drew explained.

"He kept Malyn," I noticed. "He should've taken Gideon." A mass of concern flooded my appreciation. Gideon was stronger. He would've been better protection for Luke.

"He wanted you to have the strong ones," Drew said.

"I'll ride Angus," Maddy announced as she reconnected with the grey wolf.

Drew and Keagan mounted the tigers while Gideon came to stand next to me. He was watching me, an earnest look of communication on his brow. I opened my mind to him and searched for his voice.

*If Master Luke finds the cure, he will have Malyn send me the message, and I will lead you to them.*

"Is that why he left you with me?"

*Yes. He doesn't trust Nitsua's keeper.*

For some reason, this encouraged me. *Are you able to see what they're doing now?*

Gideon turned his head sideways, a focused concentration to his stare. He was connecting with Malyn, but I couldn't hear their communication. Then he slowly brought his eyes to mine, and I felt a tug before everything around me disappeared, my surroundings replaced with a blurry scene of trees rushing past.

Through Gideon, I saw what Malyn saw. I saw nothing but trees as Malyn ran, full speed, through the mountain passages. Then Ella, atop her perfectly poised panther, caught up and passed Malyn. She looked back and flashed a beautiful smile at Malyn's rider—Luke—and said, "Bet you can't catch me!"

My heart squeezed, and Gideon closed the connection between him and Malyn.

"Thank you," I told him, and I wasn't sure if I was more thankful he opened his mind to me, or that he closed it when he did.

WE RODE THROUGH the mountain pass with our weapons readied. We could see the valley at the other end of the pass, but there was no sign of the vicious, blood-hungry creatures that had been lurking there just hours before.

As the passage let out into the valley, we surveyed the carnage left behind by Ella's army. Dozens of monsters had lost their lives in that valley. Dozens of warriors did too. I tried not to notice their bodies lying at odd angles, some missing their heads, while others torn right in two.

Gideon stayed close to my side, much to Lucia's discomfort. Keagan and his tiger took up a position on our left, and Lucia relaxed. She found comfort in knowing the wolf was now outnumbered in case he tried something he shouldn't.

Suddenly, a skull-shattering screech sounded in the distance. The trees on the mountainside swayed and broke as a massive, black-bodied creature surged down the mountain toward us.

"Get ready!" I yelled to the others as I pulled my bow and released an arrow toward the beast. The arrow stuck into the monster's chest, but didn't slow it down any. I aimed another, but just as I released it, Lucia veered right and my arrow narrowly missed the monster's head. The movement ripped me from Lucia, and I fell to the ground. As soon as I fell, Lucia roared, realizing that I had fallen into the path of the monster. She turned quickly and leaped through the air toward the beast, her claws and teeth sinking into its neck.

My head was dizzy from the fall, but I shook it off and

pulled my sword. Where had this beast come from? Hadn't Ella's army cleared them all out? Or had Ella given her army orders to leave a monster as a gift for us because she knew we would be following them through the valley? I shuddered. We could be walking right into a trap.

The monster threw itself into the base of a tree, crushing Lucia against it. She fell to the ground, and the creature turned on me. Gideon, Angus, and the two tigers stood bravely in front of me, while Drew, Maddy, and Keagan surrounded the monster. But all I could think about was Lucia lying still on the ground.

Drew leaped through the air, seemingly flying as he bent the laws of gravity, and drove his sword into the creature's back, but other than flailing and throwing Drew away, with a sword still stuck in its back, the monster didn't fall.

Maddy let out a roar and threw her hands into the ground causing the earth to erupt, throwing us all back. We were expecting it more than the monster, so our recovery was faster. Gideon and Angus attacked the monster from both sides, but they, too, were flung into the trees. Keagan mounted one of the tigers and as the tiger leaped through the air toward the monster, Keagan drove a sword into the creature's chest. But still, it lived.

Suddenly, an arrow whizzed past my ear and into the monster's eye, giving me enough time to scramble out of the way before the creature landed on me. Another arrow stuck into the monster's mane, knocking him off balance.

Keagan helped me to my feet while Maddy fought the creature with Drew by her side. So where were the arrows coming from?

As Keagan pulled me to safety, I found the shooters — Simon and Beth from the mountain cave. As relieved as I was for their assistance, my concern for them was greater. They were Yelram's people, and I was responsible for them.

The enormous monster still wasn't falling. Keagan had joined Drew, Maddy, Simon, and Beth, but even the four of them with swords and knives, were only strong enough to slow the thing down, not kill it.

"Sarah!" Maddy shouted. "Cripple him!"

*Cripple him?* It took a few seconds to register, but as the monster turned its sights on Beth and Simon — Yelram's people — I realized what she had meant.

I grabbed a hold of the monster's mind with my own and brought him the most pain I could think of because I had to if it meant saving their lives. The creature fell to the ground as if a ten ton truck had fallen on its head. It squealed in agony, the sound piercing our ears.

"Sarah, that's enough!" Drew yelled before ripping his sword from the beast's back and plunging the blade into its skull.

I fell back onto the ground, breathless and exhausted.

It had taken everything out of me.

"That's what darkness will do to you," Drew said, helping me to my feet. "There are more humane ways to kill a thing."

"At what cost?" I muttered, feeling an arousal of darkness at the comment.

He brought his mouth to my ear. "Your craft wasn't created to bring pain."

Lucia was breathing heavy at the base of the tree, her legs unsteady as she slowly stood. I ran to her and pressed my hands to her back and chest. I already knew where the pain was. I felt it too, the moment she slammed into the tree. Bones cracked and moved, and soon her breathing regulated. In a few minutes, she was pacing the forest, eager to go again. I studied my hands in awe, so thankful for the ability to heal.

"What are you doing here?" Keagan barked at Simon.

"We were following you," Beth answered. "In case you needed help."

Gideon and Angus were circling the newcomers, their heads low as they bared their teeth menacingly. Their threat was challenged by two new tigers that leaped in front of Simon and Beth, and the four animals growled and snarled at each other until I stepped between them.

"That's enough," I said. "We're all friends here."

"What the hell are those?" Simon said, a nervous edge to his voice.

"Wolves, genius," Keagan answered.

"I *meant* where did they come from? Who do they belong to?"

"You shouldn't be here," I said, ignoring Simon's question, although part of me felt comforted by having them with us. Aside from being good fighters, they had experience with the monsters, and they knew the quadrant well. They could help us.

"Go home," Keagan said.

"Not happening," Simon challenged while Beth looked to me for direction.

"Excuse me?" Drew said. "You don't get to make those types of decisions around here."

"Okay," Simon said arrogantly. "Send us back. I'm sure everyone would love to hear all about the dark army you let in here, and their vicious animals."

Gideon growled at the same time Keagan took Simon by the throat. "Your *princess* let that army in here, which means it doesn't matter what you have to say about it— you need to respect it."

Beth was watching me, and I couldn't ignore her any longer. "We needed help," I finally admitted. "Nitsua's army agreed to clear a path for us so we can look for the cure."

"Do you trust them?" she asked.

I inhaled deeply. "I may not trust Nitsua's keeper, but I do trust someone I sent with them. He will keep an eye on her."

Simon's mouth fell open. "That dark lord that I kicked out of here last night? Seriously?"

Keagan threw him to the ground, which, judging by the anger in his eyes, was generous.

"Luke," Beth recalled. "You love him, don't you?"

My eyes flickered to Keagan's, and I felt a pity for him that I couldn't justify. "I . . ."

"She does," Maddy finished.

"He is more trustworthy than any of us," Drew added. "He would fight to death for Sarah and her world."

Simon shook his head. "I don't believe this." He turned to Beth. "Are you buying this shit?"

"Simon!" she scolded. "As a matter of fact, I am. And you'd do well to hold your tongue."

Keagan chuckled. "I like her."

"Fine," Simon said. "If that's what you think is best for Yelram, princess, then we'll support it."

"You didn't have a choice," Keagan reminded him. "And you're still not coming."

Simon opened his mouth to say something, but Beth squeezed his hand, her eyes on me. Keagan's fists were clenched, his dislike for Simon too obvious. And yes, although I could easily agree that Simon's ignorance and bad attitude were characteristics that I could do without, there was no denying that he was an excellent fighter and knew this quadrant better than we did. I relayed these thoughts to Keagan, and presented them as his own.

*Simon's a good fighter. He'll be able to help protect Sarah.*

Keagan's brow furrowed, and he shook his head, as if the thought was almost too strong.

"Well," Keagan said, seemingly confused, "I guess you proved your worth out here, so if Sarah's okay with you staying . . ."

"Are you sure you *want* to come?" I asked Beth.

She answered with a huge smile. "We've been waiting for this day for a long time. We can lead the way. We know it well."

Simon grinned smugly, which was meant for Keagan.

I motioned toward the new tigers. "These are yours?" I asked.

Beth nodded. "That one's Garfunkel," she said, pointing to the large animal that Simon had just mounted. "And this is Bear." She stroked the side of her tiger. "We've been breeding tigers in the mountains for years, trying to bring back their population so they can help us kill the monsters."

"That's amazing," Maddy said.

Simon smiled at Maddy as if just noticing how pretty she was. "Those two tigers are female," he said, nodding toward the two that Lucia had summoned at the portal. "You can tell by the diamond mark on their foreheads. Females are yellow. Males are blue."

"Once the tigers are full grown," Beth continued, "Simon and I deliver them to other surviving villages."

"Wow," Maddy said. "That's really great."

"We put collars on them," Simon said, "which makes it easier to hold on when you're riding. And we carve their names into their collars."

"Really?" Maddy dismounted Angus and cautiously approached the tiger that Drew had been riding. Maddy was nervous around the big animals, and I couldn't blame her. Although I knew they wouldn't, they could easily kill her with just one wrong move.

Maddy ran her hand along the animal's shoulder and when she found the collar, she slowly turned it so that she could see the name. "Bella," she read.

Simon chuckled. "I thought so. I could tell by the white tail tip."

Keagan rotated the collar of his tiger. "Jasmine?"

Beth nodded. "She's a fierce one. From a line of fighters."

A low growl emanated from Jasmine's chest, causing Maddy to return to Angus's side.

"Don't worry," Simon assured her, "they won't hurt you. They're bred for destruction of darkness, not . . . prettiness."

"Yeah, okay, so we should get going," Drew said, instantly annoyed.

Simon grinned, and then he and Beth led their tigers

onward, and when they were out of earshot, I asked
Drew and Maddy, "Did I do the right thing letting them
come along?"

Drew nodded. "We can use all the help we can get."

Maddy nodded her approval too, and then they both
followed Simon and Beth, leaving Keagan and me
behind.

"Hey," Keagan said as Lucia and Jasmine carried us
slowly toward the others. "You did great back there."
Gideon followed closely behind, keeping a watchful,
wary eye on the forest.

"What—with Simon?"

Keagan clenched his jaw. "No. He's an idiot. I meant
with the monster."

"Well, I mean, I'd prefer not to, but there wasn't
another choice. It would've killed . . ." I shuddered.

"How did you do it?" he asked, referring to the way I
threw the monster to the ground without lifting a finger.

"I . . . I'm still not a hundred percent sure how all my
powers work here," I said, carefully constructing my
sentence so that it wasn't a lie.

Keagan nodded, slowly, deciding not to press further.

I smiled. "Thanks for being here, Keagan." And as if
on cue, Lucia started sprinting toward the others. Luke
had told me to do what I needed to do to survive. This
meant using the dark power to cripple the monsters if I
had to. Luke would've wanted me to do the same thing.

Drew may not understand it, but it was necessary for survival.

THE GARDEN OF Hope wasn't in the valley. I knew because the garden was a field of daisies surrounded by a perimeter of tall trees. I only had one memory of the garden, and that was it. But we searched anyway. Drew wasn't convinced that the garden wasn't somehow camouflaged to protect it.

The edges of the valley had more trees as the ground slowly crawled up toward the mountains. We concentrated our search in these wooded areas, and combed our way back and forth through the forest looking and listening for a secret, special garden that would carry the cure for my soul. And my world.

"I think we're going in circles," Maddy complained.

"We're not," Drew answered.

"It feels like it. I'm sure I've seen that tree before."

Drew dismounted Bella and pulled the map out of his pack. He stretched it out onto the ground as Simon, Beth, and Keagan joined him.

"We came through here," he started, "and then we came here. This is where the monster came down the hill. We've searched here . . ." I let his voice trail off as I turned my attention to Gideon. He hadn't joined the others, and he hadn't come to my side, either. He was off on his own, peering into the distance.

I slid off of Lucia and slowly made my way to Gideon. I didn't like the way his body was tense, and his eyes were narrowed.

"What's wrong?" I asked as I approached. He didn't answer, so I let myself feel his emotions, which I almost regretted immediately. A sharp sense of guilt washed over me. Guilt as though I should have been there because I was stronger, faster, and braver. This was Gideon's guilt, of course, and I knew instantly that he struggled with watching Malyn carry Luke into battle when it should have been him.

Hesitantly, I opened a connection to Gideon's mind and the edges of my vision blurred as a tunnel to his opened.

I saw a sea of monsters and warriors fighting. Bodies were being eaten with one bite and wolves were being ripped in two as if they were made of tissue.

"Where is Luke?" I pressed, searching the crowd for Luke's blue shirt.

*He is with Malyn*, Gideon told me, and I realized that Malyn wasn't in the fight. He was watching from the sidelines, and Luke was with him. Suddenly a familiar female voice shouted, "Luke, watch out!" Malyn turned his head in time to see a monster lunge toward them.

"Are you okay?" Drew was asking, and the scene before me dissipated, the trees of the forest and my friends returned to my vision. "What's wrong?"

"Gideon!" I said, frantic. "Gideon, what happened?"

Gideon looked away. *Master Luke doesn't want you to worry about him.*

"Then tell me he's okay!" I shouted.

*I can't reach Malyn right now.*

"Sarah," Drew said, stepping between me and the wolf. He didn't need to say anything else, his warning was because of Keagan, who couldn't know that I was a mindbender and telepathically communicating with Gideon.

*Why can't you reach Malyn?* I pressed Gideon, wordlessly.

*He's busy.*

*Is he still alive?*

*I feel his energy,* Gideon confirmed. *He is still alive.* But his restless movements confirmed his worry.

I tried to ignore the feeling of hopelessness and fear. I had put Luke in this position. I was responsible for whatever happened to him.

Drew led me back to Lucia and helped settle my shaking arms as I mounted her. "Everything okay?" he asked quietly.

The lump in my throat prevented me from answering. I just shook my head, shrugged, and wiped a stray tear.

Drew squeezed my leg. "It's okay," he assured me. But he didn't see what I saw. He didn't know what I knew.

"Let's keep riding," I said, refusing to think about Luke's fate any longer. Maybe if we could catch up to them, we could help. I could heal.

FINALLY WE FINISHED searching the first valley and surrounding area. Simon and Beth led us toward the next mountain pass, while Gideon took detours up the sides of the mountains, searching for some type of resistance that might suggest a charmed garden was near.

My heart quickened as we neared the end of the mountain pass. The end of the tunnel meant that there was another field of slain monsters and fallen riders.

As we rode into the valley, the scene was too familiar. It was the aftermath of what I had seen through Gideon, and my heart hammered with the suppressed concern that Luke could be one of the fallen.

Drew held out his hand for us to stop. He readied his bow with an arrow and aimed it toward the field, but nothing was moving. Lucia took us between Drew and Maddy, lowering her head as she peered intently into the field.

"What are we doing?" I asked as Beth and Simon began circling the valley.

"Waiting," Drew said, his lips barely moving.

"You think it's a trap?" I said, my heartrate accelerating. When it was just my thought, I could pass it off as irrational, but if Drew considered it too, there was merit to my suspicions.

At Drew's silence, Maddy answered, "I don't think it's a trap. Luke would never let them get away with it."

"Unless he's dead," Drew considered.

And my breath got lost in my throat. *What did he just say?* Lucia swayed. Or I swayed, I couldn't tell, but it took more effort to hold on, so I slid off her back and took a few steps toward the field, my feet working hard to ignore the imbalance in the ground.

"He's not dead," Maddy said confidently, but her voice and her thoughts didn't match.

If he was dead, it was all my fault. I had sent him in there. I paired him with Ella. It was all my fault.

"Sarah, where are you going? Drew, stop her!" It was Keagan and his voice was already far behind me. I was running into the field, empty-handed. I had left my bow on the ground next to Lucia, but she wasn't guarding it, she was running alongside me. Not so much running, as walking swiftly, since her stride was much longer than mine.

I had to find him. I had to heal him.

"Luke!" I cried.

"Sarah!" Drew shouted. "Shut-up!"

"LUKE!" I cried again.

Drew caught me by my arm and pulled me atop Bella, throwing me behind him. "Shut the hell up! If there's even one monster within a mile radius, you're asking for it to come kill us."

I tightened my arms around his waist and buried my face into him, fighting back the tears. "What if he's dead, Drew? This is all my fault."

He didn't answer, but Bella was still moving, weaving in and around bodies, and I knew Drew was checking them for me. I kept my eyes pinched closed, not wanting to see anything but dead monsters and red armour. Suddenly, we stopped.

"Oh, no," he said, his words a hush.

"What! What is it?" I pressed my face into his back. "Drew, is it Luke?" I let out a sob and clutched his shirt in my hands.

"It's not him," he said and his hand found mine. "Relax."

I pried my face from his shirt and looked down. It was a red soldier, his hands and feet bound by ropes. At least I assumed it was a male, there really was no way to tell with the head missing.

I gasped and covered my mouth. "What the hell happened?"

Drew growled. "Ella. This soldier was a diversion. She sacrificed one of her own to draw in the monsters so they could slaughter them."

"You think she would do that?"

"You got a better explanation?"

"Look over here!" Maddy called from about fifty feet

away. When we reached her, she was standing next to another warrior's body, bound and sacrificed in the same way.

"That's inhumane," I said.

"But it worked," Keagan said as he joined us. My eyes darted to his for a second and he smiled. "I checked all the bodies. Luke's not here." There was a kind jealousy in his eyes. He knew I still loved Luke, and it bothered him, but he understood—Luke and I had history. I had told him that from the beginning.

"It might have worked," Drew said, "but it still doesn't make it right."

I was too relieved that Luke was not one of the fallen to really care whether Ella sacrificed some of her own to save herself. Because I knew saving herself meant saving Luke, too. She wanted him alive. She still cared about him, which, if I had to be honest with myself, was why I knew he would be safe with her. Besides, if anything happened to Luke, the deal would be off. She would be stuck in my world with no way out.

This was what I told myself to stay brave. Luke was okay. He would have to be. I didn't send him to his death.

"The garden isn't here," Drew announced. "We need to keep moving."

As we readied to leave, I saw Beth and Simon standing over the sacrifices in the field. I steered Lucia toward them.

"You guys okay?"

Simon nodded and Beth wiped a tear. "We're fine," she said.

"I'm really sorry you had to see that."

Simon looked up at me. "We've never seen anything like this before." His face firmed. "Another reason we can't trust the dark lords."

"Luke wouldn't have been okay with this," I said.

Simon nodded, although he wasn't convinced. "Come on," he said, nodding to Beth. "We should keep moving."

The sun was starting to set, which meant we were running out of time. We had less than twenty-four hours to find the cure and end the eclipse. End the darkness of my soul. The turning of the worlds.

# Chapter 17

## A Cold Night

### ~ Sarah ~

Like the previous two, the third valley had been conquered and left littered with the bodies of monsters and warriors alike, as well as a few more sacrifices. It was clear now that this was their strategy—tie up a few disposable warriors, cut their achilles or slit their throats, then wait for the monsters to swarm and feed on their blood. It was a clever plan, I had to admit. Was it my inner darkness that allowed me to appreciate this plan?

We searched the bodies, my heart beating wildly as we did. The others, convinced that Luke was not among the dead, searched for anyone who might still be alive and in need of healing. I, on the other hand, only searched for dark jeans and a blue fitted t-shirt.

By the time we had declared the valley gardenless and absent of any survivors, the moon was high in the sky.

"We have to move faster," I said. "We're running out of time."

"Sarah," Maddy began, "these bodies are still warm. Ella's army isn't that far ahead of us. If we keep riding, we'll run into them. Besides, they'll have to stop for rest anyway, and we don't want to be stuck in the forest with them in the middle of the night."

I nodded. It was getting cold, too, and I was hungry. I needed a rest but hated the idea of wasting hours on sleep.

"Where should we rest then?" Maddy asked Drew.

Drew looked around the field. "We could pitch a tent here."

"In the middle of all these corpses?" I asked incredulously. "I don't think so."

"It's probably the safest place," Maddy said. "Among the dead. The monsters won't be able to smell us with all this blood around."

"No, of course not. We'll just wake up in the middle of a feeding frenzy."

Maddy ignored my sarcasm. "Simon, are there any settlements in these mountains that we could rest in?"

Simon shrugged. "Could be, but none that we know

of."

"Then we'll go up that mountain," Keagan decided. "And find a cave or someplace sheltered."

He started riding toward the mountain, and I gladly followed, shaking my head at Drew. *Pitch a tent in the middle of corpses! What was he thinking?*

We led the animals up through the hills until we found a ledge large enough for our tent, with another ledge, twenty feet below, that provided a good look-out spot for the animals.

"This will do," Drew said as he surveyed the dark corners of our resting place. "Keagan and I will go for wood." He looked at Simon. "You'll come with us," he ordered. His dislike for him was obvious.

"I'll come too," Beth offered. "Unless, Sarah, you'd like for me to stay with you."

I smiled. "No, that's fine. Maddy and I will try to start a fire with what we have here. We'll be fine. You go."

The night was cold, and I wondered how we would all sleep. We had only one tent, which was barely big enough for four. We would need warmth from each other, but I pushed the thought from my mind. Would Luke be stopping for rest too? Would he and Ella be sleeping under the stars together? Would he be cold? Would she comfort him? Was he even still alive? A feeling of panic churned in my chest, and I closed my eyes and tried to think of Luke happy and healthy and safe.

While the others were gone for wood, Maddy began working at starting a small fire. She gathered some sticks and leaves from nearby and placed them carefully in a circle. Then she reached into Drew's bag and pulled out a lighter. Each time a leaf caught fire, it extinguished just as quickly.

"You done? Can I try?" The fire licked at my fingertips, patiently waiting to be let out.

"No!" Maddy scorned. You're not supposed to be practicing that. Besides, if Beth or Simon see you do that, they won't be so impressed.

"It's fine. They're not here." I flicked my finger toward the fire, and a small ball of fire landed on her makeshift firepit, instantly igniting the sticks and leaves.

"Fine," she said. "Just don't tell Drew I let you do that."

"You didn't." I winked, then we both took a seat next to the fire.

The sky darkened quickly over the next half hour while we warmed up and cooked beans and hotdogs over the small fire, and I let the flickering flames and crackling sticks distract me from the cruel thoughts of what was happening elsewhere in my world.

Maddy tested her hotdog with her fingers, then hissed and licked her wounded fingers until the heat left them.

"Remember when we went to the cabin with Drew

and Luke?" she recalled.

"You mean when they kidnapped us and took us deep into the scary woods to train us?"

Maddy gave a half-smile. "Yeah. Before we knew what we were getting ourselves into."

It had been three long days of intense training where we learned how to use a sword, kill a man with our bare hands, and Maddy learned how to shoot a bow. I also learned that I could communicate with wolves, which would've been the highlight of the experience had it not been for the stolen moments in the woods with just Luke where he held me tenderly, kissed me softly, and we hid our desperate, rekindled love from Drew.

"Those woods don't seem so scary anymore, do they?"

Maddy's smile faded quickly. "Not at all."

"I would give just about anything to have Luke here right now," I admitted, my voice hushed and threatening to waiver.

"You're worried about him, aren't you?"

I nodded.

"Why did you send him then?"

"She made me. It was her only condition. And we needed her army." I put the can of beans on the ground, having lost my appetite.

"For what it's worth, I think you did the right thing."

"You do?"

"Yeah, I do. We've made good progress, and we couldn't have done it without them. Drew's been a little hard on you, but he shouldn't be. You were right."

"Then why do I feel so sick about it?"

She nudged me with her shoulder. "It's called jealousy."

I grinned, but shook my head. "It's not just that. I mean, yes, I hate the idea of the two of them together." I shuddered and pressed the image out of my mind. "But I'm also sick. Like I just pushed him away forever."

"Well, maybe you kind of did."

"That doesn't help."

"No, hear me out, Sarah. Maybe you wanted to send him away. Maybe you have feelings for Keagan and—"

"I don't have feelings—"

"*Hear . . .* me out." She rotated her hotdog over the fire. "Maybe you sent him away because deep down you wanted to see what life would be like with just Keagan. Without Luke around."

My mouth was dry, and I couldn't speak. This was, of course, not true at all, but . . . but what if it was? What if my feelings for Keagan were enough to warrant me needing some space to see if they were real? Luke had obviously felt it, or he wouldn't have told me to use this time to figure out who I wanted to be with.

But I loved Luke.

It wasn't that simple. It wasn't an easy choice. My

people rejected Luke. My world rejected him. If I wanted to be a leader here, my choices would affect my people, and I had to take their needs into consideration.

"For what it's worth, I don't think Keagan makes you happy."

I smirked. "He's a good guy."

"I didn't say he wasn't."

"When I'm with him, I feel drawn to him. He makes me happy, and I really care about him. . . . But when we're not together, like right now, all I can think about is Luke, and I feel like I've betrayed him with feelings for Keagan."

"Sounds like a dilemma," she said.

"Keagan deserves to be happy."

"But that's not your job to make sure that he is."

"But he was my first dreamer. So it kind of is."

"Oh my gosh." Maddy straightened up. "Is that what this is all about? You feel a responsibility to him because he was your first dreamer?"

I stared at her. Had I said that?

She squatted down next to me and steadied my hand that was rotating the hotdogs. "Sarah, listen to me. Your only responsibility right now is to find the cure and save the worlds." She laughed at herself. "Okay, I know that sounds like a huge responsibility, but I only meant it as perspective. Keagan is not important right now. Focus on the mission."

"Luke wants me to figure out if Keagan will make me happy," I said. "Maybe he could."

She pursed her lips and shook her head. "Only you can answer that, I guess."

"I just . . . I *want* to figure it out, but all I can do is think about Luke."

"Then that should tell you something."

"But Maddy, I can't be with him. My people reject him. I have to be the keeper that they need. They're suffering. Yelram's a world full of hurt and destruction. I need to be there for them. I need to show them that they can trust me."

"You need to show them that you are a leader, Sarah. Nothing else."

I nodded, then plucked my hotdog from the stick and ate it even though it wasn't quite heated through.

"So what do you think about Simon?" Maddy asked as I took my last bite.

I chuckled and shook my head. "He's eager," I said, choosing my words carefully.

"That's one way to put it. I don't think Drew and Keagan think much of him."

"He's just used to being alpha male," I realized. "And that doesn't go over well with Drew and Keagan."

"I just worry he's going to get himself killed," Maddy said. "He doesn't know what he's getting himself into."

"Sounds like you have a soft spot for him," I teased.

"I have a soft spot for Drew, in case that wasn't obvious."

I laughed. "Oh, it was obvious."

She shook her head. "Besides, I'm pretty sure he and Beth have a thing."

"You think?"

"Well, I mean why wouldn't they? They clearly spend a lot of time together and he's hot, and so is she."

I laughed. "Sounds like you have a soft spot for Beth, too."

"Maybe I do," Maddy teased. "Jealous?" She stood and stretched her legs, and that's when I saw a darkness lurking in the shadows of the mountainside. Before I could warn her, the figure had one arm wrapped around Maddy's body and another holding a knife to her throat.

"Easy now," I said, my hands outstretched to show that I was weaponless. "We don't want any trouble."

"Who are you? What do you want?" the man demanded. His voice was deep, and from the way he towered over Maddy, he was also much larger than even Drew and Luke.

"I'm Sarah," I said, my voice trembling slightly. The knife's edge was tight against Maddy's throat, and she was struggling to breathe. "I am Yelram's keeper."

"LIAR!" the man roared. "You're one of them!" He pointed his knife in the direction of the valley, but then returned it to Maddy's neck.

"Sarah," Maddy whimpered.

He was convinced that we were part of Nitsua's army. I had to get into his head. *These girls are clearly not one of Nitsua's,* I thought desperately, bending the thought so that it was one of his own.

"Nitsua," he repeated. "You're Nitsua's keeper, aren't you?" His voice was louder now. "You're shapebending to look like Queen Leah. How *dare* you impersonate our queen!"

Blood trickled down Maddy's neck. I had to fight harder to get through to him, but instead of pushing thoughts into his head, which clearly wasn't working, I decided to pry open his mind and listen to his own thoughts.

*But what if she's telling the truth? She does look a lot like the queen, so she could be her daughter. What if she's the lost princess? There were rumours that she survived. . . . But then what is she doing here? And how did those dark warriors get in here? . . . If she was the keeper for Nitsua, she could've bent into a dragon and killed us all by now . . . but she hasn't.*

His eyes flickered to the shadows on the mountainside, and I knew instantly that there were more of them. Waiting. Hiding.

"Please believe me," I said. "I am the lost princess." I used his words, hoping it would convince him.

Suddenly there was a cracking sound, and the man stumbled forward. Maddy took the opportunity to struggle free from his grasp, and as he fell to the ground, we saw the arrow protruding from his back.

I grabbed my bow and raised it in the direction of where the arrow came from.

"Don't move!" Simon shouted from somewhere in the darkness. "Or I'll take out another!"

Drew climbed onto the ledge and helped Maddy to her feet, while Keagan appeared next to me, his sword pointing at the two remaining villagers who were on the ground next to their fallen comrade.

"Simon!" I shouted. "What have you done?!"

Simon climbed onto the ledge, followed by Beth. "He was going to kill her, Sarah. I didn't have a choice."

"He wasn't going to kill her!" I shouted. But I couldn't explain how I knew that. How I had entered his mind and heard his menacing thoughts. He was only trying to protect his family.

I pushed past Keagan's resistance and fell to the ground next to the arrowed man. "I can heal him," I said to his friends, one of them being a woman about ten years older than me.

"Are you . . . are you really the lost princess?" she wondered aloud.

I nodded, then closed my eyes and pulled the arrow from his back, ignoring his screams. "I'm so sorry," I said to him. "Hang on." I laid my hands on his back, and they trembled with the weight of his healing.

"Please forgive him, princess," the woman said. "We saw the red army, and we were scared. We didn't know what to believe."

It took only half a minute. The wound literally sewed itself up in front of my eyes, leaving only the evidence of blood and a torn shirt behind.

The man slowly stood. "Your Highness," he said, bowing. "I beg your forgiveness."

"You had every right to wonder," I answered.

"I'm sorry," he said, this apology meant for Maddy.

Simon was on one side of Maddy with his eyes fixed on the man, and Drew was on her other side, caressing her back. Her fingers trembled as they held onto the spot where the knife dug into her neck only moments ago. I went to her and touched her neck, healing it instantly. Then we embraced, and I felt her gratitude grow while her fear slowly diminished.

"So you have a settlement here," Beth said. "How many of you are there?"

The man hesitated, so the woman answered, "Eighty-seven," she said. "We're spread out around the valley. There used to be a lot more of us, but we lose a few each year to the monsters. We lost six this year."

"Eighty-seven," Beth mused. "That's even bigger than our settlement."

"What is going on down there?" the woman asked. "Why is Nitsua's army here killing monsters?"

"They are helping us," I explained. "I've made a deal with them. We are looking for the Garden of Hope and we need their help to clear the monsters."

"Do you know where the Garden of Hope is?" Maddy asked, hopeful.

The three strangers shook their heads. "We don't venture too far."

Drew nodded. "Listen, we don't really have much time, but we do need to eat and get some rest. Can we sleep here?"

"Our cave isn't that big, but—"

"We don't want to come in," Drew clarified. "We have a tent and can sleep out here near our animals."

"Of course," the man nodded. "Did you need some food? Blankets? Weapons? Anything?"

"We could use some blankets," Simon said, realizing he hadn't packed anything.

"Simon, you and Beth should sleep in the cave," Drew said. "There isn't room in the tent."

Beth nodded. "Okay."

"But don't leave without us," Simon said.

I grinned. "We won't. I promise."

Beth and Simon disappeared into the mountain with the three villagers, leaving Drew, Maddy, Keagan, and me alone on the ledge.

"You okay?" Drew asked Maddy as they both took a seat.

"That was terrifying," she admitted. "I thought he was going to kill me."

"He wouldn't have," I assured her. "I heard his—" I paused, realizing that I was about to admit that I had been inside his mind. I glanced at Keagan and he smiled innocently. "I heard his *friends* in the shadows," I covered. "I knew they were more scared than us. I didn't think they would hurt us." I took a seat next to Maddy and picked up the can of beans. "Anyone hungry?"

"I lost my appetite," Drew said, his grip tightening on Maddy's knee.

She touched his hand with hers. "Let's go for a walk," she suggested. He didn't need any prodding; Drew was sick over seeing Maddy in such a vulnerable position, and he was more than willing to spend a few quiet moments with her.

"Having any regrets about tagging along yet?" I asked Keagan when they were gone.

He smiled and put his hand in mine. "Not even for a second."

My face flushed as my hand froze. "It's kind of a non-traditional way to spend a weekend away with friends."

Keagan laughed. "Yes, it is."

"You're doing pretty awesome, though."

"Well, for someone who has a limited skill-set."

"I'm sorry you didn't get a craft when you came over."

"Yeah, it's okay. I've just accepted the fact that I don't really belong in any of the dream worlds yet, you know?" His eyes lingered on mine for a minute, and I wondered if he wanted me to tell him he belonged here.

*Those eyes.* He had the most beautiful blue eyes, and I wondered why I hadn't noticed them until now. They were deep, soulful, and almost mesmerizing. I felt certain that if I stared at them long enough I would forget all about Luke.

*Luke.*

I quickly looked down and pulled my hand from his. "Thank you again for coming, Keagan."

"You don't need to thank me. I wanted to be here. With you." His eyes lingered on mine, and I couldn't help but notice the seductive way that he moistened his lips. He was so handsome, and kind, and as his face moved closer, all I could think about was what it would feel like to have his lips on mine.

I pulled away at the last moment, my breath heavy with desire, but my heart hammering with love for Luke. But I didn't belong to Luke. And I wanted to kiss Keagan. Why did I feel so guilty?

*Luke abandoned me. He hurt me. I can choose Keagan.* My eyes returned to Kegan's, and then lowered to his waiting lips. I reached up and ran my thumb across his bottom lip, and he closed his eyes in response.

I pulled away again. "I'm sorry," I said, my face

burning with embarrassment.

"It's okay," he assured me, but I felt his yearning desire to hold me in his arms and his disappointment at my hesitancy. But then he stood, wiped his hands on his pants, and said, "I should go get the firewood. We left it down there with the animals."

Keagan disappeared over the edge, reappearing a minute later with an armful of wood. He tossed it on the ground, then disappeared again. He continued this for several minutes until we had a sizeable pile of firewood that would keep us warm for the night.

When he settled back down by the fire, I made an excuse to leave. "I need to go check on Lucia."

"I was just down there. They're all good."

I nodded. "I'm still gonna go."

Besides, it wasn't Lucia I needed to see. It was Gideon.

# CHAPTER 18

## *A Good Alternative*

### ~ SARAH ~

THERE HADN'T BEEN an opportunity for Gideon to show me Luke again since earlier when we had witnessed the scene where Luke was being attacked. Gideon did, however, assure me that he was still alive, and I let that thought carry me through the day.

I hurried down the mountainside to where Gideon and Angus sat on the ledge overlooking the forest, eyes narrowed into the trees, and Lucia and the two male tigers, Garfunkel and Bear, kept watch on the other side. Jasmine and Bella were missing, and I guessed that they were with Drew and Maddy in the forest below.

I greeted Lucia, but she didn't leave her post. She

knew why I was there—for Gideon.

I reached my hand up and stroked Gideon's side. "How is he?" I asked quietly.

*Alive,* Gideon answered.

"Can you show me?"

Gideon took a deep breath and opened his mind to me. I saw him connecting with the other wolves in their pack. Most were resting, some were guarding, and one was pacing—Malyn.

Poor Malyn. He didn't have the luxury of running with this pack and sleeping alongside hundreds of trusted soldiers. No, he had the responsibility of protecting their master, and running alongside hundreds of soldiers that he dared not turn his back on.

Malyn stood on a rise while a blanket of red soldiers slept on the ground all around him. Luke sat off to the side, arms across his knees, his eyes on the fire.

"You coming to bed soon?" It was Ella, and I felt a growl grow in Malyn's chest. Or maybe it was my own.

Luke shook his head. Why hadn't he told her to get lost?

"What's wrong?" She came closer and sat down next to him. Malyn circled them and took a new position so that he could watch her carefully, which I appreciated.

"Nothing," Luke said. "You should get some rest."

"I will when you do." Her voice was soft and caring, and my heart raced with jealousy.

They caught eyes and he smiled, but then he looked down and moved away from her. She was tempting him, and he was trying hard to resist her.

"So what's the deal with the cute blonde guy, anyway?" She was referring to Keagan, and I wanted to reach through Malyn's eyes and strangle her for trying to cause problems.

"I don't know what you're talking about."

"Oh please, Luke. It's so obvious that he's crazy about Sarah."

"He's an idiot."

She grinned and nodded. "But super cute, right?"

"I don't see it."

"Do you think she's sleeping with him right now?"

Malyn snarled, showing his distaste for Ella.

"It doesn't matter, Ella. She doesn't belong to me." Luke stood up.

"No?" Ella followed. "So she wouldn't mind too much if you and I, you know, kept each other warm tonight?" She took his hand and brought it around her back, pulling him closer to her.

I could feel the tension, the temptation, even through Malyn's eyes. My heart beat so wildly that I wanted to scream.

"Ella," Luke said, pulling away, "it doesn't work on me anymore." He turned and left her standing by the fire with Malyn watching her suspiciously.

Ella grinned as she watched Luke walk away. "So I need to up my game, do I?" she said to herself.

And then the connection was lost as I threw up over the ledge into the forest below. Was she going to seduce him? I hurled again. Why did I send him with her? How could he possibly resist her? I was torturing him. I threw up again.

"Are you okay?" Maddy asked as she hurried up onto the ledge. "Are you throwing up?"

I nodded as Gideon backed away, letting Maddy and Drew take his place.

Maddy caressed my back. "What happened?"

I shook my head. They wouldn't understand. They would think I got what I deserved by sending him with her in the first place.

"You need some sleep," Maddy decided.

DREW TAUGHT ME how to make a force field, and together we built one around our campsite. We weren't sure if it would hold up against the monsters, but it was better than just sleeping out in the open. This way we could all get some rest. The animals took turns pacing twenty feet below our ledge, which was another security measure that I trusted even more than the force field.

Small droplets of cold spring rain began to fall just as we finished our dinner, slowly smothering our fire. Keagan stoked it a few more times, adding more firewood, then we took to the inside of the tent where at least our four bodies would generate some heat. I left my shoes and coat on as I slid into my sleeping bag between Maddy and Keagan, and laid my head down on my makeshift pillow. Drew pulled Maddy into him and kept her warm against his body, resting his chin on top of her head. It was freezing, but the pink hue in her cheeks and smile on her lips suggested she was warm and cozy. As for me, I laid awkwardly next to Keagan, staring at the tent ceiling.

"You warm enough?" Keagan asked after a moment.

"I'm fine," I said, but my teeth were chattering, and I knew he heard.

"Here." He sat up and pulled off his sweater, revealing a thin t-shirt. "Put this on. I don't need it."

"No, you'll freeze."

"I really won't," he said with a laugh. "I'd rather you be warm."

There was a shine to his biceps that suggested he was, in fact, warm enough to go without the extra layer. I took the sweater from him and slid it on over top of my coat and put the hood over my head. It was toasty warm, and my teeth stopped chattering almost immediately.

We laid like this for several minutes until I heard the deep, sleepy breaths of Maddy and Drew.

"They make a cute couple," Keagan whispered in my ear.

"They do," I agreed.

"Does it bother you to see them together?"

"Why would it?"

"Because you and Drew used to be a thing."

Used to be. Until our enchantments broke and we both realized that we didn't actually love each other.

"Drew and I are *just* friends. And barely that sometimes," I added with a chuckle.

He took my hand in his and ran his thumb across Drew's school ring. "Why do you still wear his ring?"

I smiled. Drew's ring used to mean so much more to me, but then I learned it was given not for love, but for protection. "It protects me," I explained. "It doesn't mean anything more."

"You can tell he really cares about you, though."

"Yeah." My heart smiled at this observation. Drew did care about me. All enchantments aside, he was still here for me and on this crazy mission with me.

"What about Luke?" he asked. There was an edge to his question. An edge that wasn't there when Drew was the subject of his inquiry.

"What about him?"

"Do you still care about him?"

I closed my eyes, wishing this moment would go away. Of course I still cared about him. Too much, it would seem. But was it fair to Keagan to tell him that? Luke told me to figure out if Keagan could make me happy. And once I was cured, I wouldn't be able to be with Luke. So would Keagan be a good alternative? Could I be happy with him once Luke was gone for good?

"I don't know," I finally answered.

He was quiet for a few seconds, and I reached back, found his hand, and pulled it around me. "I'm cold," I said. I had to know if Keagan could make me happy. It wasn't fair to Luke to continue this way. We all deserved to know for sure.

He moved closer until his body cradled mine, and his warm breath was on my cheek. My heart was racing, but was it with excitement? Or guilt?

"Did you give your school necklace to him?" His lips were right at my ear, and his breath tickled.

"Who?" Although I knew who he meant.

"Luke."

I shook my head, but I couldn't answer.

"Drew?"

I shook my head again.

"Why not?"

I shrugged because I didn't trust my voice.

His lips brushed my neck, and I sucked in a breath and held it. "Good," he whispered, and my breath escaped me. I couldn't breathe. Yes, Keagan brought my temperature up. He caused my heart to flutter. He was strong and protective and loving and caring. We had chemistry. That's what we had. It wasn't love . . . yet.

He brushed my hair back from my neck and laid his lips there, just below my ear. He kissed me and then slowly moved his lips down my neck, his left arm pulling me in closer.

*Figure out if Keagan can make you happy.* Luke's words repeated in my head. *And let me know.*

He wanted to know. He wanted me to figure it out. He would want me to do this.

I rolled over and Keagan smiled, then when I thought he would kiss me, he just held me against his chest. His heart was beating as wildly as mine, and the rhythm slowly made me forget about Luke. Keagan was being a gentleman. He didn't make any effort to kiss me, or move closer into me. He only held me. And I only lied still next to him, afraid to move. Could I learn to put Luke aside for the sake of having a genuine relationship with a good guy? A good guy that knew all my secrets and still cared about me? A guy that my world accepted and my people respected? I *felt* something for Keagan. Was my past with Luke getting in the way of my future with Keagan?

I relaxed in his arms and let the heat from his body and the steady drumming of his heart carry me off to sleep.

**I WOKE SUDDENLY** to the sound of rustling sleeping bags. It was still dark outside, although the sky seemed to be a deep blue instead of a pitch black. Maddy and Drew were moving around, packing up their sleeping bags.

Keagan was still lying next to me, and I was suddenly keenly aware that I was holding his arms against my chest. My eyes widened at this as I knew Drew and Maddy had seen.

"Sleep well?" Maddy said, her eyes not meeting mine.

"I was cold," I told her.

"Well, I guess it was a good thing Keagan was there to keep you warm," Drew said, his movements with the sleeping bag becoming more aggressive.

Maddy glanced at me, and I saw the sympathy in her eyes. She didn't like Drew's coldness toward me.

I carefully picked up Keagan's left hand and moved it over my body and back to his, then I sat up. "What time is it?"

"It's only early," Drew said. "You still have time for more cuddles if you want."

"Drew!" Maddy snapped. She had thrown her sleeping bag down and was staring at him with an unmatched fury. He was shocked at her outburst, but didn't apologize.

Drew's eyes moved to Keagan and then he mumbled, "Lover boy's waking up."

Maddy smacked him. "I'm not kidding," she said. "If you don't give it up right now . . ."

"Give what up?" Keagan said as he stretched and yawned.

"Nothing," Maddy barked.

Keagan sat up and rubbed my back. "Did you sleep well?"

I recoiled a little at his touch, but tried to cover it with a stretch. Drew noticed and gave me a confused look.

"I slept well, thanks."

"Warm enough?"

"I was." I nodded and quickly pushed myself out of my sleeping bag.

"She's not a morning person," Drew said, his tone softer now. "I'll go start breakfast. Sarah, you can help."

I hesitated as I knew this was just an excuse for him to talk to me in private, and I didn't want any more of his accusations, but I got up and followed him out of the tent anyway.

Drew led the way past the knapsack with food, past the fire pit with low burning embers, and down the mountainside. Lucia and Gideon followed us down to the ground and into the forest.

"You want to tell me what's going on?" he asked when we were surrounded by nothing but trees.

"That depends," I said. "Are you finished making me feel like shit?"

He sucked in a deep breath. "I'm sorry, I just—"

"You know, sometimes you can just say I'm sorry. When you add anything more, it loses its effect."

He nodded and smiled, then shook his head. "I'm

sorry."

"Thanks."

"Luke's my best friend," he said.

"I know." It was all I could say. A lump in my throat caught the intake of my next breath.

"And I know he loves you."

"I know."

"And I know you love him, Sarah."

I nodded.

"So why are you trying to make yourself fall for Keagan?"

My eyebrows pulled together as I considered him.

"I know that's what you're doing. I saw it in your eyes. You don't love him, and you feel guilty for lying with him."

My eyes were stinging, and soon there was nothing I could do—the tears just silently came, and I had to look away so that Drew couldn't see my weakness.

"Luke wanted me to," I cried softly. "He wanted me to figure out what I wanted. *Who* I wanted."

"But you already know who you want."

"But I can't have him!"

Drew put his hands on my shoulders. He knew I was right. He knew a light world keeper couldn't be with a dark world keeper. He knew it defied all logic and reason and if he had to, he would do the same as me.

"You don't need to replace him," he finally said. "You

don't need to look for the next best thing."

"He's going to move on," I said, more tears coming at this thought.

"Who? Keagan?"

"No." I shook my head. "Luke. And I don't think I can handle it. It was hard enough when he left me the first time, I can't imagine how much harder it'll be if he leaves me for good. For Ella."

"Who said he'll go back to Ella?"

"Oh, please," I said, wiping my face with my sleeve. "Who wouldn't? She's gorgeous, strong, and she's a dark world keeper. Everything he's looking for."

"He wants you, Sarah. Not her."

"Well, he can't have me. So . . . next best thing."

"So you think he'll go back to her because she's the next best thing, and so you want to have your next best thing too—Keagan."

"It might help with the pain of it."

He nodded. "Fine." His hands fell from my shoulders. "But for the record, what you have with Keagan isn't love. . . . It's self-preservation."

"Speaking of self-preservation," I said as I twisted Drew's ring from my finger. "I won't be needing this anymore." I pressed the ring into his hand.

"Sarah, you can keep—"

"I don't need to. I'm a keeper now, and I don't need protection from the dream worlds anymore." I waited for him to take him, and then I said, "Maybe you could give it to Maddy."

He blushed and pretended he didn't hear me as pushed the ring onto his pinkie finger.

"Do me a favour and think about what I said, Sarah? You don't need to jump into another relationship right away. Luke isn't moving on. He loves you."

Then Drew left, leaving me to sit in my misery for a few minutes. Gideon stood on guard while Lucia lied on the ground near my feet, taking a few more minutes of rest while I considered Drew's advice—I didn't need to move on right away. Just because Luke and I couldn't be together didn't mean I had to find a replacement for him. I could take my time getting to know Keagan, or take a break from getting to know him. The only thing we had to do right now was find the cure, so I could restore Yelram and save its people.

# CHAPTER 19

# *The Diversion*

## ~ SARAH ~

BY THE TIME we finished breakfast and packing up, the sun was rising and the Eye of Darkness was only hours away. The feeling of hopelessness enveloped me as my senses heightened to the sounds around me, hoping for a messenger to arrive from another quadrant with news that they had found the garden there after all.

"Maybe I should ride ahead with Luke and Ella and see if they've found anything yet," I heard myself say as we mounted the animals, ready to depart.

"No," Drew said. "If they found something, he'd send word." He nodded toward Gideon, which reminded me of what I had seen the night before—Ella trying desperately to tempt Luke.

What if she finally won him over? What if he finally saw her beauty and undying love for him, and he gave in to her temptations, realizing I wasn't a good match for him?

"Sarah," Maddy said. She was riding beside me.

"Yeah?"

"Stop thinking so much." She winked and then Angus moved them forward, leading the way with Gideon along the edge of the valley and into the next pass.

Part of me hoped we would catch up to Ella's army. Well, really, just Luke. It helped me to push Lucia harder and faster.

TWO HOURS LATER we reached the place where they had camped for the night, evidenced by the beaten down bushes and stray empty bottles and food wrappers. Their army was still large enough to warrant destroying a fairly large tract of land just to sleep on, which was comforting, knowing they still had enough of them to help keep Luke safe.

I wondered where Luke slept. Did he sleep in a tent of his own? Or with Ella? Would she have let him out of her sight? Did she try to seduce him in his sleep? Did he put his arms around her to keep her warm? Guilt washed over me as I remembered Keagan's arms around me.

"Sarah, let's go," Drew called over his shoulder, and I realized I had stopped in the middle of their campsite.

"You okay?" Keagan asked. He had been waiting next to me, watching my agonizing surveillance of the campsite.

I nodded.

"I'm sure he's fine," Keagan said, and I wondered if it hurt him more to say that than it did for me to think of the alternative.

This mountain pass seemed much longer than the others. Was it just me? Time was running out. The Eye of Darkness was taunting me, and it seemed as though I couldn't ride fast enough.

Soon we were ahead of the others as we rode hard to keep up with Gideon. Suddenly, Lucia slammed on her brakes and reared up on her hind legs. She came down hard, and I was surprised that I was still hanging on. Her head was low and swinging back and forth, and a growl was growing from deep in her belly.

"What is it, girl?" I asked, but before the words were completely out, a monster shrieked and came out of the woods from our right, knocking Lucia and me to the ground. I scrambled to my feet and threw my hands toward the monster, sending a blast of wind at it. Then I put a wall of fire between us, giving Lucia and me both a chance to catch our breath.

Gideon leaped through the wall of fire and sunk his

teeth into the monster's back as Drew, Maddy, Keagan, Beth, and Simon caught up to us.

Keagan jumped from Jasmine's back before she had stopped, then drew his sword. "You okay?" he asked, reaching down to help me up while keeping his eye on the monster.

"Yeah," I gasped. "Just scared the hell out of me."

"Put out the fire, Sarah," Drew ordered as he slid off Bella and released an arrow through the fire at the same time. The monster shrieked, but didn't make an effort to escape.

I sprayed the fire with a stream of water that poured from my outstretched hands, and when the fire was out, the monster came at us again, but it didn't make it far. It reached and shrieked, but couldn't get closer. It was chained!

Drew released another arrow and Maddy was in mid-swing, about to cause a ground tremor, when I yelled, "STOP!"

Everyone froze and stared at me. Everyone except the creature who was gnashing his teeth and roaring as if he was a rabid dog, and I was a piece of juicy steak.

I held my sword out and walked up to the monster. The chain rattled and creaked with the threat of breakage. I tethered his mind to mine and held him in place while I drove my sword up through his skull and watched as he fell to the ground.

"What the hell was that?" Maddy said, breathless. "Why was it tied up?"

"Ella," I said, my eyes narrowing. "We're getting close to the end, and she knows if we don't find the cure, she has to kill me."

"What do you mean? I thought she wanted an alliance with you?" Keagan asked, and I wished he hadn't.

"That's what she wants us to think, but she wants me to the find the cure because if I do, I can't be with Luke."

"Why can't you?"

"Because it's not what my people want. It's not the best thing for my world. He's a dark world keeper, and I would be a light world keeper."

Keagan considered this. "So if you find the cure, she can have Luke."

I nodded. "And if we don't find the cure, then she wants me dead so . . . she can have Luke."

Keagan drew in a long, slow breath. "Then let's find that cure and keep our eyes open for more traps." *So Ella can have Luke.*

A COUPLE HOURS later, when the sun was almost at its fullest height, and the Eye of Darkness was too close to it, the animals were starting to slow down. We had only encountered two more traps—another tethered beast, and the second trap was a trip wire that would have sent a slew of arrows in our direction. Keagan had noticed the wire first, and we carefully followed the wires and plucked out the fifteen poisonous arrows from the surrounding trees.

Eventually, we reached a river that meandered down a rolling hill and continued along the right side of the path. We stopped to give the animals a break and something to drink. Lucia lapped happily at the water, lying down as she did. She was exhausted. I petted her as she drank, trying to heal her sore muscles so she could continue on. I owed her so much already. She was a faithful companion.

No one spoke. We didn't have much time left, and it was evident even just by the somber mood. Keagan's thoughts were open for me, and I knew he wondered about my fate if I didn't find the cure. He knew I could be with Luke, and he wondered if I would choose him. But worse, he worried about Ella and what she would do to me. He stiffened, and I saw his muscles tense.

I put my hand on his forearm. "I'll be fine," I said, reassuring him.

He smiled at me and nodded. "I know you will." But he looked away too quickly. Keagan never looked away from me. It made me want to see his eyes again. His dreamy blue eyes. It made me want to touch his face and keep him close. Close like we were in the tent, with his warm body pressed against mine. I shook the memory from my head and stood up. It wasn't fair that I kept him close. I was still too vested in Luke.

Suddenly, Lucia lifted her head, her ears twisting and turning to make sense of something she heard in the distance. Then she leaped over the river and into the forest, releasing a roar as she did.

"LUCIA!" I yelled after her, but she was already too far.

I grabbed my bow and ran through the river after her, ignoring the warnings of the others behind me. Keagan caught up with me a few seconds later. He was riding Jasmine, and he reached down and pulled me up. Soon we were close enough to Lucia to see what she saw—two enormous monsters, both tethered by the same chain that wrapped around a fat tree, tearing away at the ground as they tried desperately to reach us.

I freed an arrow, but it didn't do much—only angered the monster on the right. More arrows flew past me, and Drew and Simon were there helping to kill the monster that was closest to Lucia.

Soon, the monster fell, but unfortunately that was our mistake. Without the resistance from this monster, the other monster was able to drag its body as it ran toward us. He would run out of chain length soon, so we kept our distance as we released more arrows.

But then the chain broke, causing the creature to fall toward us. I only had time to pull my daggers as it came down on us. Lucia jumped at it from the side, sending it off course slightly, but not enough to miss me entirely. One gigantic paw landed on my ribs, and its claws ripped into my chest. I screamed in pain as I drove a dagger into its heart, but it didn't penetrate far enough to kill it.

Drew flew through the air, landing on the beast with his sword in hand. Keagan was pulling me out from under the monster while Lucia held onto its side, claws dug in dee,p and her teeth ripping at its face. Maddy made the ground shake, causing the monster to collapse, while Beth and Simon attacked from the sides. Then Keagan ran toward the monster, made a roar of his own, and drove his sword right between the creature's eyes.

And it was finally dead.

I was on my back staring at the sky, my hands clasped over my chest as my body shook from the pain of it. My ribs were broken, my lung was punctured, and the world was spinning so crazily that I could think of nothing but the pain.

"Come on, Sarah," Drew said, urging me to focus.

"Take her back to Earth and heal her, Drew," Maddy yelled.

*No,* I thought, desperately. *We can't leave.*

"Then heal yourself!" Drew shouted.

I tried to take a deep breath, but the air wasn't there. My lungs burned, so I just closed my eyes and didn't try. I laid my shaky fingers over my chest and soon my hands were hot, and I felt the energy leaving through them and entering into my chest. My vision was black from lack of oxygen, and as I tried to gasp for breath, I realized that I finally could. Air filled my lungs, and I rolled onto my side, breathing deep breaths of the crisp, spring air. I had never before been so grateful for the ability to breathe.

Keagan helped me up, and I steadied myself with his arms. "I thought I lost you," he said, an unnatural waiver to his voice.

"I'm okay," I assured him.

"Come on," Drew said, leading us back to the path.

"Wait," I said. "Why do you think Ella tethered those monsters into the woods, off the path?

"To kill you?" Drew said. "I thought we established that already."

"No, she's right," Maddy stopped and held onto Drew's arm. "Why *off* the path? Why not right in the middle?"

Drew shook his head. "She probably has more up ahead. Covering the bases, maybe."

Maddy shook her head. "I don't think so. I think she was protecting something back there. Trying to steer us away from a certain area."

I nodded. This had been my thought too.

"You think the garden could be that way?" Keagan asked, pointing back toward the monsters.

I nodded. "Only one way to find out."

I climbed onto Lucia, and she carefully carried me

back through the woods, meandering back and forth so as not to miss anything. The others followed closely behind, evidenced by the thundering of the animals' heavy footfalls on the hardened ground.

And then everything changed. Suddenly, we were in a quiet meadow—a place framed by a circle of tall birch trees, surrounding a field of wild daisies, and filled with a soothing light that covered me like a warm hug.

The Garden of Hope.

I ignored the black shapes that were gathering on the other side of the birch trees—lurking monsters. We were now safe inside the Garden of Hope.

I closed my eyes, and a memory floated into my mind of running through this field, the daisies up past my waist. I was holding a hand. A soft, warm hand that was much larger than my own little hand. I smiled as I remembered the laughter, the games, the love. The memory of this touch, so gentle and sure, reminded me of Luke. How he had always been there for me. How just the simple touch of his hand was enough to fill me with an exuberant love.

I could almost feel his hands on me now. The way they moved around my waist and onto my stomach. I could almost taste his lips. And then I could. They were soft and needy and . . . not at all how I remembered them.

My eyelids burst open, and I was standing in front of Keagan, our lips having just parted. I stepped back and covered my mouth. He held onto my waist in an effort to bring me back to him.

"Keagan," I said, recoiling from his touch again. "I'm sorry."

"Don't apologize," he said. "I've been waiting for that kiss for far too long."

"I shouldn't have done that."

"Why not?"

"It's not fair to you. I . . . I still love Luke."

"I know," he said, a mask of pain hidden beneath his bright blue eyes and sweet smile. "But, you've found the cure. So . . . Luke's not an option anymore."

I swallowed hard. He was right. Drew and Maddy exchanged a look, and then Maddy pulled him back a step, giving us more privacy.

"Keagan, you are such a good guy—"

"Don't," he said, cutting me off. "Don't give me that speech. Please."

"You could have any girl you want—"

"I don't want any girl. I just want you." He pulled me closer to him. "Don't you feel this? We have chemistry, Sarah."

I nodded. "I know we do. But chemistry isn't love."

He was shaking his head. "No," he said. "We can make this work. Just give it a chance. Please, Sarah."

But before I could answer, or perhaps instead of my answer, I noticed the monsters beyond the barrier lifting their heads all at once to something they heard, or smelled, in the distance. They all took off at once, heading back to the path.

I pushed away from Keagan. "What's happening?" I shouted.

"I don't know," Drew admitted as he pulled his bow.

Drew and Simon led the way to the perimeter of the meadow, both holding their bows high, while Maddy, Beth, Keagan, and I followed. But then I realized that Gideon and Angus were outside the circle. They hadn't been able to enter the garden. Both wolves were franticly pacing the perimeter as the monsters closed in on them.

And then we heard it. Hollers from the distance. Someone desperately screaming my name.

"SARAH! SARAH, HELP!"

Without hesitation, I started to run. Keagan grabbed a hold of my arm. "Sarah, it's a trap! Don't go!"

I looked to Drew and Maddy who were contemplating the same.

"What if it's not?" I pressed.

"SARAH!" And then I recognized her voice. It was Ella. "SARAH, IT'S LUKE! HE NEEDS YOU!"

I ripped my arm from Keagan and ran as fast as I could. As soon as I broke through the protective barrier, Gideon swept me up onto his back, and we raced in the same direction that the monsters were running—toward Ella's screams.

I hurled fireballs at the monsters as arrows flew past me, into the creatures, and I knew the others were not far behind. Then the ground in front of me shook violently, causing the monsters who were now within my visual, to stumble.

"Again, Maddy!" I yelled. We both threw our hands toward the ground, and another earthquake shook the earth, this time jarring the monsters enough for us to catch up to them.

I leaped from Gideon so he could attack a monster, while I attacked another with fire. When the monster's eyes found mine, I gripped his mind and threw him into the ground while Maddy finished him with her sword.

There were now only five ferocious, blood-hungry beasts left to kill before we reached Ella and Luke.

Keagan was alongside me now, putting himself between me and the next monster. He threw his sword into the monster's chest and quickly jumped out of the way, taking me with him, as the beast fell hard on the ground where I just stood.

"Thanks," I said, breathless, as I swung my sword at the monster who was giving Beth and Simon a hard time.

Now there was only one monster left—and it was fighting Ella.

Ella had bent into a monster too, except that she was red, while the real monster was black. They were wrestling each other, clawing and biting and throwing each other to the ground. Drew carefully aimed an arrow and held it steady as he followed the black monster, then finally released the arrow, and it pierced the creature in the skull. It stumbled to the ground next to Ella, who ripped the monsters head off with her teeth, then turned back into her beautiful self.

She was breathless and bleeding from her battle wounds. "It's Luke," she said, gasping. "You need to come with me."

"No," Keagan said, putting his arm in front of me. "She's lying."

Ella's eyes glistened and screamed for me to believe her. "He's dying, Sarah. He'll be dead if you wait any longer. . . . *Please*."

"You set traps for us!" Drew roared. "You tried to kill Sarah."

Ella donned a look of ignorance, but then shook her head. "Sarah, if you love him, you'll come with me now."

"Where is he?" I demanded.

"Not far from here!"

Gideon appeared next to me and pushed his body into mine. When I looked up at him, his dark eyes narrowed, and he opened his mind to me, letting me see what Malyn saw—Luke was on the ground, bleeding out. Red soldiers stood all around him, watching and waiting.

"No!" I cried. Without hesitation, I mounted Gideon. "Take me to him."

*But the cure,* Gideon thought, hesitantly. His orders were to protect and help me find the cure. But his loyalties lied with Luke.

"Sarah, wait," Drew said.

"It's not a trap, Drew. He's really dying."

Gideon took one last look back toward The Garden of Hope, and then started sprinting to wear his master lied. Never had the wind whipped at my hair quite that hard, nor the trees blur past me quite so fast.

*Faster, Gideon. Faster.*

# CHAPTER 20

# *The Choosing*

## ~ SARAH ~

"**WHERE IS HE?!**" I shouted at the red soldiers who were gathered in a crowd. Gideon pushed through the crowd, ignoring their dark stares, clenched fists, and bloody swords.

I slid off Gideon's back and thanked him. "I'll take care of him," I promised. "Go back for the others."

I pulled my sword and held it to one of the warrior's chest. "Where is he?"

The warrior smiled. She had a brave face. One that suggested she wasn't afraid to die. I supposed when you were faced with death every day and never knew when you might be killed or sacrificed, you might start to become immune to the fear of it.

Eventually she inclined her head and stepped aside. The others did too, leaving a path through the field. I ran as fast and hard as I could, slipping once or twice when my foot caught an arm or hand of one of their fallen warriors, but then someone stepped in my way, and I nearly ran into her.

"Dana," I gasped when I saw her. I stood up and sheathed my sword. "Where's Luke? Ella came for me. Is he okay? . . . Is he OKAY?"

Her mouth tightened into a firm line and her eyes narrowed. "She wasted her time," Dana said slowly, with a dark menace to the edge of her words.

"What do you mean?" I said, my legs buckling beneath my weight. Was it too late?

"He's not worth her energy or time. I don't know why she still fights for him. I would've killed him myself if I didn't think it would destroy her." Her voice was cold and dry, but I sensed there was more to it than that. She hated Luke, I could tell this, but not because he hurt Ella once before. It was a deep loathing, driven by jealousy.

"And if I weren't under orders to let you save his life right now," she continued, "you wouldn't be alive, either." She stepped aside, and I pushed past her, feeling her cold stare on my back.

Luke wasn't the only one lying in his own blood. Next to him was the body of a young warrior—bound at his hands and feet. Luke was still holding a dagger in one hand and a piece of rope in the other. A piece of rope that was missing from the young warrior's wrists. He had been trying to free the sacrifice, and the act of bravery nearly got him killed!

"Luke," I cried as I ran to him.

He was on his back, his eyes closed and unmoving, shirt torn, claw marks across his chest, and three sizable gouges in his side, possible bite marks. There was a monster lying only ten feet from him, claws bared and teeth glinting in the sun, and Ella's unmistakable sword with the red handle protruding from its head. She had saved Luke. He had tried to save the sacrifice, and Ella had saved him. Or tried to.

I dropped to my knees, my hands shaking as they found his lacerations. His battle wounds. His sacrifice for me.

A sob escaped as I pushed his hair from his forehead. I kissed him, my lips quivering. "Come back to me, Luke."

Ella arrived a second later, her panther making a hard stop as she slid off the animal's back, landing next to us.

"What's the matter?" she shouted. "Why haven't you saved him yet? Heal him!"

Dana tried to restrain Ella, but Ella pulled her arm from her. "Get away from me!" she hissed.

Luke's eyes remained closed, his lips parted, but I

could still feel the warmth from his last breath on my face. I lowered my lips to his and kissed him as my tears fell onto his face.

"I'm so sorry," I cried softly. "This is all my fault." I pulled his heavy head into my lap and cried as my trembling hands tried to find a place to heal. But my heart was shattered, and the ability to heal seemed lost to me. "I love you," I sobbed. "I only ever wanted you."

"It's about time you realized it." His voice was strained and weak, but it was his. I nearly dropped his head as I moved to his side.

"You're alive!" I said, half laughing, half crying. My face and nose were wet with tears, but I didn't care—he was alive! His fingers twitched next to me, and I took his hand with mine, bringing it to my chest.

"I didn't know if I would ever see you again," he said, wincing as he did.

I brought my mouth to his again. "Shh," I said. "You're okay. We're okay."

He smiled, but then his eyes widened as if just remembering something. "The cure," he coughed as he tried to sit up.

"Relax," I said, holding him in place. "I need to heal you first. And anyway, we found the garden."

His eyes lit up. "You did? Did you take the cure?"

"Not exactly. Ella came with the news that you were dying. I left the garden and came as fast as I could."

"Forget about me, Sarah! Go get the cure!"

I ignored him and laid my hands on him. "I earned my healing powers," I said proudly. "Now sit back and shut up so I can save your life already." My hands began to release the hot energy that was the sign of healing. It still surprised me.

Luke smiled as my hands hovered over his chest. "I'm proud of you," he said.

"My people finally trust me. They believe in me." I didn't want to tell him why they trusted me—because they thought I banished Luke.

Luke's eyes widened to something in the sky. "Sarah," he said. "You need to go!"

The sky was darkening quickly as if black clouds were rolling in. I turned in time to see the Eye of Darkness begin to glide easily over the sun, blocking its path to my world. Blocking my path to freedom.

My three days were up.

Luke was on his feet now. "What have you *done*?" he shouted, but his words were aimed at Ella. "I *told* you not to get her! I *told* you!"

Ella backed away, her eyes glistening. "I . . . I had to."

"This is the ultimate act of betrayal, Ella," Luke shouted. "And I will *never* forgive you for this!"

Ella swallowed. Her hands shook but her eyes were wide, glossy, and fixated on Luke. Her inhale was quaked as she slowly turned to Dana, her second-in-command. "Finish your mission and then go home." She took her key, and her eyes moved from Luke's to mine for just a split second, then she said, "Take me home."

Dana threw her sword into the air, shouting something that I couldn't hear through the ringing in my ears, and then the army, or what was left of them, thundered through the valley, leaving us alone for my turning.

At first it didn't feel any different. I knew the Eye of Darkness had taken over and my time was up, but everything still felt the same. Better, actually, as now Luke was safe, and Ella had left my world.

I held onto him as we stood to face the eclipse together. "Luke," I said, because he was too quiet, "I'm sorry I sent you away."

"Forget about it," he said. "I know why you did it. It's okay."

"I didn't do it because I wanted to be alone with Keagan."

He said nothing.

"You know that, right?"

"I honestly didn't think you'd ever choose Keagan. But I did think you would pick your world over me."

Even though I knew now that I couldn't choose Keagan over Luke, I hadn't yet considered what I would do about him not being accepted by my people. Would it even matter? Yelram would be a dark world now, so Luke was now one of us.

I clutched my chest. Was this what guilt felt like? Or was it dread? Defeat? My head threw itself back, and I screamed from the pain that coursed through my body. It was like every tiny vein in my body was gushing with poison, and every single cell was exploding. Soon, I couldn't bare the pain, and I let myself collapse, the edges of my vision blackening until I saw nothing. My ears only registered a dull ringing sound, muffled voices, and my own drowned out scream. But I could do nothing. I was paralyzed. I was turning.

# CHAPTER 21

## The Turning

### ~ SARAH ~

THE GROUND WAS cold and hard, but comfortable. I tasted blood in my mouth, and it made me thirst for more. A small handful of daisies laid next to me on the ground, and I pressed them into the dirt as I pushed myself up and realized I was alone.

Alone, but not alone. My friends were near, but their eyes weren't on me. Their focus was on the two dragon-like creatures attacking them. Luke was closest to me. He was strong and incredibly sexy. His muscles bulged from his shirt as he swung his sword at the beast. His dark, sweaty hair bounced with every thrust and pull of his body. And all I could do was watch.

Maddy had just made the ground shake, and I was once again lying on the dirt. Drew had jumped over one of the monsters at the same time and was driving his sword into the creature's back. Keagan, Beth, and Simon were also attacking from the side, and Luke . . . he was still close to me, holding his hands up and shielding the monster from me.

But then the monsters, as if united in mind, turned on him, and there was no time for him to get out of the way. One of the beasts swung its bladed tail at Luke, sending him flying.

Away from me.

I locked eyes with the monster, and as soon as I did, he couldn't look away. I slowly stood, gripping his mind and paralyzing the both of them with my darkness. I reached out my hands, my fingers spread wide to transfer all the power inside me into the brains of these creatures that were out to kill my friends. They withered in pain, and I loved it. I kept pouring my power into their minds, the euphoric feeling like a volcanic eruption, until their screeches were ear-splitting, and then, with one definitive movement, I squeezed my hands together, and the monsters' heads exploded.

My insides erupted with pleasure. It was an adrenalin rush like I had never felt before. It was exhilarating and beautiful, and the satisfaction was almost overwhelming.

Silence followed as Drew returned his sword to its

holster, and Keagan pulled his dagger from the monster's back.

"What . . . the hell . . . was that?" Simon said, breaking the silence. Beth shushed him.

"Did anyone else just see that?" Simon asked, breathless.

"Simon," Beth hissed as Lucia let out a roar of disapproval.

"She killed those monsters," Simon continued, "just by squeezing the freaking air!" He mimicked my movements. "Just like that. Their heads just like . . . exploded!"

Maddy went to him and put her hand on his arm, silencing him immediately as he was more interested in her hand on his arm than the decapitated creatures on the ground.

"You turned," Drew said. "Didn't you?"

"I think so," I admitted.

Maddy looked back at the executed monsters. "I'd say she did."

"Does that mean . . ." Beth started, "that Yelram is a dark world now?"

No one answered, but they didn't need to. There was a new energy surrounding us. One that slayed all hope and light.

"At least clearing the quadrants shouldn't be that hard anymore," Simon said, a small joke at the edge of a desperate situation.

"I'm sorry," I said to them. "I never wanted this for Yelram."

Beth nodded. "We know."

"I promise to make Yelram a safe place again."

Simon nodded. "And we'll be there to help you." He seemed almost fortified by Yelram's new fate, a stark contrast to Beth's apparent disappointment.

"We will ride back to the caves," Beth said. "And we'll tell the people you have everything under control and that it should soon be safe to start rebuilding Yelram." She smiled weakly, an attempt to reassure me that she believed everything would be okay.

"Take Bella and Jasmine with you," I offered. "You may need them for protection."

"But—" Beth started to protest, but Lucia let out a roar, and Jasmine and Bella hurried to join Garfunkel and Bear.

With that, Simon and Beth mounted their tigers and raced each other back in the direction of their home.

"That was tough," I admitted.

"They seem supportive," Keagan said.

"Yeah, especially Simon," Maddy added.

Drew made a face and a small noise of disgust, which made Maddy grin.

"Are you okay?" Luke's question was for me.

The minute I heard his voice, I wanted to be in his

arms. I threw myself into him, and he caught me. He held me there for a long time, stroking my hair and caressing my back. The race was over. I hadn't won, but the prize was better than if I had. I had Luke now, and as a dark lord, I was filled with a desire and love for him that was hard to control.

But what about Keagan? I knew he was watching us, and I felt a longing to be near him. But it wasn't a satisfying longing; it was desperate and needy. I pulled away from Luke and reached for Keagan. His thoughtful eyes were penetrating mine, and I got lost in them. I wanted to be near him, too. How was I ever going to choose between the two? I paused and listened to my thoughts.

My eyes drifted to Keagan's as he came closer. *That face. That sexy grin. Those full lips. Kiss him.*

"Sarah?" he said, reaching his hand out.

*Touch me. Keagan, I choose you.*

These thoughts were strong, but they weren't my own. They were in my head, but I didn't put them there. . . . Keagan was planting them! It wasn't true that he hadn't gained a craft when coming here. He gained *my* craft! Keagan was a mindbender. But did he know what he was doing?

I resisted the thoughts and soon they were coming stronger: *Keagan is better for me. He loves me and can protect me. I want him, not Luke.*

I shook my head, impressed that he was so good at it. He knew what he was doing. He knew how to bend my mind so that he could twist my own desires.

"Go, Keagan," I said, tears prickling my eyes. "Drew, take him home."

"Sarah," Keagan pleaded.

"Go home and don't ever come back."

"Sarah," Maddy said softly. "Easy."

"Sarah, please," Keagan tried.

"You've been bending my mind, haven't you?" I shouted.

He didn't answer right away as he considered a way out of it.

"That's why even though I knew I didn't want to be with you, I couldn't help it when you were close. You knew I had to make a decision, and you planted thoughts in my head to make me choose you." He stayed quiet as my mind swirled with other scenarios that he probably had a hand in. "You made me want to be in your arms last night." He still didn't say anything, but I saw the guilt all over his face. "You made me . . . kiss you."

Luke had Keagan by the throat now.

"I'm sorry," Keagan gasped. "I didn't know what I was doing at first, but you seemed to say everything I was thinking, and then I saw you take down that monster just by staring at him, and I wondered if your power was in your mind. So I just . . . gave it a try."

"And instead of telling me, you thought you should confuse me further?"

"Sarah, we could be happy together if you just stop thinking about him for two minutes!" Keagan shouted. Luke threw him down, then Drew held Luke back.

"The difference between you and Luke, Keagan, is that Luke gave me space to make my choice. But you . . . you got inside my head." I turned to Drew. "Take him back to Earth. I don't ever want to see him again."

Keagan lunged toward Luke, throwing his fist into the side of Luke's head. Luke wasn't expecting it, but he recovered quickly. He swiped Keagan's leg as Keagan came after him again, and as Keagan jumped back up, Luke kicked him hard in his stomach, elbowed him in the face, and finished him off with a right hook that knocked him near unconscious.

"There's your warning," he growled. "If you ever talk to Sarah again, there'll be more where that came from."

Keagan didn't get up immediately. He wiped the blood from his face and tried to get into my head again. I blocked him, knowing it was coming, and all I had was a throbbing headache. He had gotten good at mindbending, and I was mad at myself for not having seen it before.

Drew hauled Keagan up from the ground while taking Maddy's wrist with his free hand, then he took them out of my world and back to Earth.

Luke put his hands on my waist. "Are you okay?"

"I'm so sorry." My hands shook with Keagan's betrayal. "I didn't know he was in my head."

"I don't want to talk about it," he said. "We've all done things we're not proud of."

My stomach lurched. "What do you mean? What did you do?" Was he about to confess about his actions while he was alone with Ella? My breathing was quick and shallow, and I didn't know if I could bear to hear it.

"If it weren't for my stupid mistake, you would've had the cure," he confessed.

"What stupid mistake?"

"Almost dying."

Okay, so it wasn't Ella. My body sighed with relief. "Do you call trying to save that warrior a stupid mistake?"

He looked down. "It didn't seem stupid at the time."

"Because it wasn't stupid. It was brave. It was . . . you." I took his hands in mine. "Besides, if I could do it all over again, I would still choose you. This whole time, I only wanted to find you. Not the cure. I just wanted you."

He winced as if this hurt. "I don't think you realize what this means for you."

"So I'm a dark lord now," I said. "Sure, it's not ideal, but guess what?" I put my hand on his cheek and brought his eyes back to mine. "You and I can be together now."

He nodded and forced a smile, but it was just that. Forced.

I pulled away. "What is it? Do you not want to be with me now?"

He grinned while shaking his head. "Hardly. I want to be with you more than ever. That's sort of the problem."

"What do you mean?"

"Can't you feel that? The physical attraction?"

"Yes, but I'm not sure it's any stronger than it normally is."

"Oh, it is," he assured me.

"How do you know?"

"It's just the way of the dark side. Temptation, lust, and greed. Give it time—you'll feel it too."

"Did you have those feelings with Ella?" I asked, my gut wrenching so hard that I had to cross my arms over top of it.

"And *that* is jealousy," Luke teased.

"I'll kill her," I said. "Did she try to seduce you?"

He shook his head. "Whatever she tried, it didn't work."

"What did she try? What do you mean it didn't work?"

He took my face in his hands and hushed me. "She tried everything, but it didn't work because I love you, and I knew a moment of pleasure with her would mean a lifetime of pain with you." He smiled, but I didn't.

"Not funny," I said.

"I didn't want her, babe. It doesn't matter if she looks like you, she's not you. I didn't fall in love with your wild hair, your little freckled nose, or your crazy eyes. I fell in love with the girl inside. And no matter how hard Ella tries, she can't copy that."

Satisfied with his answer, I laid my head against his chest. The jealousy was subsiding, but the guilt still lingered. "I kissed Keagan."

"I heard."

"And I let him hold me last night while we slept."

"I figured as much."

"I thought . . . I thought I had feelings for him."

He didn't say anything, but his body tensed.

"I'm sorry."

"It's not your fault," he assured me. "If I ever see him again, I can't promise I won't kill him, but I can't blame you. Mindbending is easy to fall for."

"Will you forgive me? For everything—for sending you away with Ella, for Keagan—"

"How about you promise never talk about him again, and I'll forget about everything?" There was a sly smile on his lips that begged for my mouth to meet his, but I resisted. It didn't seem right. Not at the close of that discussion.

"I promise," I said.

Luke lowered his mouth to mine, and I melted inside his embrace. It was the kiss that I had missed for far too long. It was the kiss that wasn't contrived from an enchantment, wasn't given out of fear for his life, or need for his forgiveness. It was a kiss that meant we were free to love, and we belonged together.

His lips slowed, and he pulled away, his eyes still closed. "I have a question," he whispered.

I worried that he wanted to revisit details about my time with Keagan. I closed my eyes. "Yes?"

He took a deep breath, then moved away and slowly crouched down on one knee. He reached into his pocket and pulled out a stunning ring with a breathtaking blue sapphire in the centre. My heart hammered loudly as he asked, "Will you marry me?"

My surprise showed itself as a giggle, but I tried to regain my poise as I looked into his eyes. "Yes! Yes! A hundred times yes!"

He slid the ring onto my finger, and I nearly jumped into his waiting arms. He buried his face into my neck, and I felt his relief and happiness in his warm exhale.

I finally pulled away and fingered the ring. "Where did this come from?"

"It was my mother's ring," he answered.

"And you've just been carrying it around with you?"

He nodded. "In case we didn't find the cure."

My eyes watered. "And if I had taken the cure?"

He shook his head. "I never wanted to hold you back."

I felt his sadness, his regret for the way things turned out, but more than that, I felt his love.

"Let's get married tomorrow," I declared.

"Tomorrow?" He seemed a little surprised by that.

"Why wait?"

"Don't get me wrong, I definitely want to marry you, and I would do it today if I thought it was the right thing to do, but Sarah, you've only *just* turned. I think we should see how the darkness settles in you first. It might be a hard few days for you."

Under normal circumstances I might wonder if he had reservations about marrying me, but I was still able to see inside his mind, and it was clear that he was genuinely concerned about how the darkness would affect me.

It was a good thing he couldn't see inside my mind, though. Because the darkness that now dominated my body was so heavy and harrowing that I wondered if my soul could ever find peace and happiness again.

# CHAPTER 22

# *Change of Plans*

## ~ MADDY ~

THE MOMENT WE landed in his living room, Drew
shoved Keagan toward the door. "Get out," he hissed.

"Drew," I said, feeling like there was no sense in
making an enemy. Especially one that knew far too much
about the other worlds.

"Drew, I'm really sorry," Keagan started. "I didn't
mean to hurt Sarah."

"She's been through a lot today," I said before Drew
could react. "Let's just give her some space."

"You think she'll forgive me?"

"Who knows," I said honestly. The old Sarah would.
But the new Sarah might not. He had used her and almost

made her give up on Luke.

"If you don't get out of my effing house right now," Drew said, "I will make sure you never see Sarah again."

Keagan nodded. His eyes were red and small, and I wondered if he was about to cry. He turned away and left through the front door.

"You were hard on him," I said when the door closed.

"I was *easy* on him. If he shows up here again while Luke's here, he won't be walking out the front door."

"I feel bad for him," I admitted. "He didn't know the power behind the craft. He didn't fully understand what he was doing. It's our fault, you know. We didn't tell him about mindbending. Maybe if we had, then he would have—"

"Maddy, please don't defend him. What he did—took advantage of Sarah when she wasn't in her right mind—that was wrong on every level."

"Drew—"

"And I am *not* okay with that." His eyes were so firm that I didn't dare argue with him. The truth was, I didn't agree with what Keagan did, either, but I knew what it was like to be an outsider in a world that was so different. And I knew what it was like to love someone that wasn't sure of their feelings for you.

"So what happens now?" I asked, avoiding the thoughts that were wrestling inside my head.

"I don't know. It's never been done before."

"Will she be like evil now?"

"I don't know. She'll still be her, but she'll have stronger feelings. Jealousy, hate, anger. She'll have a much harder time being good." He pursed his lips. "But the bigger problem is that with Yelram becoming a dark world, it tips the scales in favour of the dark side, which leaves Earth extremely vulnerable."

"Is there anything we can do to stop it? Or reverse it?"

"Not anymore," Drew said as his eyes glossed over and drifted to a thought in the distance.

"Do you think she'll stay in Yelram?" I asked. "I always thought she would, but it's not exactly a light world."

"I think she will," Drew said. "She's really connected with her people. She'll still want to bring them some sort of normalcy."

I nodded, then took a seat on the sofa. I wasn't sure how I felt about Sarah staying in Yelram. Sure, it was her world, and yes, she was certainly powerful enough to take care of herself, but . . . what if it *changed* her? What if the Sarah that I knew and loved was gone forever?

"How are you feeling?" Drew asked, his voice low and comforting as he took a seat next to me.

"Tired," I admitted. "How about you?"

"Same. And a little sore. The last few days have been rough. I'm not sorry to be finished."

"I'm a little sad, actually," I confessed. "I finally found

the thing in life that makes me happy."

"Well, you can't go back there now," he said.

"Why not? Sarah will be there."

"Yeah, but she's better equipped. You're not. It'll be far too dangerous for you."

"Drew," I said, sitting up. "Tell me you're not serious right now."

"Maddy, I lost my mother to this. I won't lose you, too."

His words stopped my protest. Whenever Drew made even the tiniest mention of his feelings, it was hard not to be stopped by them. His eyes were watching my lips, and I realized that we were moving closer to each other.

"Drew," I said, my eyes falling from his. "I'm just going to lay it all out there." I swallowed as he watched me curiously. "I . . . really like you."

He smiled, a light pink blushing his cheeks. Just when I was beginning to think he wasn't going to respond, he slid his school ring off his finger and held it out for me. "I want you to have this."

My heart beat wildly. Traditionally, giving a girl your school ring meant that you wanted to be in a relationship. But with Drew, it could mean something entirely different.

"Why?" I asked, hoping for clarification.

He smiled. "Because I want to protect you from the

dream worlds," he said, "and because I . . . really like you, too."

It took every bit of self-control not to squeal with excitement and leap into his arms, but I managed to maintain composure while I took the ring from his fingers and slid it onto my own hand.

Our faces moved closer together, and soon our lips met. It was our first kiss, and it was exactly how I imagined it would be. Steady, sure, and perfect. I resisted every urge to rush the kiss and instead just let myself get lost in the magic of the moment.

His fingers touched my face, then slowly wrapped around the back of my neck, causing an exhale that I didn't know I was holding in until that moment. The buildup of anticipation over the last few months had been intense, I realized it now that this kiss was finally happening.

It was such a crazy feeling being with Drew Spencer. The same Drew I thought my best friend would end up marrying one day. The same Drew that annoyed the hell out of me when he was Sarah's boyfriend. But now he was mine. Or half of mine. I wasn't exactly sure what we were, but whatever it was, I didn't want it to end.

But as quickly as it started, Drew pulled away, a drunken look of pleasure plastered on his face.

I ran my finger along my lower lip, which felt too exposed without his lips covering them.

And then a breeze passed through the room as if a door was suddenly opened. Luke appeared just feet from us, and I was grateful for his interruption.

"Are you okay? Where's Sarah?" I said, jumping to my feet.

"She's at her home in Yelram. She wants to stay there." His face contorted, as if he bore the weight of Sarah's transition. I admired that about him. And envied it about Sarah. He loved her so deeply that it showed in everything he said and did.

"But it's not safe there yet," I argued. "She shouldn't be alone."

Drew and Luke just stared at me blankly. "Sarah's turned," Drew explained. "There's not much that can hurt her now."

"I'm going back," Luke said. "I just wanted to tell you where you can find us, preferably tomorrow as she needs some rest. And I also wanted to thank you for everything."

I looked down, trying to hide my disappointment over our loss.

"Hey, man," Drew said, "I'm really sorry about Keagan. I had no idea what he was doing. If I had known, I would've killed him."

Luke nodded his thanks. "It's okay, man. Thanks for keeping her alive. Worst thirty hours of my life being away from her. I just wish it would've ended in the cure so it could've all been worthwhile."

"Well, you're still alive," I pointed out. "So that's something."

"I would rather have died."

"But now you two can be together," I reminded him.

He nodded, and a small smile showed at the corner of his mouth. "I asked her to marry me." He looked at me, then Drew. "And she said yes."

"Really?" I screeched. "Are you messing with me right now?"

Luke laughed. "No, I'm not messing with you. We're getting married."

"When?" Drew asked as he shook Luke's hand.

"Ah, maybe soon." Luke scratched the back of his neck. "She wants to do it right away, but I think we should wait till she can manage the darkness. I'm just concerned that she only wants to get married because it's reckless, and adrenalin rushes are kind of a drug for people covered in darkness."

"Luke, Sarah loves you," I told him. "It's not like this is new."

Luke nodded, then a smile swept his face. He was skeptically elated about marrying Sarah, and I loved witnessing his excitement.

Suddenly, the back door opened, and Mr. Spencer appeared in the entrance to the living room.

Drew straightened. "What is it, Dad?"

"A virus outbreak in Europe," Mr. Spencer began, "Three hundred and sixty confirmed dead since this afternoon."

Silence.

We all knew what this meant. Yelram's turning tipped the scales of balance, and Earth was going to suffer for it.

Drew's eyes bounced around the room. "Luke, take Maddy to Yelram."

"Wait," I interjected. "Why can't I stay here?"

Drew shook his head, but his eyes were still moving. "No. I'm going to need to help find a vaccination." He turned his attention to Luke. "Keep her safe."

Luke didn't need any more instructions. He slipped his hand into mine and said the three words that took Drew from my sight: "Take us to Yelram."

WE LANDED IN the upstairs hallway of Sarah's palace. It took me a moment to get my bearings, but Luke immediately left me and went into the room on the right—Sarah's parents' bedroom. Then I heard him call Sarah's name.

"How did we get in here?" I wondered aloud. The last time we had been here, this section of the palace had been protected.

"Sarah took down the protection." Luke crossed the hall to Sarah's nursery. "Sarah!" he called as I entered the master bedroom and looked around.

"Was she supposed to be here?"

"Yes. This is where I left her. I told her to stay here."

"Maybe she isn't far," I hoped.

"Lucia's gone too." He pushed his hand through his hair. "I shouldn't have left her."

"Did she seem okay?"

He shrugged. "She's restless."

"She's probably miserable. We should go look for her."

He was lost in thought, as if deciding whether or not he should ignore Drew's request to keep me safe, and instead take me out into Yelram in search of Sarah. But I knew he wanted to go. It was written all over his eager face as he paced the hallway.

Gideon appeared suddenly on the upper landing, confirming his allegiance to his master. Luke jogged down the hall to the great wolf.

"Where is she, Gideon?"

Gideon made some noises, but none that Luke understood.

"I still have my weapons," I told him. "Let's go find her, Luke."

"Drew told me to keep you safe. It's not safe out there. Especially now." He stroked Gideon's side as he considered my offer.

"But what if she needs us? She could be in danger!"

"She's stronger than anything in this world right

now." He said it with certainty, but I knew he still worried.

Suddenly, Luke's eyes went to his chest. He pulled his key from his shirt. It was glowing.

"What is it?" I pressed.

"It's Devon. He's calling me."

"Where is he? You should go, right?"

"I can't leave you."

"So take me with you."

He shook his head. "Too dangerous."

"But what if it has something to do with Sarah?"

I knew this was his concern, too. His jaw clenched as he took my hand, then we disappeared, reappearing seconds later on the side of a hill next to Luke's second-in-command. Devon, along with Luke's army, all had their weapons drawn and eyes fixated in the same direction.

"Sarah."

# CHAPTER 23

# A Deeper Darkness

## ~ SARAH ~

THE CREATURE WAS all mine. Although I could see Devon's army readying their bows behind me, their orders were to hold their fire because this monster was mine.

I gripped the thing's mind and menacingly squeezed it with my desperate craving to taste its death. I stretched my left arm out wide, then gripped the air as the monster faltered from the breath that I choked from its lungs. I threw my hand down, and the creature's head crashed into the ground.

I could've killed him in seconds, but I enjoyed this game. It made me feel alive. There were so many heightened emotions running through my veins—my own excitement, the monster's fear, Devon's concern, the army's surprise . . .

"Just kill it!"

It was Luke, and as I turned, reacting to his voice, I found him standing next to Devon with Maddy clinging to his arm.

A spike of jealousy rushed through me as my eyes fell to her hand gripping his. But then Luke gave a signal to his army and hundreds of arrows flew through the air, causing the beast to fall to the ground, taking my excitement with it.

"That was *my* monster," I hissed. When he didn't apologize, I added, "What are you doing here?"

"Devon called me." He eyed his second-in-command. "You okay?"

Devon nodded. "I thought you might want to know where she was, and . . . what she was doing."

"Thanks, man."

Devon gave Luke a strange look of sympathy, one that I had a hard time interpreting, but then I decided I didn't care what he meant by it. In the short time I had to explore my world post-darkness, I saw what I needed to see—I had lost. My people were worse off now than when we began this quest.

Luke and Devon exchanged a few private words while Maddy came to my side, then Devon departed with their army of wolves and warriors, their heavy footfalls thundering through the woods.

"I'm sorry," I said. "I shouldn't have left the palace."

Luke nodded. "Yeah, you kind of promised you'd wait there for me."

"I know," I said. "I just kept thinking about Riley, and how he came here and killed Louisa, and I just . . . I just wanted—"

"You wanted revenge," Luke finished for me.

I nodded and rubbed my head, realizing that this wasn't something I would've done before my turning.

"Devon said Riley is back in Etak," Luke said. "I don't want you to spend another second thinking about that piece of shit."

I nodded. "I want to kill him."

"I'm sure you do. Just let *me* worry about him." He tried to comfort me with a smile. "I probably shouldn't have left you." He came to me and brushed the hair from my face. "I remember when the key chose me. It wasn't easy."

"Did you feel this way too?"

He chuckled. "It took some time to learn how to control the urges to lash out and hurt everything and everyone around me. But it's like a drug, Sarah. It might feel impossibly good for a short time, but the better you feel now, the worse you'll feel later. And soon, reality will seem like it sucks, and you'll want that high more and more before you lose all control."

"But it feels so good," I admitted. My head was still blissfully light. To hold the life of the monster in my hands and feel its fear and know that I had complete control over it was better than feeling nothing. And better than feeling miserable over how I let everyone down.

"The greater the high, the harder the fall," Luke said. "You need to learn to control your urges."

"But on a positive note," Maddy began excitedly, "you're getting married! Congrats! I'm so excited for you." She gathered me in her arms and squeezed, reminding me that I still had a lot to be thankful for.

"Thank you. I'm pretty excited too." I searched my brain for the happy emotion that was supposed to accompany the situation, but I failed to find it.

Maddy pulled away. "Are you okay?"

I nodded. "I'm really happy." I tried again to find evidence of that claim.

Maddy flashed her eyes to Luke before saying, "Well, let's get you back to the palace. We can talk more there."

"Where's Drew?" I asked.

They exchanged another private glance and then Maddy said, "Home. I thought I'd come stay with you for a bit. Is that okay?"

I nodded, although I wasn't much in the mood for company. I just wanted to curl up under the covers of my new bed and sleep off this lonely, restless gnawing feeling at the edge of my brain.

AFTER MUCH DELIBERATION Maddy decided that she would claim one of the abandoned bedrooms in the west wing as her own. She wasn't far from us, but Luke insisted that both Malyn and Angus be assigned to protect her throughout the night. And the wolves took their new assignment very seriously.

Maddy spent the evening sweeping the floor, shaking the dust from the drapes, and discovering all the hidden treasures in each nook and cranny of her new apartment. Luke and I, perched together in the window seat, mostly watched her putter around the room, making herself feel at home.

But my thoughts kept wandering to the world on the other side of the window pane. The world where monsters now tormented dreamers, and dreamers frantically searched for a way out. My thirst for revenge on Riley was what pulled me into the woods earlier, but the screams from dreamers were what kept me there. I had tried to help them, but it was always too late. I tried waving my arms like I had done to wake Keagan. I tried killing the monsters that tormented them. . . . But it always ended the same. Before the nightmare was over, the dreamer would collapse, and their body would vanish. I couldn't help but wonder if they were even still alive. How dark had my world become?

Eventually, we said good night to Maddy and waited until Angus curled up comfortably by her bed and Malyn positioned himself in the hallway outside her bedroom door.

Gideon and Lucia led us back down the hallway of the west wing and through the corridor toward our own bedroom. Luke motioned for me to go in first, then he closed the door, but not before whispering to Gideon and Lucia, "She'll be safe with me. You can just man the hallway."

Gideon let out what I was sure was a chuckle, while Lucia sighed heavily, and I could almost feel her eyes rolling.

"You were quiet tonight," Luke noticed.

I pressed a smile but struggled with how to answer. Instead, I just focused my attention on getting undressed, the warmth of the bed calling my name.

He took my hand before I could climb under the covers. "What were you thinking about?"

"I saw dreamers today," I finally admitted. I hadn't wanted to bring it up in front of Maddy for fear of upsetting her.

I felt Luke's sympathy before he said, "I was afraid of that." He pulled me into him, and I rested my head against his chest, feeling his heartbeat.

"I just let my key take me to them and one after another I saw them terrorized and then . . . vanish. It was like they died. Right there in front of me. Screaming for someone to help them."

"They woke up," he tried to assure me.

"It didn't feel like it."

"They're just dreams, Sarah. No one is really getting hurt. Okay?"

I nodded, but I wasn't convinced. I saw the horror and desperation on their faces. Even if they were just dreaming, there was no way those feelings would just leave when they woke.

"I know what you need," Luke said, his breath tickling my ear.

"To kill something?" The darkness answered for me.

"Ummm, no, that's not what I was thinking." He ran his fingers down my side, causing me to shiver. Then he lifted my chin and brought his mouth to mine. My body immediately reacted, and a flood of tingling sensations covered my body. I tried to control the urges, but my mind and body weren't friends, and one betrayed the other. My hands gripped his face, holding it close to mine so that he couldn't pull away, but he didn't want to. I felt his energy pulsing inside him, and he was having an even harder time than me with control. Our bodies slammed into the armoire and he pinned me against the heavy mahogany, his body full of intent. He slid his leg between mine and propped me up as he kissed my neck, and I let my head fall back as I relished the tingly sensation as we moved together. I fumbled for his shirt, but he took my hands and held them above my head.

"Control yourself," he whispered, but the way his breath tickled my ear, combined with the way his thigh felt against mine, I lost myself. He held me in his arms while I desperately tried to regain my composure and control.

"What was that for?" I said, breathless.

"I'd rather you get your highs from me than from killing things."

"I'm okay with that." I reached for a kiss, which he let me have.

"But can you promise me you'll at least *try* to control how the darkness affects you?"

"I'll try," I promised.

I wanted to be able to assure him that the darkness wouldn't make me kill things, but was it the darkness? Or was it just me? And what was so bad about killing monsters anyway? We needed to get rid of them, why not let me have my fun with them? The darkness wasn't controlling me. I was controlling the darkness. I knew it was in me, I knew it wanted me to suffer, but I found a way to make sure I didn't suffer—I found a way to turn my pain into pleasure.

## CHAPTER 24

# *Sarah's Sadness*

## ~ MADDY ~

IT HAD BEEN three long days since the virus outbreak, which meant it had been three long days since I had spent any amount of time with Drew. The waiting was the worst. I relied on Luke for updates, but we were hardly ever alone, and he was adamant he didn't want Sarah to know yet. The only information he was able to relay was that the virus had spread to every continent, and countries were literally shutting down. In some areas where the virus had spread, no one was even permitted to leave their homes.

So when Luke returned one afternoon, and Sarah was

having a nap, I ushered him into the hallway and quietly closed the door behind us.

"Did you go to Earth?"

"Yes, Maddy, I went to Earth." He smirked, amused by my eager concern for Drew.

"Well??"

"There's no real update. Drew's still trying to figure out where the virus came from so he can work on a vaccination."

"But he's okay?"

"Yeah, of course he's okay. I told you he can't catch this."

I sighed, relieved. "Well, you keep saying that, but what if you're wrong, Luke? What if I never see him again?" My heart raced with this terrifying thought.

"Just trust me. Keepers are immune. He'll be fine."

"What's taking them so long?"

Luke ran his hand through his hair, something he did when he was stressed. "It's an airborne virus," he began, "which made us suspect it came from Etak, but we've checked. There's no trace of the virus there. I think it has Ella written all over it."

"What do you mean? Isn't Nitsua's mark shapebending?"

Luke nodded. "Yeah, and in the later stages of the illness, the victims all believe they're either an alien, or animal, or something else. Their final hours are spent in excruciating pain while acting like these . . . shapes."

I shuddered. "It sounds so cruel."

Luke's face hardened. "It is, which is another reason I suspect Ella."

I wondered what motive Ella would have for sending a virus into Earth and killing hundreds of thousands, if not millions, of people. Maybe she was feeling extra murderous after Sarah failed to find the cure, thus being free to marry Luke.

"I'm going back in there," Luke said, nodding toward the bedroom. "I don't want her to know I left. She'll ask questions, and I don't think I could lie."

I agreed. "She doesn't need to know about the virus. I'm actually really worried about her state of mind right now."

He nodded. "Me too." Then he disappeared into her bedroom, leaving me alone in the empty and cold hallway to ponder our future and think longingly of Drew.

TWO DAYS LATER Sarah's mood was still not improving. Her thoughts were consistently anywhere but here, and when she wasn't staring gloomily out her bedroom window with fire flickering at her fingertips, she was demanding that Luke take her hunting. On occasion he would take her, but he was usually able to convince her to leave the monsters to his army, and if Sarah got too restless, he would have Angus and Malyn take me for a walk through the palace. Whenever we came back, Sarah was asleep and Luke was pacing her bedroom uneasily.

This time, as Angus, Malyn, and I approached their bedroom door after a thirty minute exploration of the palace, the door opened and Luke met us in the hallway holding his glowing key in his hand.

"She's asleep," Luke said. "Devon just called for me. I don't know how long I'll be, but if she wakes up while I'm gone, just tell her I'll be back. And if she wants to leave the palace, make sure you bring the wolves." Lucia growled. "And Lucia," Luke added before petting the loyal tiger.

"Okay," I said. "We'll be fine. Go."

AN HOUR LATER Sarah began to stir. I waited until she was definitely awake before moving from my chair in the corner.

"Hey," she moaned as she stretched.

"Hey. Did you sleep well?"

She nodded while yawning. Her eyes searched the room, and I knew she wondered where Luke had gone.

"Devon needed him for something," I explained.

Sarah whipped the covers off of her and hopped out of bed. "Let's go hunting."

"Huh?" I went to her, my heart suddenly racing. "Why?"

"'Cause they're not gonna kill themselves."

"Shouldn't we wait for Luke?"

"Ideally, yes, but for some reason he hates it when I want to kill stuff."

"He just worries about you."

"I know." She waved her hand, dismissing my comment. "But I'm stronger now, and this is my world, so I need to protect it." She had her shoes on and was belting up her sword. "Are you in or not?" She headed for the door, clearly not waiting for my answer.

"I'm in," I said as I rushed to get ready too. "Wait up."

SARAH RODE LUCIA, while Angus and I stayed close to her right. Gideon flanked Sarah's left side, and Malyn trailed closely behind. The animals' eyes were wide and waiting as we raced through the meadow that surrounded the palace.

Sarah was alive with the air rushing at her face and adrenalin pumping through her veins. It felt more natural to watch her like this than to see her cooped up in the palace. But of course I had also seen her after the hunt when she came crashing down. I just hoped that Luke would be back by then so he could magically bring her back down and put her to sleep.

As we crested a hill, the air suddenly changed and Keagan appeared in front of us. Lucia and Angus both slammed on their brakes, and I nearly slid over Angus's head.

"Keagan," Sarah said, surprised. She slid off Lucia's back and greeted him. "What are you doing here?"

I hurried to Sarah's side and pulled my sword. "Keagan, you need to go." The wolves, with heads low, slowly circled him.

"I didn't come for a fight," Keagan explained. "I want to help you." He turned his attention to Sarah while I nervously stood guard, worried Luke would show up.

"I don't need your help anymore, Keagan," Sarah said, her face hardening.

"There's gotta be something I can do, Sarah. Please. Let me help you kill the monsters."

"You've helped enough," Sarah told him. "I got this."

"I don't think you do," he said.

"Excuse me?"

"Things are crazy on Earth right now. That virus is out of control. And I feel like it has something to with Yelram's turning."

I groaned as Sarah asked, "What virus?"

"Keagan, you need to go *now!*" I said, pushing my hand into his chest.

"Wait," Sarah said. "What virus? What is he talking about, Maddy?"

"Sarah, if Luke finds him here—"

"Who the hell cares what Luke thinks?" Keagan sneered.

"Um, he's her *fiancé*!" I snapped. "So yeah, shut the hell up."

"Fiancé? Sarah, is that true?" When she didn't answer, he took a step closer. "Tell me you're not going to marry that piece of shit."

Before Sarah could answer, Gideon was on top of him, and then Keagan was gone.

"Where'd he go?!" Sarah shouted.

"He woke up."

"Gideon, that was bad!" Sarah scorned as Gideon growled his disapproval, but then lowered his eyes. "Maddy, what virus is he talking about?"

"Earth is infected, Sarah. Drew's working on a vaccination. You don't need to worry about it."

"Do you know what the worst thing about being like this is? . . . How delicate you all treat me. . . . Take me to Earth."

"Sarah, no!"

But she was gone. The air whipped around us, and the four animals circled me, realizing the vulnerable state Sarah had just left me in. Then Angus nudged me to climb onto his back, and we raced for the palace. I had never felt so defenseless and scared in my life. Angus wasn't the fastest runner in the pack, but Gideon and Lucia never got too far ahead. Malyn stayed behind, and I tried not to let my thoughts wander to what lurked in the nearby forests.

As we approached the palace, I could see Luke standing at the top of the stairs, waiting. I dreaded telling him what had happened. When we got close enough, and he saw that Sarah wasn't with us, he ran down the steps and met us at the ground.

"Where is she?!" he demanded.

Gideon roared angrily, as I swallowed hard. "Keagan showed up. She knows about the virus."

# CHAPTER 25

# *The Apology*

## ~ SARAH ~

HESITANTLY, I RAISED my fist and rapped my knuckles against the wooden door. My heart was racing and my palms were sweating, knowing I shouldn't be there.

I knocked again, this time a little louder, then wiped my palms on my pants. A light turned on inside, and then the curtains drew back, and Keagan peered out. He quickly unlocked the door and opened it wide.

"Hi! Come in." He ushered me in as if it wasn't safe to be outside. "What are you doing here?"

"Tell me more about the virus."

Keagan motioned for me to follow him into the living room. He reached for the remote and turned on the TV, then flicked through the stations. Every channel was "Breaking News" on the spread of the virus that they were calling the Sunrise Fever, on account of the victims falling asleep healthy and waking up delirious.

Journalists reported from helicopters above, showing deserted roads and highways as they described whole cities being quarantined. Hospitals were overflowing, while linen-covered bodies laid in rows in farmers' fields. And in the bottom left hand corner of the screen was a counter.

626,468 confirmed dead.

I sat heavily onto the sofa. "What have I done?"

Keagan sat down next to me and reached for my hand. "It's not your fault, Sarah." His face hardened, and I saw that he blamed Luke more than anyone. He turned the TV off and set the remote down on the table in front of us. "Sarah, I should never have tried to alter your thoughts. I'm really sorry."

I nodded. "I know you are."

"I just . . . I really do love you, Sarah. And I would do *anything* for you."

"Thanks," I said, unmoved by his gesture.

"Sarah, are you really going to marry him?" He looked both disappointed and disheartened at the same time.

I let our eyes meet until I felt his every emotion. Then I nodded, and slowly drank his despair.

"Then why are you really here?" His desire to hold me moved him closer.

"I don't know."

As he closed the distance between us, my heart began to beat faster, bringing back that familiar, liberating feeling of being alive. But it wasn't my desire to be with him that caused this surge of adrenalin, it was the thrill of knowing it was forbidden. I didn't want to be with him, but more than that, I knew Luke didn't want me to be with him. And this adrenalin rush helped me to forget the pain and suffering that I had caused hundreds of thousands of people.

Keagan reached for my hand, but I pulled it away too quickly. "I should go," I said, although I didn't move.

"Don't go," he begged. "Stay. Let's just talk."

"Where are your parents?" I looked around, realizing that no one had come inquiring about the late night visitor.

"They went to Cape Breton to get my grandparents. They're bringing them here until this whole virus thing is under control."

"I'm sorry."

"I told you, it's not your fault."

Suddenly, there was a knock at the front door. Reluctantly, Keagan left me and went to the door.

"Is Sarah here?" It was Luke's voice.

"Wouldn't you love to know," Keagan retorted as I

hurried to the door.

"What are you doing here?" I demanded.

"I'd like to ask you the same question," Luke said as Maddy stood, hands on her hips, at his side.

I crossed my arms. "Why didn't you tell me about the virus?"

"I didn't want to upset you. Sarah, can we please just go home and talk about this?" The vein in his forehead was throbbing, his fists were clenched, and every ounce of his self-control was being spent on not beating Keagan into the ground.

And all of this excited me. I loved his jealousy. I loved the collection of emotions swirling in every direction. Not just with Luke, but Keagan was also jealous, angry, bitter, resentful, and wanted just as badly to fight Luke. Maddy was upset with me for leaving her, but also worried about the impending fight.

The adrenalin poured through my veins, awakening every cell in my body.

"Sarah?" Luke asked again.

"She doesn't want to go," Keagan answered, and although this wasn't my answer, I was curious how it would play out.

"Keagan, I'm trying really hard not to kill you right now, so I'd *strongly* suggest that you back the fuck off and leave us alone right now."

It happened quickly, but the next thing I knew, I was

on the ground, having been shoved aside by Keagan before he threw himself at Luke. Both tumbled down the front steps onto the driveway, and fists were being pounded into each other's faces. Maddy was screaming for them to stop, but my body had already exploded with excitement, and I was coming down hard, suddenly filled with regret and self-loathing for what I had caused.

Stumbling, I found my way down the lawn, and my feet carried me swiftly to the sidewalk. I wasn't sure where I was going, but I also didn't care.

I KNEW LUKE would be okay. I didn't have the same confidence about Kegan's fate, but I was pretty sure Maddy could break up the fight once she told them I was gone.

I sat at the base of the old apple tree, breathing heavily, still reeling from the adrenalin rush of the last ten minutes. I wasn't sure what brought me back here — to the safety and security of Earth's portal, but my time alone was short-lived.

A rustling of trees and bushes in the distance alerted me to the arrival of company. It was dark, but I wasn't afraid. Fire warmed my palms, and I welcomed a threat. But a minute later, I recognized Luke's silhouette walking toward me, followed by Drew and Maddy.

"How'd you find me?" I asked.

"Better question—" Luke started, "what the hell were

you thinking?"

I pressed my heated hands into the ground and pushed myself up. Luke was close enough now that I could see his split lip and torn shirt. Drew and Maddy came up on either side of him.

"Why the hell would you go see *Keagan* of all people?!" Luke boomed.

"Because I *wanted* to! And because you don't *own* me!"

"What is your problem, Sarah?!"

"I DON'T KNOW!" I wailed. "Stop yelling at me!" The floodgates burst open as my tears just began pouring out.

A long minute later, he ran his hand down my arm and then folded me in his arms. "I'm sorry," he said. "I just hate seeing you like this. I hate feeling so helpless."

"At least you feel something."

His embrace relaxed. "Is that why you did it? Did you go see Keagan because he made you feel something?"

I nodded. "But I don't like Keagan. I just knew . . . I knew I shouldn't go there. I knew it would hurt you." It was his turn to be silent. "I'm sorry. I don't know what's wrong with me," I cried. "I just hate feeling so numb all the time. When I kill monsters, I feel something. When I make you jealous, I feel something. And when I feel something, I feel alive. I like feeling alive, Luke. I do. I like it."

"I know, babe. We all do," he said softly. "But you

can't keep looking for those highs. Because the greater the high, the harder the fall. Remember?"

I nodded. "Is he dead?" I meant Keagan, and he knew it.

"No. There's enough darkness on Earth right now, they don't need a random murder on their hands."

I pulled away and looked past him to Maddy and Drew. "I'm sorry, Maddy. I shouldn't have left you in Yelram."

Drew looked down quickly at Maddy, then back at me. "You left her?"

"All I could think about was finding out more about the virus, and I . . . I just left her."

Drew breathed in slowly, but deeply, then he turned his attention to Maddy, "You'll stay with me tonight."

Her face lit up, but she tried to conceal her excitement. "Um, sure, I guess. Whatever."

"Drew," I said, "where did this virus come from?"

Luke and Drew exchanged one of their famous looks of unease before Drew answered, "We're not sure yet."

"It's an airborne disease, which is Etak's mark," Luke said, and I knew this was information Drew hadn't planned to share. "But I've checked, and it's not coming from my world."

"What other world could create a virus that is airborne?" I wondered.

Drew shrugged. "We're still looking."

"I know where it came from," Luke said, teeth clenched. "It has Ella written all over it."

"Why Ella?" I asked.

"Why *not* Ella?" Luke growled.

"Plus," Maddy began, "when the victims wake up with the illness, they all believe they're different. Like some believe they're monsters, some believe they're dragons, or animals."

"So it's like shapebending," Luke finished.

"Drew?" I asked, waiting for him to chime in on this theory.

"Ella isn't really being cooperative right now, so it's definitely a possibility. It'll take some time to get some people in there to investigate. If we can find the source, we can kill the virus."

"How long will that take?"

"That's all we know right now, Sarah," Drew said. "But I need to get back to the house. Maddy will stay with me tonight, and we'll touch base tomorrow, okay?"

I nodded while Luke put his arm around me. Then without another word, he said, "Take us to Yelram," and we were gone.

I WAITED FOR the sunrise. For that bright strip of sunshine that I imagined would filter through the space between the drapes and fill the room with light. Had I even slept three hours? I had fallen asleep quickly, but woke at some point during the night, a sadness gnawing at the edge of my thoughts, and as much as I tried to ignore it, it wouldn't vacate.

626,468 people were dead because of me. Or maybe because of Ella, but really because of me. Because I chose Luke over the cure.

Carefully, I moved Luke's arm from my side and laid it gently on the bed as I slid out of the silk sheets unnoticed. I watched him sleep for a moment, smiling at the way his face softened, and how the corner of his mouth turned up just a little as if he were dreaming. He was a good man, and I loved him.

I turned away and went to the window. Quietly, I pulled open the drapes and peered out over the grey meadows and fields. Would the blanket of dark clouds ever go away? Would sunshine ever touch the mountains again? This was my fault. I had the cure. It was within reach, and I chose Luke. Of course, at the time, I didn't feel as though I had a choice. The draw to him was so fierce that if anyone had tried to stop me, I probably would've killed them. I wondered if this was what Ella felt like. Was this why she defied Luke's orders in the mountains and came for me anyway?

For some reason, I found it hard to convince myself that Luke was right, and that Ella had started the virus. She had fought for the balance of the worlds. She had wanted me to find the cure. Because finding the cure and restoring Yelram meant that Luke and I wouldn't have a future together. But I hadn't taken the cure—I chose Luke instead. Whether or not it was a conscious decision, that's what I had done. It was all on me. The imbalance of the worlds was all on me. It wasn't on Ella—she tried to save Yelram (and keep Luke and me apart). And now that I was familiar with how the darkness wreaked havoc on your thoughts and emotions, I could imagine how desperately sad Ella was now that she lost Luke for good this time.

Maybe she did start the virus. Maybe after losing Luke she wanted to destroy everything around her. I couldn't deny that I would feel the same.

I was thumbing my key nervously. I knew what I had to do. I had promised Ella an alliance if I failed to find the cure. I would have to honour that alliance, and then hopefully be able to somehow convince her to stop the virus. But she hated me. She had no reason to help me. Would she just kill me on sight?

With my heart beating wildly, I searched the desk drawers for a notepad and pen. Then I went to the window, sat down, and penned a note for Luke. Maybe I would be back before he woke. Maybe I wouldn't be back at all.

IT WAS PROBABLY foolish to arrive in Nitsua without a weapon, but I didn't want to look confrontational, so, with only the clothes on my back, I departed Yelram and resurfaced at Ella's portal.

"It's Sarah of Yelram," I announced into the eerily calm darkness.

A second later, Dana appeared, a hateful look on her face. "What do you want?" she spat.

"I need to see Ella." I pressed my fingertips into my palms, willing the heat to dissipate.

She studied me carefully, taking notice that I carried no weapon. "Why?"

My jaw clenched, along with my fists, as I tried desperately to control the urge to bring her to her knees. "Just bring me to Ella. . . . Please."

"And why should I listen to you?"

"Because Ella told you to. Otherwise you would've killed me by now." I smirked, and her knuckles whitened on the hilt of her sword as my fingers brightened with the flames that promised a fight.

She approached quickly, grabbed my arm with an intense strength, and then we disappeared, reappearing a few seconds later in the same room that Ella had brought me to when I had asked for her help in Yelram only a week before.

Dana shoved me toward Ella, and I reacted with producing a ball of fire in my right hand. I squeezed my hand closed, extinguishing the flame, but it wasn't unnoticed.

"Have some respect, Dana," Ella said calmly. "She's one of us now."

"She'll never be one of us," Dana hissed. She glared at me once more and then left the room. There was a beast inside my chest that hammered to get out, but I kept him subdued, knowing that it wasn't the time or place to make enemies.

"Here." Ella motioned for me to take a seat. "Ignore her. She's very protective."

"I came to apologize," I said, deciding to just jump right into business. "Luke was hard on you back in Yelram. He never should have blamed you for what happened."

She watched me curiously. "I deserved it," she said slowly. "I cost you the cure."

"I don't think it was your intention."

Ella was silent, but her thoughts were too sensitive not to hear. She had desperately wanted me to find the cure so that I couldn't be with Luke. She turned away, her emotions hardening.

"I know you love him," I said. "And I'm so sorry that he doesn't see that."

"He sees it," she said coldly. "He just chooses you." She said it with disgust, as if she didn't see what he saw in me. "And now he can have you. His precious little princess has joined the dark side."

"Luke will see that you were on our side," I said. "He

just needs time."

She shrugged. "Whatever." Although she tried to show her indifference, I felt her pain.

"I do have one question, though," I started. "Why did you put the monsters in my way?"

"What do you mean?"

"The monsters tethered to the trees along the path and near the Garden of Hope. If you wanted to help me find the cure, why would you do that?"

Her eyes focused on a thought in the distance, then a look of realization took over. "It wasn't me."

"Then who was it?"

She nodded toward the door where Dana had just exited. "She has a mind of her own sometimes." Ella's face hardened. "She didn't agree with the mission."

"So she did this behind your back?"

Her face tightened, an angry set to her eyes. "It would appear so."

"I believe you," I said. "And I'll convince Luke, too. Eventually."

She offered a nod, which suggested it didn't matter what I said to Luke, she knew he would never be hers again.

"Anyway, I just wanted you to know that I appreciate your help, and I don't blame you for how it turned out."

Her face contorted in a show of confusion. "How do you do that?"

"Do what?"

"Forgive. I've been trying for years to just . . . let it go, but I can't." She looked down as if straining to find the words for something. "There's always been this rumour that it wasn't Leah who killed my mother."

"What do you mean?"

"My mother's trusted guard, Rayna Wile, was the only witness to her death. Naturally, we all assumed it was Leah who killed her, and Rayna was summoned to testify under the truth serum, but then she disappeared."

My mouth was dry. Rayna had been my mother's loyal friend who had helped us immeasurably while in Nitsua. "Did you ever find this Rayna woman?" I asked, secretly hoping they hadn't.

Ella nodded. "Recently. And we finally got the truth. Rayna was a traitor to my mother. She was a loyal friend of Leah's. It was Rayna. Rayna killed my mother."

"What?" I heard myself gasp.

Ella nodded. "She testified that my mother had found out that Leah had a child—you—and that my mother was going to have you found and killed." She swallowed. "So then Rayna killed my mother in order to protect the secret. She said she knew Leah would never do it—she was too kind." Ella hung her head and shook it gently. "So your mother was innocent after all."

My mouth had fallen slack, and I tried to recover quickly from the shock. "Ella, I'm so sorry."

"For once, it's not your fault." She said this with a grin, but there was still suffering behind it. "I've finally been able to avenge my mother's death, but it doesn't change anything."

My heart sank. I knew what this meant. Rayna was dead.

"Do you know what this means?" she asked. "It means I've hated you for all the wrong reasons. Well, I won't lie—taking Luke from me was still a stinger. I still don't love you for that, but at least I can finally let go of the need for revenge. But it still doesn't change anything, you know? Sure it takes away some of my resentment, but I'm still a dark lord. Some things will never change."

*Some things will never change.* This thought bounced around in my mind, as if trying to unlock a distant memory.

I shook the confusion from my head. "Ella, do you know anything about Earth's virus? About where it came from?"

"I wish I could take credit for it, but it's not mine." She eyed me suspiciously. "Did you think it was me?"

"Not really," I answered honestly. "But Luke said it wasn't Etak's."

She grinned. "Well, it is an airborne virus, but if you want to believe your boyfriend, then who am I to argue?"

"It wasn't him," I said.

She poured me a drink and then one for herself.

"What else do we know about the virus?"

"It makes people believe they're something or someone else," I told her.

Her eyebrows puckered. "So it's airborne *and* it affects the mind," she said thoughtfully.

"The mind," I repeated, and a heavy sense of reality hit me hard in the chest. The virus affected the mind. Mindbending was Yelram's mark. My thoughts pinballed, trying to figure out if it was possible. Then my heart sank when I realized—Riley had been in Yelram. Had he brought the airborne virus from Etak and left it in Yelram to morph into something more powerful?

"What's wrong with you?" Ella was next to me now, and I realized I was bent over, trying desperately to catch my breath.

"It's from Yelram," I heard myself say.

Ella considered my clues, and I wondered if she would catch on that Yelram's craft was mindbending.

"How did you release a virus and not know?" She chuckled, but I saw her confusion. When I didn't answer she added, "Well, there's no sense in crying about it. There's nothing you can do to change it now."

*Change. Change.*

How could I have let this happen? My world continued to cause more problems than it was worth. I closed my eyes and tried desperately to suppress the sobs that shortened my breath.

"Don't worry, your friends will find a way to stop it," Ella continued. "You're lucky to have such good friends."

I *was* lucky to have my friends. But what good was I to them in this state? What good was I doing for them as a dark lord of a dark world? With the imbalance of the worlds, it was only a matter of time before Earth collapsed, and my darkness was the cause. The evil inside me was the reason for everyone's misery. My dark world was responsible for distributing a virus to hundreds of thousands of people. I had to *change* it. How could I *change* it?

"What are you thinking?" Ella asked, a look of suspicion and curiosity on her pretty face.

"You just gave me an idea." I stood up, my cells awakening with a new mission.

"Wait. Where are you going? What are you doing?"

"Saving the worlds."

"How? Sarah, it's too late—"

"Ella," I said as I took my key, "it's never too late to change a world."

# CHAPTER 26

# *Ella's Story*

## ~ MADDY ~

"DREW! . . . DREW!"

It was Luke, and although we had been in a deep sleep, wrapped up in each other's arms, Drew and I both jumped when we heard the urgency in his voice.

"Drew!" Luke shouted again before the bedroom door burst open.

"What's wrong?" Drew was out of bed and pulling on a t-shirt.

"Sarah," Luke said, breathless. "She's gone." He held a piece of paper in his hand.

Drew snatched the paper and read the note. "Shit."

"We need to go," Luke said.

"Yeah." Drew hurried out of the room while Luke followed, leaving me alone with the worn paper on the end of the bed. I hesitated, fear making it that much harder to reach for the note.

> *Luke,*
>
> *I've gone to see Ella. If the virus is from Nitsua, I will find a way to stop it. If I don't come back, please know that I love you more than anything.*
>
> *I'm sorry. I need to do something. I can't keep going on like this.*
>
> *xo*
>
> *Sarah*

I found the guys in the dining room where Drew was now stocking up on weapons.

"Why?" I asked Luke. "Why would she do this?"

Luke shook his head. "I don't fucking know. Apparently she's lost her freaking mind!" He made fists and brought them to his head as if he wanted to break something.

"She'll be killed," I realized.

"No, I don't think so." Drew shook his head. "She's on the dark side now. Ella will want her as an ally. She won't kill her."

"So should we wait then? Do we really need to go after her?" Both looked at me as if I were some sort of traitor. "Sorry," I said, "but if Ella won't want her dead, then why risk our lives going after her? Ella doesn't have a soft spot for you and I, Drew."

"You can stay," Luke said, "but I'm go—"

Before the words were out of his mouth, there was a knock at the door. Luke's eyes narrowed and darkened. He sensed it too. It was Ella.

Luke whipped open the door, grabbed her by the throat, and pulled her into the house. He threw her against the wall as she struggled for air. She didn't struggle, but she could have. Drew pulled Luke back and Ella fell to the ground.

"Where is she?" Luke demanded, his fists vibrating with rage.

"She . . ." Ella gasped as she clutched her throat. "She . . . came to see me."

"Where is she *now*?!" Luke roared.

"I don't know," Ella said, and then winced at the punishment she expected.

I pushed past Luke, pulled Ella to her feet, and drew my knife. I dug it into her chin, the same way she had done to me when I was her prisoner. "Why are you here?"

Drew positioned himself close to my side, and I knew he didn't trust my strength if this went to battle.

"She came to make peace." Ella had tears in her eyes, which confused me. I hadn't thought she was capable of feeling anything other than hate. "And then we talked about the virus, and she thinks it came from Yelram." She waited for Drew and Luke to exchange glances, and then continued, "But then she got weird and said she had to go, and that it was never too late to change a world." Her eyes met Luke's, and I saw the fear in them.

*It's never too late to change a world.* Everything around me slowed to a near halt. This was unsettlingly familiar. . . . The prophecy! *In the darkest world a soul will burn, and from dark to light a world will turn.* Was this what Sarah meant? Had she really decided to sacrifice her own life to change Yelram and stop the virus?

"Where'd she go?!" Luke boomed again.

I fell back, my dagger slipping from my hand.

"What?" Luke pressed as Drew caught me.

"She's gone to Leviathan," I said, turning to Drew. He steadied me with his arm. "To change Yelram from dark to light. 'In the darkest world a soul will burn, and from dark to light a world will turn.'"

Drew finished the prophecy, "'Peace be restored and darkness diminished, by a sacrifice and the words 'It is finished."'

"No," Luke said, shaking his head. "She wouldn't do that."

"I think she's right, Luke," Ella said softly. "That's why I came here. To warn you guys."

# CHAPTER 27

# *The Sacrifice*

## ~ SARAH ~

I KNEW THIS meant I was choosing the future of Yelram and Earth's people over Luke. That knowledge was probably what made me suffer the most.

I let memories of Luke torture me as I made my way through Leviathan. I remembered the way too well. It had only been a couple of months since I walked this exact path in search of the final clue that would lead me to my key. But this time it was different. The dragons didn't come after me. The lava river barely flowed. It was much easier this time. Too easy.

My legs burned as I climbed the sweaty walls of the pit. Just a few more feet and then I would be there—on the ledge overlooking the inferno below. The inferno that would gladly accept my soul, but in exchange, I would be giving life and promise to the worlds.

I pulled myself up onto the ledge. Almost directly across from me was the same firefall that concealed my kiss with Drew; my betrayal of Luke. This seemed like a fitting place to end it all. A sob escaped, surprising me as I didn't know it was there.

"I'm so sorry, Luke," I cried into the air, my voice echoing off the orange walls.

He would forgive me. He would. He would understand why I had to do it. He would move on eventually, and he would be happy again. As happy as a dark lord could be.

# CHAPTER 28

# *It Is Finished*

## ~ MADDY ~

"YOU'RE COMING WITH us," Luke said as he pulled Ella to her feet. "Because if you're lying, I'll kill you myself and leave your body to burn in Leviathan."

Her eyes widened, but it wasn't fear I saw—it was heartbreak and suffering.

Drew tied Ella's wrists with a thick, coarse rope, and Luke held onto it as we stood together, then Drew said, "Take us to Leviathan."

We landed on a narrow ledge behind a firefall. The hot lava burned my face as it flowed effortlessly past us.

"This is it," Ella said. "This is the pit." She frowned at Drew. "How did you get us here? Have you been here before?"

Luke clenched his jaw and pushed Ella forward. Drew only caught my eyes for a second before following Luke along the ledge. And then I remembered—he *had* been here before. With Sarah. This was where they had kissed. This was where Luke and I found them, right before Sarah collapsed in his arms. Drew used his connection—the memory of kissing Sarah—to get us here.

I followed him out of the firefall and swallowed my jealousy. I should have been thankful for his connection now as it saved us a lot of time dodging dragons, crossing a ferocious lava river, and meandering through the mountain pass.

I ran into Drew who had stopped once we were clear of the firefall. On the other side of the pit stood Sarah, her eyes closed, arms out, standing on the cliff's edge.

"Sarah." Luke's voice echoed off the pit walls, startling Sarah.

"What are you doing here!" she demanded.

"Sarah, come down," Luke said. "This is a mistake." He started making his way around the path toward her.

"Luke, you are the reason that this was the hardest decision I've ever had to make. But I need to do this. For my people. My world. And for you. I love you so much, but if I can't bring you light, then I am nothing for you."

"Sarah, you are *everything* to me. Don't do this," Luke

pleaded. "Please come down. I love you. Let's talk this through."

She returned her stare to the lava below. "There's no other way. This will kill the virus. This will change Yelram."

Luke, desperate, fell to his knees. "Please, Sarah," he begged. "Let me hold you. We'll do this together. If you go, I go."

"No," she said. "I'll need you here to help Maddy and Drew. Don't abandon them."

"Don't *you* abandon them!" he shouted out of desperation.

"I *have* to do this," she said, her own desperation attached to her words. "Not just for Yelram, but for Earth. For everyone. For balance."

"Sarah—" Drew tried next, but she cut him off.

"Drew, thank you," she continued, as if on auto-pilot. "Thank you for being my protector all these years. Thank you for sticking beside me and still loving me even when you didn't have to."

"Sarah, come down," Drew begged.

"And Maddy," she continued, a sob escaping as she said my name, "I could not have done this without you. Everything. Life. School. Finding the key. Going to Yelram. You were there through it all, and I owe you. I am naming you my second-in-command." She chuckled when she said this. "And on my death, you will take over

Yelram. I just hope that after this, Yelram will be a light world once again, and you can find happiness there."

A tingling sensation on my chest pulled my eyes down to where I found my very own key appearing out of thin air. Begging and pleading were useless now and I knew it. Nothing we could say would stop her, and the more we begged her to stay, the worse the goodbye would be. I couldn't hold back the tears, though, and I didn't have the strength to wipe them away.

"It's my turn to be the hero," she said. "You have each done more for me and Yelram than I could ever repay you for. But this—this is my task. This is my duty. I know now what it means to be a leader—to sacrifice yourself for the greater good."

"Baby, please don't do this," Luke cried. He was on his knees, hands clasped in front of him as he pleaded for her to stay. "I can't . . . I can't live without you."

She couldn't make herself look at him. Her heart was crumbling at the pain she was causing him, but she couldn't tell him.

She took a step closer to the edge and closed her eyes as she mentally prepared herself for the fall.

"Sarah," Ella said quickly, stepping forward.

I had almost forgotten she was there, and evidently, so had Luke.

Ella continued, "The worlds need you, Sarah. You have brought more hope and balance than anyone before you." Ella's tears slipped down her face too, but with her hands bound, she wasn't able to wipe them away. "It's my turn to do something good for the worlds." She stepped toward the cliff's edge.

"NO, ELLA!" Sarah screamed as she quickly scrambled down from her perch. She knew. She felt it. Or she heard it in Ella's thoughts. However she knew—she just knew. "Don't do it, Ella! It's not your fight."

"It *is* my fight," Ella said calmly. "It's everyone's fight." She took another step forward. "Balance doesn't have to be about separating the good and the bad. You don't belong at the bottom of a firefall, Sarah. You belong with Luke." She took off her key and dropped it on the ground at Drew's feet. "This is for you, Sarah. For the worlds. . . . And for Yelram." She turned toward the pit, took a deep breath, then fell forward while saying, "It is finished."

"NO!" Sarah yelled as she watched Ella fall into the fiery pit of lava below. Luke caught Sarah and held her against his body as she struggled fiercely, trying desperately to break free. She wailed in his arms, and then suddenly she gasped as if her very soul was being ripped from her body. She screamed demonically, thrashing in Luke's rigid arms, and then she collapsed.

IT HAD BEEN the longest three days of my life. Drew kept assuring me that this was normal, but to watch Sarah sleep so deeply, made me wonder. At least the tremors had stopped and the shadows under her eyes were nearly gone. When she had turned to the dark side, the turning had been so quick, although, she had been turning slowly for months.

I sighed, walked away from her bed, and went to the window. The sun was high over the kingdom, and the tigers frolicked playfully and freely in the fields—all but one beautiful, multi-coloured tiger who was just outside the bedroom door, pacing back and forth about as much as I was inside the room.

"Would you relax?" Drew said, catching my arm.

"It's been three days," I pointed out. "I thought you said it would be three days."

"Maddy, why don't you go for a walk," Drew suggested.

"A walk? Are you kidding me right now?"

He came to me at the window and brought his mouth to my ear so that Luke wouldn't hear. "You're making it worse."

I glanced back at Luke who hadn't moved from her side since he carried her home from the firefall. His silence was a sore reminder that for every moment he spent in this world, the weaker he became. As light transferred into her, life sucked itself out of him.

After a few minutes, Luke spoke for the first time all day. "Maddy, will you promise to take good care of her?"

"First of all," I said, "I will be the best damn second-in-command any of the worlds have ever seen." I waited for him to smile, but he just kept his sunken eyes on Sarah's face. "But, seriously, why'd you say that?"

"I have to go." There was a quiet surrender in his voice that was painful to hear.

"But she'll want to see you, Luke. You can't leave yet."

"Look at me." He turned his ashen face toward us. "I don't belong here now. *She* belongs here, but I don't."

I sat down next to him on Sarah's bed. "Aren't you happy for her?"

"Of course I am. I hated seeing her suffer. I even considered doing the sacrifice myself to save her world, but . . . I just couldn't bring myself to leave her. Forever." He brushed a strand of hair from her forehead.

It was time to address the elephant in the room. It had been there since we brought her back to Yelram after she attempted the sacrifice, but no one wanted to talk about it. Especially with Luke. But now it was time. She would wake soon (according to Drew), and Luke was ready to leave her.

"You're hurt that she did that, aren't you? That she was going to sacrifice herself and leave you?"

"I can't be mad," he admitted. "I know she did it for the worlds, and I love her even more for how selfless she really is, but I . . ." he trailed off, unwilling to finish his thought.

"You're still hurt."

He let silence fill the room before he added, "We were going to get married."

"Sarah loves you, Luke." I wasn't sure what else I could say.

He nodded. He knew she loved him. "But I can't survive here, and she won't be able to survive in my world. There isn't anything left to say." He leaned over and kissed Sarah on the forehead, his lips lingering there as a tear fell onto her face. "I love you," he whispered.

Before I could object and convince him to stay at least until she woke, he was gone. The wind carried through the room, and soon it was just Drew and me left with Sarah.

"What the hell!" I shouted.

"I saw it coming." Drew was leaning against the window, seemingly unmoved by it all.

"What? Why didn't you say anything?"

"Think about it, Maddy. They were finally able to be together, and then she goes off to kill herself."

"To save her world! And Earth!" I corrected. "To free herself from the darkness!"

"Regardless, what kind of message does that send him? 'Turns out you didn't make me happy after all. I'd rather die than be with you.' And now that Yelram is a light world, there's no future for them. You saw what being here did to him. Another hour and he'd be dead.

Etak will do the same to her. There's no future for them now."

"But Earth," I challenged. "They can be together on Earth."

"Sure," Drew shrugged. "Whenever they're not busy ruling their own worlds."

My heart squeezed with the pain Luke felt. I closed my eyes, and a few tears fell. Drew came to me and wrapped his arms around me.

"Do you think she'll still love him when she wakes?"

His silence confirmed my fear. Even if she did love him, she had chosen her path.

AN HOUR LATER Sarah's fingers twitched, her eyelids flickered, and then she squinted from the light in the room. She inhaled deeply, then exhaled slowly as if appreciating her very first breath in a world liberated from darkness.

Drew joined me at her side. "Good morning, sunshine," he said.

Her eyebrows came down. "Luke?" she said, her voice weak.

Drew glanced at me. "You've been asleep for a few days," he said, avoiding her question. "I suppose you needed it."

"Where's Luke?" She tried to sit up, her muscles straining under the pressure.

"Home," Drew finally answered.

"But he was here," I added when her face fell from disappointment. "He had things to take care of."

"You were right about Ella," Drew diverted. "She wasn't as bad as we all thought. Her sacrifice changed Yelram."

"Really?" Sarah's face brightened with relief.

Drew nodded. "She gave her dark soul so that Yelram would receive the light it needed to change. She made Yelram stronger."

"What about Nitsua? What will they do without her?"

"Dana's in charge now," Drew explained. "She blames us for Ella's death. She doesn't believe Ella willingly sacrificed herself."

"Ella's legacy will be forgotten," Sarah realized, distraught with frustration. "Her selfless sacrifice will be dismissed as murder."

"We know the difference," Drew assured her. "We'll carry that legacy for her."

Sarah nodded, seemingly content with this. She would carry on Ella's legacy, and if nothing else, she taught us all how to see the good in even the darkest person.

"We're having a party tonight," I told her. "To celebrate Yelram's reform. We could honour Ella in the ceremony."

"I'd love that," Sarah said. "What's this party thing?"

"Your people have been celebrating for the last few days, but they have a big event planned for tonight—for when you wake up."

"When will Luke be back?" Sarah asked.

I hesitated with the right wording, but Drew answered instead, "Sarah, I'll be honest, he probably won't be back."

"What?"

"He can't really come here. Your world doesn't accept him. And he knows you belong here, so . . ."

"So that's it? He's going to just take off again?"

"This isn't easy for him," Drew countered. "But when he realized that you would rather die than be with him, he got the picture."

Sarah gasped, taken aback by his insensitivity. "It was meant to be a sacrifice! For the worlds! For balance!" At her last word, her face contorted in confusion as if she was trying to grasp at a memory. "Balance," she said to herself.

"Right. Sorry. Sacrifice," Drew went on. "Which I believe ends in death, no?"

"Is that what he thinks? Does he think I would rather die than be with him?"

Drew shrugged. "It was kind of a strong message."

"No, Sarah," I said, glaring at Drew, "Luke is not upset with you. He understands why you did what you did."

"I was in a dark place," Sarah defended. "Earth's people were dying. My people were miserable. I couldn't just . . . I had to do something!"

"It's okay," I assured her, putting my arms around her. "Luke knows you love him. And he loves you."

"Then why isn't he here?" she cried.

I paused, giving Drew ample time to answer the question for me, but he didn't. "Being here," I started slowly, "is quite toxic for him . . . now."

She watched me, unwilling to accept this new truth.

"You'll have to see him on Earth," Drew added.

"No." She shook her head. "But you said he was here."

"He was," I said, "and it took everything from him. The stronger you became, the weaker he got. He had to go . . . or die."

Sarah clutched her chest. "What have I done?" she cried.

"You saved your world," I reminded her. "And Earth. Sarah, don't forget that. Regardless of what this means for you and Luke, your people are safe now. And the worlds have balance again. Okay?"

"Balance," she said again, her eyes wandering around the room as if the word meant something more. Then her eyes lit up and she said, "I need to go see him."

Drew considered her for a moment, a softness to his

eyes. He loved her—but not in the way I used to envy; he loved her like a sister, and I enjoyed watching how tender he could be toward her. "Etak's not the safest place for you anymore, either."

She nodded, but she had a look of determination on her brow that concerned me. What was she thinking?

"If he came here, how long would he have before . . . you know . . . he had to go?"

Drew studied her carefully before answering. "Probably thirty minutes or less."

"That's all I need," she declared. "Drew, I need you to go find Luke and bring him here in one hour"—she looked at the grandfather clock in the corner of the room—"at six o'clock sharp. Okay?"

Drew studied her carefully, then shrugged. "It's your day. I'll do my best."

# CHAPTER 29

# The Princess' Tribute

## ~ SARAH ~

ALTHOUGH I WAS keenly aware of the minutes that passed, I took my time getting ready, enjoying the way my body felt—new, whole, and powerful. I had gotten used to the pain in my legs every time I walked, but now it felt as though I had a brand new pair of healthy, strong legs built for any task I needed to do. It no longer took effort to shower or get dressed, although doing my hair was still something to complain about. Maddy was convinced that leaving my hair down, taming the curls, and inserting some daisies would be the best look for the event.

Music and laughter floated in through the open

windows, and I enjoyed listening to the celebrations unfold.

"What should we wear?" Maddy asked.

I had been eyeing the double closet doors, trying to work up the nerve to open them and discover the types of clothes my mother would've worn when she was alive. This was the moment. It was now time to slide the large wooden doors apart and see what dresses waited within.

Maddy entered the wide tunnel of clothes with me. The closet was a rainbow of colour. I ran my hand along the entire row of dresses, admiring each one—pitch black . . . blood red . . . golden yellow . . . emerald green . . . brilliant blue (which caught my breath) . . . stunning purple . . . whimsical white.

And then the rainbow repeated itself in different hues of the same colours—deep grey . . . softer red, almost pink . . . pale yellow (embroidered with tiny daisy petals) . . . mint green . . . sky blue . . . pale lavender . . . and antique ivory. They were all stunning, each one a unique design.

"This is insane," Maddy said after a minute. "Which colour do you want to wear?"

I was drawn to the yellows, knowing this was the colour of Yelram, and the colour my people would expect me to wear. There would be a lot of yellow in the crowd already, though, and when my fingers brushed against the royal blue dress, I stopped. It was the same blue that his army wore in battle. The same bright blue as the flecks in his eyes. It was the only colour in the whole closet that filled me with a sense of belonging and love.

"This one," I decided.

I removed the dress from the hanger, let my robe fall to the floor, and stepped into the ocean of blue. Maddy helped with the zipper, and we both stood in front of the floor-to-ceiling mirror admiring the dress. It wasn't as fancy as some of the others, but its soft silk, brilliant colour, and simple lines made me ache with pleasure. The wide straps came off the shoulders and down to a perfect dip in the centre. The rest was simple and sleek, but touched the floor with a ribbon of flare.

"It's perfect," I breathed.

"It is," Maddy agreed.

While Maddy decided between two gorgeous green gowns, I wandered into the hallway where Lucia waited patiently. She made an affectionate noise of approval when she saw me. Then she lowered her head, and we shared a hug.

"I miss Luke," I confided.

Lucia groaned her understanding.

"I still want to marry him, Lucia. Am I crazy?"

Lucia purred, then thought, *Your father asked me the same thing when he fell for your mother.*

"He did?"

*The people were wary of her, too,* Lucia continued. *She wasn't destined for Yelram, you know. She was more of a wild spirit.*

I caught the laugh that jumped from my belly. "Really? My mother was a wild child?"

*She sure shook things up here,* Lucia recalled. *But your father loved her so deeply that, in the end, it didn't matter what his people thought. He knew he loved her, and what was good for him was good for his world. And the people learned to trust and love her.*

"Why have you never told me this before?"

*You never asked.* She let out a grunt meant to be a chuckle. *Besides, you weren't ready to hear it before. Now you know what it feels like to have it all but still be missing something.*

I put my arms as far around her as I could. "Thank you, Lucia! That is *exactly* what I needed to hear."

LUCIA PROUDLY LED Maddy and me down the left staircase and into the foyer. When we reached the large wooden doors, two guards pulled them open, and the noise from the crowd outside filled my ears. There were hundreds, maybe even thousands, of people in the square, and my heart hammered from the love and energy I felt from each one of them. Slowly, one by one, they noticed us at the top of the stairs, and they turned to give their full attention.

Along the side of the sprawling steps stood three familiar figures. As I got closer, I recognized the smiles

from each—Trinity, Eli, and Mr. Spencer.
They greeted us on the steps, each taking turns
embracing me.

"What are you doing here?" I wondered aloud.

"It's an historical event," Eli laughed. "And an
honour to be here." He bowed dramatically.

Trinity smiled warmly. "I'm not sure how you did it,
but we sure are grateful for your many talents."

"Earth is on the mend now," Mr. Spencer added. "All
thanks to you."

I wasn't able to offer any thanks or appreciation for
their kind words. Because they weren't meant for me. I
shouldn't have been the one listening to them. It was
Ella's sacrifice that saved the worlds, not mine.

Nervously, I scanned the sea of well-wishers. Some I
recognized from the mountains—Beth, Simon, the old
man with the cane (although he no longer carried one),
Elizabeth (my first intentional healing in the mountains),
and her daughter, Rachel. It filled my heart with joy to
see that they were all alive and well and had made the
journey safely.

The crowd was quiet now, and I knew this was my
opportunity to say what I came to say. Maddy handed
me a microphone, and I climbed the steps so that
everyone could see me. I cleared my throat and raised the
microphone to my lips. "Thank you everyone for coming.
I am overwhelmed with gratitude for the love and

support you've shown me. It's very clear that my parents were well loved here, and those are big shoes to fill, but I plan to do my very best to continue making this world a safe and happy place for everyone."

The crowd erupted in applause and cheers, which helped chase away the nervous butterflies.

"That said, I want to thank my best friends, Drew and Maddy, for everything they've done to help take back Yelram. I wouldn't be here today if it weren't for them." I took a deep breath, deciding to jump right into my tribute to Ella's sacrifice. "Just like we wouldn't be here today if it weren't for the help of the other world leaders. I love that we were able to transcend boundaries and come together to bring back the balance of the worlds. So I want to make sure I give proper thanks to Nevaeh, Lorendale, Etak, and Nitsua." There was an awkward silence at the mention of these dark worlds, which I ignored and continued, "I know most of you weren't thrilled about my decision to involve Etak and Nitsua, but I have no regrets. Nitsua's keeper, Ella, gave her life for Yelram, and we should never forget that." I paused, swallowing the lump in my throat. "And Etak's keeper, Luke, has been my rock. He believed in me, challenged me, supported me, protected me . . . and loved me."

The crowd was quiet, surprised, no doubt, that I would use my celebration speech to honour the dark worlds. But their silence, and reluctance, was what moved me to continue.

"When my soul transitioned to the dark side, my judgment was clouded, and it felt like there was this veil of darkness over me that I couldn't lift. It was . . . awful. No matter how hard I tried to fill the void, there was always this empty feeling. A feeling like I was missing something. Something that only death could find."

My thoughts carried me back to the cold, sleepless nights where I laid in a fetal position, blanketed only by the lonely, debilitating feeling of being completely alone, even though I wasn't alone—Luke was with me. How had I felt so lost? It scared me to think that this was the feeling Luke battled every day. This was the same darkness that plagued souls in the dark worlds, and souls on Earth.

"I know you all sit her singing my praises for saving Yelram, but it wasn't me. Ella saved Yelram. She did it consciously, and out of hope for our world. My sacrifice would have been out of desperation. Desperation to free myself, and all of you, from the dark cloud of depression. I believed that all of you would be better off without me. That my sacrifice would bring you light. But what I didn't consider was what it would've done to my friends. My family. And what I realize now is that happiness can't be bought with a sacrifice, and sadness can't be erased with death. Hope, faith, and love are the only things that can truly balance a world, and without these things, darkness still lingers."

I lowered the microphone. The mood of the crowd had plummeted. I should've stopped, but I never felt more alive by being truthful. Truthful to my people, but more to myself. I had blamed the darkness for my sadness, and I thought I could fix it by changing my world. But in bringing light to my world, I shut Luke out, and that had been my biggest mistake. I needed my people to know that. I needed them to appreciate and respect my love for him.

"You know, before Ella gave her life for our world, she said something to me. . . . She said, 'Balance doesn't have to be about separating the good and the bad." I grinned, appreciating the irony. "Balance can be about joining the good and the bad and making it neutral. . . . Balanced. If I've learned anything over these past few months, it's that light and dark belong together. Without one, the other loses balance. Together, we are stronger."

I lifted my head high, never feeling so sure of my next words. "There will be a change in tonight's plans. With or without your blessing, I intend to marry Prince Luke of Etak. Obviously, I would much rather have your blessing, but ultimately, this is my decision. I realize that a union with Etak will mean Yelram will lose some light and gain some darkness, but it also means that Etak will lose some darkness and gain some light. The worlds will still be balanced."

There was a small murmur of protest or surprise at the back of the crowd, but it was quickly silenced. I closed my eyes, and a tear escaped. I felt the surprise of my people, the respect of Drew and Maddy, the proud approval of Lucia, and the love of my parents.

When I opened my eyes, I found Trinity first. Her arm was raised, three fingers held high. "You have Nevaeh's love and support," she said.

Eli and Mr. Spencer both raised their hands too, and as my eyes fell over the crowd, I was moved to find countless hands in the air. I couldn't contain my laughter and gratitude. Tears flowed from my eyes. "Thank you," I cried.

Then Maddy touched my arm, bringing my attention back to her. She nodded behind us and when I turned, I found Drew and Luke standing at the top of the stairs.

He was more handsome than I ever remembered, which made me realize that a small part of me was worried I wouldn't be attracted to him in the same way. But I was wrong. As he stood fifty steps away from me, in a navy blue suit and yellow bow tie, my whole body filled with the strongest desire to be connected with him forever.

I raced up the stairs, careful not to trip on my gown, and when I reached the top, Luke gathered me in his arms.

"How long have you been here?" I asked, concerned

for his health and the thirty minutes that Drew guessed we had.

"Long enough to hear your speech." He squeezed harder. "I'm sorry I had to go."

"I'm sorry for what I put you through."

"I know."

I had a violent flashback of him on his knees begging me to come down off the ledge. My heart squeezed with guilt until his lips came to my forehead, releasing me from my momentary lapse in happiness.

"You were right about Ella," he said. "She wasn't all bad."

I nodded. "Good can be found in anyone if you look hard enough."

"You're stunning," he said. "The dress is beautiful on you."

"I wore it for you."

He smiled as he gave a little tug on his bow tie. "I wore this for you."

Mr. Spencer appeared next to us, reminding me that we weren't alone. "Sorry to interrupt. I just wanted to offer my services if you two planned to marry tonight."

I looked up into Luke's deep blue eyes. "What do you say? Are you ready to marry me now?"

"Yeah." His voice had softened with the water from his eyes.

Mr. Spencer cleared his throat, drawing our attention

to him. "I've only officiated a handful of weddings in my lifetime, but this one . . ." he started, but had to swallow a lump, "this one is a true honour."

We were moments away from being united for eternity, but it didn't scare me nearly as much as I thought it would. The moment my eyes found Luke's again, the beating settled, and I let myself get lost in his deep blue eyes. He laced his fingers with mine and caressed my thumb with his, reminding me that we were in this together.

The rest was a blur. I only saw Luke, and he only saw me. Our minds were open to each other, and I shared my thoughts, and he shared his. Our lips moved in rhythm as we repeated the words laid out for us, and we meant them entirely. Later, we would fail to remember a single word, but I would remember the way his fingers felt against my palms, and the way his eyes softened to such a pale blue that I was sure they sparkled, and how our hearts beat in unison. I would remember the fresh fall air that moved freely around us, and the flicker of flames from the sconces that lined the staircase. I would remember Drew and Maddy standing proudly next to us, the village square filled with Yelram's people waiting to witness our union, and Mr. Spencer's melodic voice bringing us closer and closer to the moment of completeness. I would remember all of that, but not the specific words we said. Because it wasn't about the words. It was about us, in that very moment, making a promise with our hearts for eternity.

Luke finished his scripted vows and then cleared his throat before adding, "Sarah, from the day I met you, I knew my life would never be the same again. And every moment thereafter was either pure bliss or complete torture—depending on whether we were together or apart. I promise to bring you hope, faith, and love for the rest of our lives." He raised my hand to his lips. "And I promise to keep you balanced . . . for eternity."

I hadn't noticed I was crying until he reached for my cheek and brushed away a tear.

Mr. Spencer spread his arms out wide. "By the power entrusted in Earth, I now pronounce you forever united."

Luke grinned, and I found it hard to breathe as he slowly lowered his face to mine. The moment our lips met, a burst of light exploded from our keys, sending millions of tiny little blue and yellow sparkles into the air. At the same time, ribbons of blue and yellow light twisted and danced around us.

As the crowd below us celebrated, and the music began to play, Luke gathered me in his arms, and we danced to the soft hum of the new balanced energy that now rested in both our souls.

# CHAPTER 30

## A Brave New World

### ~ SARAH ~

**MAYBE THINGS DIDN'T** work out the way everyone had hoped or planned. Maybe Yelram would never be the world it was intended to be. But maybe it would be better. Maybe the darkness would make it stronger in some way. All I knew was that this was the new Yelram. This was the new me. And I was right where I belonged.

Dear Reader,

Thank you for reading *Eye of Darkness*. The next book, *When Worlds Collide*, is the epic finale that you won't want to miss!

Please consider leaving a review for *Eye of Darkness* on Amazon. Reviews help other readers decide if a book is worth their investment in time, which, in turn, helps the author. So, in advance, thank you.

And finally, if you would like to be notified of upcoming book releases, please sign up for my newsletter on my website at **www.klhawker.com**.

Thank you so much!

*Kimberley*

K.L. Hawker
www.KLHawker.com

**P.S. Turn the page for a look at the final book in this series, *When Worlds Collide*.**

LEVIATHAN AND NITSUA have joined forces to begin the War of the Worlds—with Earth as their prize. As the armies begin preparing for the greatest battle in the history of the worlds, Sarah discovers a truth that would prevent her from joining the fight. But with humans being forced to kill, and creatures being unleashed to destroy, Earth is crushing under the weight of the war, and Sarah may be the only one who can tip the scales in their favour. With her friends preoccupied on Earth, and her people looking to her for hope, Sarah has a difficult choice to make—play it safe and secure on the sidelines . . . or risk a merciless death on the battlegrounds. The future of her kingdom is at stake, and Earth hangs in the balance.

A grand finale to The Dream Keeper series, *When Worlds Collide* defies the laws of traditional storytelling and will leave you questioning your own existence.

# PROLOGUE

# War of the Worlds

## ~ RILEY ~

DANA PUSHED THROUGH the double doors, and we entered the meeting place. She was holding onto my arm as if she expected me to change my mind. But even if I were to change my mind, where would I go? I was in her world now, without a key to get back to my own. I was at her mercy.

But I trusted her. We had the same agenda. We both wanted nothing more than to see my brother dead. With Luke gone, that meant I would become Etak's keeper. But for Dana, she stood to gain nothing but the satisfaction that the man who was responsible for her lover's death would exist no more.

Keagan, Dana's new second-in-command, was already seated at the round table when we arrived. He had poured us each a drink, which I hesitated to take. There were few people in the seven worlds that I trusted, and Keagan was not one of them. Maybe it was because I knew he had a soft spot for Sarah. Although we did have one thing in common—he hated Luke almost as much as I did.

I took a seat across from Keagan. Dana sat down next to me, and there was still one unattended seat where a drink was placed.

"Riley," Keagan said, nodding his greeting.

I lifted my head with a short nod. "Who are we waiting for?"

Dana smiled. "Victor," she said, and there was a mixture of excitement and jealousy in her eye.

"Of Leviathan?" I said, although it was clear that this was who she meant. What other Victor was there? The only Victor that mattered was Leviathan's keeper. The darkest lord of all of the seven worlds. Suddenly I realized that whatever plan Dana had in mind was going to include more than just getting rid of my brother. If Victor was involved, there would be much more to it.

The door opened, and Victor walked in. At least I assumed it was Victor, having never met him face to face before. He was tall and thicker than I had pictured. His hair was kept short and his eyes were the darkest black I had ever seen. He wore dark clothing with big black boots and walked with an air of defiance and importance. I felt myself stand as he approached the table, but realized I wasn't alone as Dana and Keagan were both standing now too.

Victor pulled the chair and sat down. He pushed the drink away and folded his hands in its place. "So you want to start a war." His deep, commanding voice seemingly echoed off the walls.

"It's time we take Earth," Dana said, keeping her eyes on Victor as she spoke. "They're weak. They turn on each other every chance they get."

Victor nodded, thoughtfully, but kept silent.

"And how do you propose we do that?" I asked, causing Keagan to grin and Dana to break her stare with Victor. "I mean, I thought we were just here to discuss how to get rid of my brother."

"We'll get to that part," Dana said. "Right now we make a plan to take over and rule Earth."

"Who will rule Earth?" Victor asked.

"Both of us, of course," Dana answered. "We'll share it."

"Share it," Victor repeated with a grin. I could tell sharing wasn't something he was used to doing.

"We'll set fire to every inch of that planet," Dana started, "and then when it's burned to the ground, we'll—"

"I have a better plan," Victor said, ignoring what he clearly thought was a juvenile, ill-thought-out plan. "And in the end, *I* will rule Earth, and *you* will benefit from my generosity for sparing your life right now."

Dana opened her mouth to refute, but the fire at the ends of Victor's fingertips made her close it.

Victor leaned forward, pressing his forearms into the table. "There is only one way to take Earth," he began, "and you're going to need a lot more firepower than you currently have." Flames erupted from his shoulders as if proving his point. "But as dark world allies, I think we all stand to gain from this . . . merger."

Dana visibly relaxed, and a smile formed at her lips. "Yes," she agreed. "I like the sound of that."

"Okay, so you take Earth," I interrupted. "Then what? How does Luke die? How do I become keeper of my world?"

"No one wants Luke dead more than me," Keagan said, "so don't worry—it will happen."

"I'm pretty sure your anger toward him because he embarrassed you in front of Sarah isn't as strong as my hate for how he took away my honour and threw me into prison," I said.

"Keagan is my second-in-command, Riley," Dana said. "He shares my hate for Luke as well. Your brother is the reason Ella is dead. We loved each other, but somehow your brother snaked his way into her mind and made her believe her purpose was to die for Sarah." She spat the last words.

"Sounds like you all have reason," Victor said. "So I

assume by killing Etak's keeper, you plan to turn Etak back into the dark world it was intended to be?" His question was for me, but I still couldn't make my eyes meet his.

"That's the plan," I said. "And because Yelram and Etak are united now, it won't be long before Yelram's mine, too."

"You're not to touch Sarah," Keagan said under his breath but loud enough for all of us to hear.

"Got a soft spot for her, do you?" Victor asked.

"She's never done anything to any of us," Keagan said.

"Sarah's not our target," Dana clarified, "but if she gets in the way, or dies trying to save Luke, that's not on me."

Keagan frowned but didn't dare backtalk his new master.

"Seems like she has you all under a spell," Victor noted. "I look forward to meeting this temptress and seeing what she's capable of once she loses Luke."

"Speaking of which," Dana said, "how about we go take a walk and I'll show you just how we plan to make his death happen."

"Is it ready?" I asked eagerly.

"Just about," Dana said. "All we need is a key." She turned to Victor. "I was hoping that once you saw our weapon, you would be willing to loan us your second-in-command key."

Victor narrowed his eyes on her. "You're asking a lot."

"Wait 'till you see what it's for."

And with her eyes alight with excitement, we all followed her out of the room, through the passageways, down a long narrow staircase, and into the solid steel wing of the castle where she kept the beast tethered.

# ABOUT THE AUTHOR

**K.L. HAWKER** grew up in Nova Scotia, Canada, where she spent her childhood writing stores that took her imagination all over the world. All grown up, Hawker is still an avid daydreamer and writer, and enjoys travelling the globe with her family, visiting all the places she once only dreamed about.

For more information, please visit:

**WWW.KLHAWKER.COM**

# ABOUT THE DAISIES

SEVENTEEN-YEAR-OLD Alexis Fletcher is the artist and creator of this beautiful trio of daisies that you will find at every chapter heading in this book series. In December 2015, after an unforgiving struggle with mental illness, Alexis ended her life. A close friend of my son's, Alexis was a beautiful, caring, outgoing, funny, smart and very talented girl. She is loved by all who knew her. As light and delicate as a daisy, Alexis's spirit now blooms freely and without suffering.

MY HOPE IS that you will consider educating yourself on mental illness and suicide prevention. If not for yourself, then for someone you care about, because we all struggle at one point or another. Alexis's family started a non-profit foundation in Alexis's memory wherein they help to provide much-needed support for other young people like Alexis. You can find out more about this foundation by following the link below. You can also purchase a piece of jewellery for just $20CDN and wear this trio of daisies proudly in support of mental health. All proceeds will go to the foundation to ensure youth get the help they need.

WWW.BELIEVEINHOPEFORALEXIS.COM

# ACKNOWLEDGMENTS

First thanks goes to God. For everything.

Many thanks to my readers for continuing this awesome journey with me.

A big thanks to my amazing, supportive husband, Stuart. I couldn't do it without your love and support. Thanks, babe.

Thank you to my three amazing kids—Austin, for inspiring me way back then (my first trilogy was for him!). Kate, for your honest feedback and love of my books. And Marley, for keeping my creative juices flowing by having me tell you bedtime stories every night.

Thank you, Mom (aka Linda), for being all-around perfect. I really hope some of your awesomeness rubs off on me someday. Thank you for always being there and listening, and for not <u>always</u> quoting the Bible when you have advice to give (although, it is sometimes nice to know what Jesus would do). Thanks, Mom. You're the best.

A big thanks to my editors / beta readers / feedback specialists—Janet, Melanie, and Annette. Thank you for always being ready and willing to help!

Made in the USA
Columbia, SC
27 March 2020